Sleuthing the Klondike
Canadian Historical Mysteries – Yukon

Joan Donaldson-Yarmey

Print ISBNs
Amazon Print 9780228624769
Ingram Spark 9780228625612
B&N Print 9780228625469
BWL Print 9780228624790

BWL Publishing

Books we love to write
Authors around the world

http://bwlpublishing.ca

I0523881

Canadian Historical Mysteries Collection

Rum Bullets and Cod Fish - Nova Scotia

Sleuthing the Klondike – Yukon

Who Buried Sarah- New Brunswick

The Flying Dutchman – British Columbia

Bad Omen - Nunavut

Spectral Evidence – Newfoundland

The Seance Murders – Saskatchewan

The Canoe Brigade – Quebec

Discarded – Manitoba

Twice Hung - Prince Edward Island

Jessie James' Gold – Ontario

A Killer Whisky – Alberta

Dedication

With Love to Oliver and Sherry, Sally and
Phil,
Elizabeth and Terry, and Matthew.
And to Michael

* * *

Acknowledgement

BWL Publishing Inc. acknowledges the
Government of Canada and the Canada
Book Fund for their financial support in
creating the Canadian Historical Mysteries.

Funded by the
Government
of Canada

Table of Contents

Chapter One
Summer 1897

After midnight, the man who sometimes called himself Stanley Noland shuffled the deck of cards while waiting for punters to step up to the table with their chips. He wore a white shirt with long sleeves, the cuffs held up by sleeve garters around his biceps. While the other dealers wore black waistcoats and black bow ties, he preferred a red waistcoat and tie, thinking it lent him an air of sophistication. He shuffled methodically and carefully, knowing that Ernest, the owner of the saloon, was watching him. Stupid man. Accusing him of cheating and in front of the other dealers.

"We run honest games here," Ernest stated a week ago and had watched Stanley ever since. The saloon made most of its money from selling spirits but offered card games to its patrons to make sure they spent their money in the house.

Stanley knew there were some complaints about his dealing. Foolish punters who lost their money made themselves feel better by saying he occasionally stacked the deck, but no one had proven it so far.

He stood in the cut-out at the back of the oval table, leaning against the edge. He hated his job as a house dealer. The only reason he'd taken it was that the owner of the Belmont Saloon caught him dealing off the bottom of the deck. The owner kicked him off the poker table he rented to run his game. He'd paid the owner a percentage of his winnings at the Belmont, and the rest of the profits had been his. Here he was paid a measly seven dollars an hour by the owner to operate the faro board in front of him on the green baize that covered the table. He straightened the board pasted with the suit of spades running from ace to king.

The room was large, noisy, and filled with smoke. A band, made up of a fiddle, a piano, and a flute player, did their best to make their din sound like music. Stanley wondered why the owner didn't hire a decent band, at least on Friday and Saturday nights when they were the busiest.

Men stood three deep at the bar, talking or laughing as they swapped stories while drinking beer or cheap liquor. There were a few tables, and patrons sat in threes or fours at these and chin-wagged as they downed their drinks. Everyone talked loudly to be heard over the band and each other. Waiters pushed their way through the crowd carrying trays with full mugs to the tables and picking up the empties on their way back to the bar.

Three men came and stood at his table. They looked at the row of spades, and each put a chip on one of the cards.

"Evening, gents." He nodded a greeting as he continued shuffling. He wanted more than just three men.

Two more arrived, and when they had put their chip or chips on the card number of their choice, he quit shuffling. While the five men watched carefully, Stanley placed the deck into the dealing box or shoe, as it was commonly termed. The shoe was supposed to prevent the dealer from cheating, but that was a laugh. All he had to do was make sure two cards of the same number were paired in the deck and then drawn together. The rule was that the saloon won half the winnings on that number. He'd also gotten quite good at distracting the players and surreptitiously moving a chip from a winning card to a losing card. And a good player could use the same technique of distracting the dealer to move his chip from a losing number to a winning one.

Stanley removed the top card, or soda as it was called, and set it aside, also known as burning it. He now worked with a deck of fifty-one.

"How is the game going?" Ernest asked, stepping up to Stanley's right elbow.

Stanley turned and glared at him. What the hell? If Ernest thought to catch him cheating, he could watch all he wanted and see only an honest deal.

"The game is fine, right, gentlemen?" Stanley looked at the men across from him.

Two mumbled a yes while the others nodded.

"Then carry on." Ernest stepped back a few paces but remained close.

The next card was the dealer's card, and Stanley set it to the right of the box. The third card was the player's card, and he placed it on the left. He looked at the placement of the chips on the board. Regardless of the suit, any chip put on the same number as the dealer's card was a loss for the punter and a win for the house. Any chip on the player's card was a win, and the house had to pay dollar for dollar. If the number the player bet on was higher than the dealer's number, he also won. The bets that neither won nor lost could remain on the table if the owner desired.

Stanley waited while the men set their chips down, then dealt out the following two cards and went through the same process of seeing who won or lost their money. In his two years in Victoria, he'd learned that most men who gambled liked to play faro. It was faster-paced, had better odds, and the rules were easier to learn. He, however, liked to deal poker. It was easier to cheat.

The men who had lost grumbled and placed more chips on the cards. Those who won laughed and, buoyed by their success, made heavier bets. Ernest left, but Stanley didn't try any sleight of hand. Tonight was his last here at the saloon and in Victoria. Tomorrow he was boarding a steamer and heading to the Klondike gold fields. If half the stories he'd heard were true, money could be earned either from staking a rich gold claim or working in the saloons in Dawson City. Since hard manual labour wasn't part of his life's plan, he hoped to rent a table and make his fortune winning some gold from the prospectors.

The night continued with Stanley dealing an honest hand each time. When his nine-hour shift was up, he set the cards down, picked up his single-breasted, black frock coat from the shelf under the table and put it on. The coat was a little big, having once belonged to a man taller and broader than him. The man carelessly forgot he'd draped it over the back of his chair when he left a table in a saloon Stanley played poker. Stanley walked over to the table and lifted the jacket while the other men were busy ordering another round of beer from the waiter. He now patted the side pocket to make sure the two steamer tickets and tag for his ton of supplies were still there. They were, and beside them was the diamond stick pin. He caressed the pin he'd won back at a poker game before starting work. It had taken some fancy card hustling, but he'd done it. Then, with a smile, he walked away from the table.

Stanley went up to Ernest with his hand out. Ernest counted sixty-three dollars in tens, fives, and ones and placed them in Stanley's palm. Stanley clamped his fingers around them and stuffed them in his pocket. Neither man said a word. Any other night, he might have stayed and played a few games but not tonight. And if Ernest weren't such a jerk, Stanley would have told him he was leaving for good. But he just walked out the door, knowing he would never return. Let Ernest scramble to find someone else to run his table.

The summer air was warm, even in the middle of the night. Wisps of fog had rolled in off the ocean, and the three-quarter moon barely lit the street. It was a long walk from the saloon to the boarding house where Stanley had rented a room for the past year. He walked down the street for three blocks and stopped at the edge of the woods. It was a nice stroll along the path during the day, with sunlight filtering down between the tree branches and leaves. And it was shorter than going around but more dangerous, especially at night. Many a man had been rolled for money or jewellery, some even by him.

Stanley debated taking the shortcut. He only did it when he was in a hurry, and tonight, he was in a hurry. He had to finish packing his clothes and be at the docks by early morning so he could load his ton of supplies onto the steamship. The Northwest Mounted Police required that ton for anyone going to Dawson City to prospect for gold in the late summer of 1897.

Stanley listened hard as he peered into the dark forest. It was quiet, with no sound of men talking, no boot steps, no smell of a fire indicating that someone camped out for the night. Stanley pulled his collar up against the cooler air in the trees and hurried along the well-worn path. He watched ahead of him and occasionally turned to look over his shoulder. Just when he started to relax and think he might make it, he heard footsteps behind him. He walked faster, and the steps kept up. Maybe it was someone he knew, someone who was trying to catch up to him.

Stanley abruptly stopped and started to turn. When the first blow landed on his head he knew he'd made a big mistake. His legs gave out, and he fell to the ground. He tried to yell as he raised his arms to ward off the next blow, but his voice was just a croak. The large tree branch came down on his head again, and he verged on the edge of consciousness. It wasn't the first time he was on the receiving end of a beating and robbery, and he prayed that the mugger just took his money and left. The third blow knocked him unconscious.

* * *

The man stood over Stanley, ready to hit him again if he moved. When he didn't, the man bent and searched his pockets. He found Stanley's wallet with his earnings for the evening, his tickets to Dawson City, his supply tag, and the tie pin. He held the pin in his hand, glad it was back where it belonged. He stuck everything in his pocket, picked up Stanley's arms, and dragged him into the bush.

The man found some sticks, pulled some small branches off the trees in the dim light and covered Stanley as best he could. Then he returned to the path and hurried out of the woods. It wasn't safe to be in here at night never knowing who might be waiting in the shadows.

The man had no place to stay that night. He couldn't go home because he didn't have a home anymore. His new wife, Louise, had just found out about his past two wives, both of whom he'd never gotten around to divorcing. And the worst part was that he hadn't had time to get into her savings account. Sure, she'd been paying for everything so far, and he'd almost had her convinced to give him access to her money so he could invest in the restaurant he'd told her about, the restaurant that didn't exist, but she didn't need to know that. He'd taken her to a building and shown her what he planned to do with the money—the redecoration, the new tables and chairs, and the upgraded kitchen to satisfy the chef, the one he told her he was purloining from one of the better restaurants in Victoria.

"It's all set," he'd said. "I just need the financing to pull it all together. I have two investors, but they won't accept my expertise as my share of the investment. They want me to put up one-third of the money needed to get the bank financing."

"Let's go home and discuss it," she'd said with a smile. "You might be able to convince me."

The next day there'd been a knock at the door. He'd answered it and stared in surprise and shock and fear.

"Who is it?" Louise called, coming up behind him.

"I'm his wife, Brenda. I heard he was living with another woman."

"He's not living with me. We're married."

"No, you're not. Because he and I never were divorced. And I've also learned that he has a wife in Calgary."

Louise stared at Brenda and then turned to him. "Get out!" she roared. "Get out now!"

Brenda smiled at him and left.

Louise hadn't allowed him back in the house. She'd pushed him out the door, slammed it shut and locked it.

That had been two days ago. He'd had no place to stay since then. It was only when he remembered Stanley boasting about going to the gold fields with a friend that he'd formed his plan, a plan he'd just put into effect.

He was now a gold prospector, and decided to call himself Frederick Alden.

Chapter Two
Summer 1898

Helen Gastrell finished the breakfast the Colonial Hotel staff delivered and waited for her maid, Mattie, to clear away the tray of dishes.

"What would you like to wear today, Miss?" Mattie asked after she'd set the tray on the trolley left in the hallway outside the room.

It was the third week of July 1898, and Helen and Mattie had arrived in Victoria the day before after a long journey by sea and land from London, England. She immediately phoned the Davenport & Son Detective Agency to make an appointment and was meeting Mr. Davenport this morning. She hoped to hire him to find her brother on her father's behalf. She needed to present a professional air since she needed to convince him to go with her to Dawson City.

"My gray skirt, white shirtwaist, and black jacket."

"Yes, Miss."

Helen went into the powder room and did her toilet while Mattie laid out her clothes on the bed. She declined the corset Mattie picked off the bed and settled for her combination, which was a chemise and drawers in one garment. Mattie helped her into the shirtwaist with its long sleeves and then her skirt, which reached below her ankles. Helen preferred the sportier and freer bicycling outfits and bloomers of the new age but, had brought along a few full-length dresses and skirts at her father's insistence because, as he put it, she was representing him and his company and needed to look like a businesswoman.

Helen wasn't sure how coming to Victoria in search of her errant brother was representing her father's company, but she'd gone along with his request. So far, she'd cruised the Atlantic Ocean on a luxury liner from London to Toronto, taken a train from there to Vancouver, followed by a ferry ride to Victoria. And once she'd hired the detective, she would be on a steamship north to the exciting gold fields.

Thinking about her journey, plus looking ahead to the next part of it, made her smile. Since childhood, her parents had instilled in her the knowledge that she could do anything she wanted in her life. They'd wanted her to learn the family textile business, but she'd chosen to attend the London School of Medicine for Women instead. She'd trained at the Royal Free

Hospital, the first training hospital in London to admit women.

She'd graduated this past spring and wanted an adventure before opening her practice. She'd envied David when she heard he was headed to the famous Klondike gold fields so when her father started talking about sending someone to find David, she volunteered. Her father refused to listen to her, citing the long trip might be hazardous to her health. She countered that by stating she was the embodiment of health and very seldom sick. Then he said she should be looking to put her education to work and apply for a position at a hospital. She reminded him that he'd promised her a reward if she graduated in the top ten of her class. She'd been number seven and wanted this trip as her gift. That education had bolstered her confidence in herself, and that confidence made her insist she could do this, that she could travel halfway around the world, find David, and deliver her father's message.

Finally, since no one else in the family was able to go, he agreed.

After Mattie braided and coiled Helen's long brunette hair into a bun at the nape of her neck, Helen set a straw boatman hat with one upturned side on her head and studied herself in the mirror. She was twenty-one years old, tall, and slim. Did she look like the businesswoman her father expected?

Helen left her suite on the third floor of the hotel, rode the elevator to the ground floor and walked out onto Johnston Street. The concierge had given her directions, and rather than take the horse-drawn Hansom cab the doorman offered to summon, she chose to walk. It was a warm, sunny day, and she'd left early to tour this colonial city she'd heard so much about. She was surprised at how modern this capital of the province of British Columbia was with its street cars, paved streets, and tall brick or sandstone buildings.

It was more like cities in other parts of the world she'd visited with her parents than expected. After all, it was out in the far west area of the country of Canada. From the stories she heard, she'd half expected a wooden fort surrounded by natives.

She did have to step around some horse droppings as she crossed a street, but it was no different than in London, where she'd grown up. Here, as there, men scoured the streets, scooping up the droppings and putting them in wagons to be taken somewhere for disposal.

After a block, Helen turned right onto Government Street and came to Yates Street. She continued along Government past View, Fort, and Broughton Streets to the inner harbour. Across the water, she could see the British Columbia Parliament Buildings, which were officially opened last year on Queen Victoria's Diamond Jubilee. As she neared the grounds, she spotted the statue of Queen Victoria on the Parliamentary lawns. Looking at the top of the building, Helen saw the gold-gilded statue of George Vancouver, a great navigator and map maker for whom Vancouver Island and the city of Vancouver were named.

Helen returned on Government Street to Fort Street and turned right. She immediately saw the brick building the concierge had described halfway down the street. Her heart skipped a beat as she neared the detective agency's office. She was going to meet a real detective who solved real mysteries. Helen was an avid reader of mystery stories. When she was sixteen, she started reading Edgar Allen Poe's short stories and poems. He was considered the creator of the detective fiction genre in the early to mid-1800s. It was too bad that he died at the age of forty in 1849. His death was still a mystery. No one knew for sure if he died from a disease, if he was an alcoholic, used opium, or if he'd committed suicide.

What stories could he have written if he'd lived longer.

Another of her favourite authors was Arthur Conan Doyle with his Sherlock Holmes character. That Sherlock figured out any mystery brought to him amazed her.

She'd wanted to solve a mystery like Sherlock Holmes in her childhood mind. She'd even contemplated writing a mystery story, but as an adult, her desire to be a doctor had overridden that thought. She still liked reading mysteries. She wondered if she could consider herself a detective since she was ready to plunge herself into finding out what had happened to her brother? She smiled. She would be sleuthing in the Klondike.

Helen pushed open the door and entered a hallway. The door to the right was half glass with the name Davenport & Son Detective Agency painted on it. She knocked gently, and when she heard someone yell, "Come in," she opened the door. She was immediately in a small office. It had a desk with a chair behind it and one in front in the centre, a filing cabinet against one wall and a smaller desk and tall coat rack along the other. A well-built man with bushy, blond hair and a faint scar on his left cheek sat behind the larger desk, talking on the telephone. He gestured for Helen to sit in the other chair.

"Yes, yes. I know," the man said into the mouthpiece of the upright, candlestick telephone. "I have tried all those suggestions, and none have contributed to finding your husband." He listened in the receiver. "Yes, I will continue to watch for him. Goodbye." He set the receiver in the fork of the switch hook sticking out the side of the stand and looked at her.

"Miss Gastrell, I presume."

Helen nodded. "And you are Mr. Davenport?" She wondered if he was the father or son.

"Private Detective Baxter Davenport at your service." He rustled through some papers on his desk and found a piece of folded paper. He opened it and read, "Your father, Algernon Gastrell, sent me this telegram over a month ago letting me know you were coming. According to it, he wants to hire me to go to Dawson City and find your brother."

"That's right," Helen nodded.

"Why?"

Helen tilted her head to the side, not understanding his question.

"Why does he want to find your brother?"

"That's a personal matter."

Baxter Davenport stared at her. "How long has it been since he's seen or heard from him?"

"The last time Father, or any of us for that matter, saw David was when Father sent him to Canada ten years ago. The last time Father heard from him was when David picked up his August allowance here in Victoria last summer."

"Allowance?" Davenport raised an eyebrow.

"David is referred to as a remittance man. Father sends him a monthly bribe to keep him away from England."

"Ah, the black sheep, sent here because he was an embarrassment to the family. Why did it take your father so long to start looking for him?"

Helen wasn't sure if she liked this man. His questions were abrupt and almost accusing. She also wasn't sure how much she should tell him. After all, until he agreed to go to Dawson City, it was none of his business.

"Before I tell you any more, you have to agree to accept me, as a client, on my father's behalf."

"And go to Dawson City looking for your brother."

Helen nodded.

"Why Dawson City?"

"When David picked up his last allowance, he sent a telegram to Father saying he was going to the gold fields and would send a letter when he was settled. He never did."

"Does your father know how far away that is and how long it will take to get there? Does he know how much it will cost for the passage? Does he know that a gold rush is going on and everyone is heading north? Booking passage on one of the steamships is going to be difficult."

Helen stared at him. So far, he hadn't answered her, just asked a lot of questions. Was he stalling? If so, why? She knew her father offered Davenport & Son a hefty retainer which she had in her purse. He would also have all his expenses paid for on the trip.

"My father is a very smart businessman. He knows what is happening in the Yukon and that this past June, the Canadian Government passed the Yukon Act, separating the Yukon Territory from the Northwest Territories. Dawson, although not having city status yet, is called Dawson City by most people and is the capital of the Yukon." She stared at him, daring him to contradict her. What made him think that because they lived so far away, she and her father knew nothing about what happened in the rest of the world?

"I see you've done your homework."

"And I already have three rooms booked on the steamship *Bristol*. It leaves in two days."

"Three?" Baxter demanded. "I would only need one."

"I'm going too," Helen stated.

"What?" he sputtered. "Even if I was going, which I haven't decided yet, I wouldn't take a woman with me."

"I'm afraid you have no choice, Mr. Davenport," Helen said tightly. "I haven't travelled all this way just to go back home.

I'm going north." Now she knew she didn't like the man.

The door opened and a striking, older woman walked in, limping slightly. She wore an emerald green, velvet skirt with matching jacket. Her rich, reddish-brown hair was tightly coiled at the nape of her neck and small, light green trilby hat perched on the top of her head.

"Miss Gastrell?" she asked as removed her hat and hung it on one of the arms of the coat rack.

"Yes," Helen replied.

"I'm Private Detective Muriel Davenport, the senior partner in this agency."

"Oh," Helen said, flustered. And then she felt embarrassed. She hadn't even thought about there being a woman partner. "I'm very pleased to meet you."

Helen felt a growing excitement. Not only was she meeting real detectives, but one of them was a woman. Maybe her childhood desire to solve a mystery hadn't been so peculiar.

"Has my son explained our position on your matter?"

Helen looked at Baxter, but before she could answer, he said, "We were just discussing it, Mother. Apparently, Miss Gastrell has already booked our passage to leave in two days."

"You're going also?" Muriel asked, sitting down at the smaller desk.

"Yes. And my maid."

"Your maid?" Baxter stammered. "I'd have to look after two women?"

"Baxter!" Muriel warned.

"We don't need looking after," Helen said haughtily. "And certainly not by a man like you. I don't think we need your services." She stood and stormed out the door. She couldn't believe there were still men who thought women needed looking after. Hadn't this past decade of women getting jobs, living on their own, and travelling alone proved anything? Her two sisters had jobs, one as a telephone operator and the other as a music teacher, and she recently graduated from the London School of Medicine for Women and was a doctor.

Helen headed down the street, wondering if there was another detective agency in the city that would help her on such short notice.

"Just a minute, Miss Gastrell," Muriel Davenport called, limping up to Helen. "I have to apologize for my son."

Helen stopped, tempted to ask why. He was the one who insulted her and should be the one apologizing.

"May I buy you a cup of coffee or tea?" Muriel pointed to a small café beside them.

Helen hesitated. She could use something to drink. "I don't think we have anything to discuss. Your son made it perfectly clear that he didn't want to take the job."

"Please."

"All right." Helen nodded and followed Muriel into the café. The smell of soup and homemade bread greeted them.

"Welcome, Mrs. Davenport," a waitress said. She smiled shyly at Helen. "Please follow me to your table."

She led them to a small table in the corner and placed menus in front of them.

"I'll just have a cup of coffee and a piece of apple pie," Muriel said. She looked at Helen.

"Tea and a scone," Helen said. "I haven't had a good scone since leaving London."

"Well, these are considered the best in the city," Muriel said as the waitress picked up the menus and left to fill their order.

Helen looked around and saw there were only women in the room. This must be an all-woman café since most restaurants and cafés still required that a man accompany a woman before she could enter.

"Again, I have to apologize for my son. You caught him off guard by saying you and your maid would go with him. He hadn't expected that."

"I don't see how us going has anything to do with him finding my brother."

"It doesn't, and he will see that. I just want you to know that he has been quite excited about handling your father's request. That's all he's talked about since we received the telegram. He can't wait to start for the gold fields. He is so obsessed that he almost bought a steamer ticket two days ago."

"I'm surprised my father didn't mention that I would also be going. It was decided even before he sent the telegram." Helen wasn't sure how to take this news. Baxter Davenport did want to go and find her brother. He just didn't want to do it with her.

The waitress brought a tray with two steaming cups, and two plates, one with a piece of pie and the other with a scone, a bowl of clotted cream, and one of jam. She set them all on the table and carried the tray away.

Helen cut her scone in half and then spooned clotted cream and jam onto her plate.

"Tell me about your brother," Muriel said as she took a bite of her pie.

Again, Helen didn't know how much to tell her. She still wasn't sure whether Davenport & Son were taking the job. Much had been said over the past hour, but not the words, 'Yes, we will go to Dawson City and find your brother.'

"As I told your son, David is a remittance man. Father sent him here ten years ago when I was eleven and David twenty-one and has sent him money each month to help him support himself. Father received a telegram last summer telling him David was going to the gold fields and would mail him a letter with his address. That letter never came."

"And your father is wondering if he is dead."

"Yes, he thinks he must be because David has never missed picking up his allowance in all the years he's been gone."

"May I ask why your father sent David away?"

"From what I was told, he was a bit of a confidence man and kept swindling people out of their money. Father got tired of making restitution." Helen decided that was all Mrs. Davenport needed to know.

"Do you have a picture of him?"

"Just an old one from before he left." Helen dug the black and white photograph her father had given her from her purse and handed it to Muriel. "It's not very good and taken when he was twenty."

Muriel studied the photograph and then handed it back to Helen. "That's not much to go on. And from what I've heard, thousands of men are in the gold fields. He might be hard to find."

"I have to make an effort for Father's sake."

"Did your father try contacting the Northwest Mounted Police in Dawson? Or put an advertisement in the newspaper?"

"There isn't a telegraph office in Dawson City, so Father sent letters to the police and the *Klondike Nugget* but received no response. He also sent a letter to David. After waiting four months, he decided to send me to find him."

"Could you come back to the office in about an hour? It will give me time to speak with Baxter."

"Will it do any good? He seemed quite adamant."

"I think he'll have had enough time by then to cool down and realize his mistake."

"If he decides not to go, would you consider coming?" Helen blurted out. So far, Mrs. Davenport had asked all the right questions. She might be better at finding David than her son.

"I'm afraid I can't do that. I broke my leg last year, and it didn't heal right. I'm limited to working in the city where it is easier to get around. Baxter is the one who handles our out-of-town cases." She tilted her head. "So, will you come to the office later?"

"I do have some shopping to do." Helen thought of the toiletries she needed for the voyage. She'd have to go back to the hotel and get Mattie to come with her. "Then I'll return."

Chapter Three

Baxter sat and listened to his mother as she pointed out the need for him to go to Dawson City: business had been slow lately as most people had the Klondike gold rush on their minds; they needed the money; it was a chance for him to fulfill his wish to go to the gold fields, a wish he'd had ever since last year when news broke about the big gold strike.

He knew she was right. He'd decided to go to the gold fields last summer, even had his steamer ticket and was ready to leave when his mother fell and broke her leg. He'd sold the ticket and stayed to look after her. He knew she felt bad that her injury prevented him from going, and this was a way to make it up to him. And he had thought so, too, until he found out he'd have to take two women with him.

"I wouldn't mind them coming if it was a holiday," Baxter said. He rather liked the feisty young woman with the English accent who'd come to the office. "But this is our first international case and it could make our name as international investigators. I'll have a job to do and I don't need a rich, spoiled woman who has been pampered all her life coming along. What if she wants to be part of the investigation? What if she gets in my way of asking questions? And her maid will probably flit around, wanting to do everything for her and possibly for me, too. I won't have any time to myself to ask questions or be able to go to saloons and meet men who may know David Gastrell, or even meet up with Gastrell himself. It would be easier to speak with David without his sister hovering around and trying to find out why he hadn't contacted his father."

"I understand all that," Muriel said. "But as our paying client, she can do as she pleases."

"And I don't know if she realizes that we could be gone three months," Baxter said. "It'll take about a month to get there, so we should arrive around the third week in August. We may only have two weeks to find him. We'd have to leave Dawson City by the first week of September to get to St. Michael before the freeze-up of the Yukon River. Plus, you will be running the agency alone."

Muriel looked at him. "You know it's what you want to do. Having two women with you, one being the sister of the man you're looking for, should not be a hindrance. And I'll be able to operate the business while you're gone."

"Is Max Golding still willing to help you?" Baxter smiled. He knew it was a silly question. Max was in love with his mother and always stopped by under the guise of offering his expertise. After all, he'd been a policeman for twenty years. More than once, he'd aided them in solving the mystery of jewellery disappearing or a mysterious death that the police ruled natural but a family member thought was murder.

"Yes, he'll be here anytime I need him."

Did she blush a little at the mention of his name? Baxter wasn't sure. In the three years since his father died, many men had come courting. But she turned them all away, and for some of them, he was glad. But when Max started coming around last year after his retirement, offering his services if they needed them, Baxter had seen a spark in his mother's eyes that hadn't been there since his father died. The two of them might take their budding romance further if Baxter was in the Klondike.

"And just so you know, if you don't go, I will."

"Mother!"

"What? It's a case that needs solving. Someone has to do it. It might as well be us."

"All right, Mother, I'll do it," Baxter sighed. "And I'll do it with Miss Gastrell and her maid tagging along. But I want to speak with people who may have known him here before we go."

Half an hour later, Helen knocked on the door and opened it.

"Come in," Muriel smiled.

Helen did as asked but stood just inside the door, ready to leave if Baxter had another outburst.

Baxter felt a little regretful at his actions earlier. After all, she would want to go to Dawson City and see the brother who had left home so long ago.

"I'll be happy to go to Dawson City and find your brother," Baxter said.

Miss Gastrell stood taller. "My maid and I are still going," she said, her voice defiant.

"Yes," Baxter nodded. He decided to get right to work. "Mother said you have a photograph of him. May I see it?"

Helen took the picture out of her purse and handed it to him.

Baxter studied the black and white photograph of a young man staring at the camera. His head cocked to one side, and a slight smirk on his face looked like he found the picture-taking amusing. It was impossible to tell the colour of his eyes or that of his thick, unruly hair, but it was impossible to tell what colour it was, and also the colour of his eyes. He would need a good description from Miss Gastrell and anyone who knew him while he lived here in Victoria. David Gastrell could have changed a lot in ten years.

"His hair is light brown and his eyes are a sparkling blue," Helen said.

"Sparkling? What kind of blue is that?"

"That's the way I remember them. They seemed to sparkle when he laughed."

"It's probably a good thing you're going," Baxter said grudgingly. "You'd have a better chance of recognizing him in person than I would with just this photograph."

Helen looked at Muriel. "Let me know how much money you need right now as a retainer, and I can pay you. I also have access to all the necessary funds for our stay in Dawson. I booked the passage for the day after tomorrow because I didn't think there would be any difficulty between us."

"There isn't any problem," Baxter said. "I can pack quickly. But I have some things to check before we leave. Do you know where he stayed while he lived here? Did he have any friends we could talk to?"

"David never mentioned any friends to Father. He did tell him once that he was renting a room in Mrs. Grimley's Boarding House."

"I know where that is." He wasn't sure how to tactfully say the next words. "If there's been nothing since that telegram, then maybe he didn't go north. Maybe he didn't leave Victoria."

"If he was still here, he'd have let Father know."

Baxter saw the moment when she realized what he meant.

"We have considered the possibility that he might be dead," Helen said. "The problem is: how would we be able to find out if he died here?"

"I could check with the police and then go to the newspaper offices and look at back issues from that time."

"You mean we could do that."

Baxter swore under his breath. He had been right. She already wanted to help in the search and it was only day one.

"Where is the police station?"

"In Bastion Square, which is just a couple of blocks over on Langley Street. We could go now and talk with them."

"We will need two hundred dollars as a retainer, Miss Gastrell," Muriel said. "I'll draw up the paperwork, and you can sign it when you get back."

Helen nodded and waited as Baxter took his straw hat from the hat rack and plopped it on his head. He held the door open for her. "I'll be back later, Mother."

They walked to the corner of Government and Yates Streets, turned down Yates and then onto Langley where they reached and the three-storey brick building police station.

"Good afternoon, Mr. Davenport," the constable behind the desk said. "How may I help you today?"

"Afternoon, Constable Daffern. I'm looking for a man named David Gastrell. He was last heard from in August of last year." Baxter showed the constable the photograph. "He's ten years older than in this picture."

The constable studied the photograph. "No. I don't recognize this man."

"He never spent time in your jail?" Helen asked. "He wasn't known for his honesty."

Constable Daffern looked at her.

"This is Miss Gastrell, David's sister from London, England," Baxter said, trying to keep the anger from his voice. This was his investigation. He was the one who should be asking the questions.

"As I said, I don't recognize him. Why are you asking?"

"He was supposed to have gone north to the Klondike gold fields, but no one has heard from him. I'm wondering if he even left the city." Baxter put emphasis on the word "I'm" for Miss Gastrell's benefit. "Do you know if anyone who looks like him may have been killed last summer?"

"We've had a transient population since the gold strike in the Klondike last year. Hundreds of men pass through here every day, buying their supplies and boarding steamboats to Dyea in Alaska so they can hike over the Chilkoot Pass to Dawson. Or some go by steamer all the way to St. Michael, Alaska, and sail up the Yukon River to Dawson. A number of men were killed, but most have been identified."

"Were there any unclaimed bodies around the month of August?" Baxter asked.

He knew that was an indelicate way to ask in front of a lady, but he didn't have time to be delicate. They only had today and tomorrow to learn all they could about David and his life here.

"I'd have to go back over the files. If there were, they'd have been buried a long time ago. Come back in two hours."

Baxter escorted Helen out of the building.

"Where are we going now?" she asked.

"We'll go to one of the newspaper offices." This was something she could help him with that didn't involve any interference on her part. "They may have written an article last August about someone dying and not being identified."

They walked the short distance to the Victoria Daily Times building.

"Good afternoon," the man behind the desk said. "Do you wish to place an ad?"

"No, thank you," Baxter replied. "I'm looking for some information about a man who may have died last August."

"Why come here? Why not go to the police?"

"I have, and they are checking. I'd like to read your articles from last August to see if any unidentified bodies were found."

"It would be the same information as the police have."

"Yes, but I could find it now instead of waiting for them to look through their files."

The man pointed over his shoulder. "We have stacks of old newspapers in the back room. They're in order by week."

Baxter and Helen went through the door into a small room with tall stacks of newspapers.

"This isn't going to be easy," Helen muttered.

Baxter smiled as reached up and took the top newspaper off one pile. Could she be changing her mind this quickly? After all, she didn't have her maid to do the job for her. Then he had a horrible thought. What if she decided her maid would help him on his quest instead of her? He shuddered at the idea.

Baxter looked at the date. It was from January of this year. He tried the stack beside it. November of 1897.

"It could be this one." Baxter grabbed a handful of newspapers and set them on the floor. He looked at the top date. October 1897. He set the next handful crossways on the first and kept going until he found the stack published in August. Luckily the papers weren't very thick.

They each picked up one and scanned the headlines. When there was nothing about a death in them, they went through the rest of the newspaper. When that one yielded nothing, they continued looking through the others.

"I found something," Helen said. She read the small headline. "**Body Found In Woods.** The body of a man who went under the name of Stanley Noland was found in the woods between the business district and the lower income area. His head had been beaten in. It looked like robbery, since his money was missing. He was identified by his boss at the saloon where he worked. According to a friend, a steamship ticket to Dawson City was also missing." Helen looked at Baxter. "From the description given, he could be David."

"Well, it sounds like they knew who he was," Baxter said.

"Except that they worded it 'who went under the name of Stanley Noland.' It doesn't sound like they think that's his real name. And David was known for using different names, especially when courting women. He didn't want them to know that he came from a rich family."

"Maybe Constable Daffern can tell us more about him. Let's keep looking."

It was slow reading, and Baxter found the next one. "The body of a man was found in the harbour Friday night. It is estimated that he had been in the water for about three days. There was nothing for identification, and no one reported anyone matching his description as missing. He will be buried in Potter's Field if no one comes forward by this coming Friday."

"What is his description?"

"He was about five foot nine inches with a slim build."

"Again, that could be David."

"So, that's two possibilities. Let's continue to the end of August."

They only found one more prospect. Baxter read: "Early in the morning of August 25, the dead bodies of a man and a woman were found in the cabin of a deserted barge moored in the harbour. The woman was identified as Julie Mason, of no fixed abode. The barge was laden with gas lime, and it is believed the pair climbed into the barge and died of suffocation by the fumes of the gas lime, which is used to purify gas and for the clearing of land. Up to a late hour last evening, the man had not been identified."

"That might be something David would do," Helen said.

"I'll ask Daffern if the man was ever identified."

They finished with the paper for the month with no more bodies being discovered. They stacked them up again and went to the front.

"Did you find what you needed?"

"Yes, thank you," Baxter said.

They headed back to the police station on Bastion Square. "Did you find anything?" Baxter asked Constable Daffern.

"There were three unsolved deaths in August," Daffern said. "A man named

44

Stanley Noland and two others who are as yet unnamed."

"We read the newspaper's account of Mr. Noland's death," Baxter said. "It implied that Stanley Noland wasn't his name."

"We had three witnesses identify him by three different names: Stanley Noland, Charles Fairfax, and Oscar Gilroy."

"So his real name could be one of those or even a different one."

"Yes. Very few men carry any type of identification. We have to rely on family or friends to tell us who they are." Constable Daffern looked at some papers. "The other two were a man who died on a barge and one who drowned."

Baxter nodded. "Were they ever identified?"

"No."

"Thank you, Constable Daffern."

Daffern nodded and went back to the other paperwork on his counter.

Baxter and Helen stepped out of the police station. It was almost dusk, and Baxter was hungry.

"One of those men could be your brother," Baxter said as they walked back to the hotel.

"Yes, that's true."

Baxter had to ask her. "Do you want to accept that one is your brother and he's dead and go back home with the news?"

Helen stopped and looked up at him. "What makes you think I'd do that? I have no proof that any of them is David, and I'll keep looking until I have proof that he is dead."

"I just wanted to know for sure."

"Well, now you know. What do we do next?"

Baxter noticed the word 'we.' He decided to ignore it. "I'll walk you to your hotel, and you can have supper. Tomorrow, I'll go see Mrs. Grimley."

"Why can't we go now?"

Baxter sighed inwardly. Obviously, she wasn't about to be put off. Knowing he wouldn't be able to dissuade her, he decided he might as well prepare her. "Because it's an unsavoury part of the city that you don't want to visit at night."

"Then I'll go with you tomorrow."

"It's not a very savoury neighbourhood to visit during the day either."

"Mr. Davenport," Helen said, crisply. "In my training to be a doctor, I attended to men and women in the very bowels of London. Nothing in this city will shock me."

Baxter was taken aback by her statement. The lady was a doctor? He knew getting a doctor's degree wasn't an easy feat. And it was harder for a woman. No wonder she was adamant about going north with him and being part of the investigation.

She was tougher than she looked. He decided that to argue further would be pointless.

"I'll pick you up at ten o'clock tomorrow morning."

"I'll be ready in the lobby."

Chapter Four

Helen watched Baxter Davenport leave and then walked to the nearby bank. She cashed two of the numerous letters of deposit her father had given her for the trip. She'd gotten used to the exorbitant fees of up to two dollars and a half for the privilege of exchange she had to pay for Canadian money.

Helen went to the detective agency office and entered. Mrs. Davenport was at her desk.

"Please, sit down, Miss Gastrell," Mrs. Davenport smiled.

"I have your retainer fee." Helen set the two hundred dollars on the desk and then sat down. "And please call me Helen."

"Thank you, Helen. And I'm Muriel." Muriel took the money and put it in the top drawer of the desk. She pushed a piece of paper toward Helen.

"This is the contract and a list of the expenses usually paid by the client. And since Baxter will be staying out of town, you will also be responsible for his room and board."

Helen read over the contract that stated Davenport & Son had been hired by Mr. Algernon Gastrell and Miss Helen Gastrell to find or at least, make an effort to find, David Gastrell in Dawson City. She then looked over the expense list: Hansom cab or streetcar fare; meals; compensation for information; rental of any horse and wagon or cart. She wasn't sure if those expenses were fair, but it didn't matter. Picking up the quill pen, she dipped it in the ink well, and wrote: *Mr. Davenport is to report all his findings to me at the end of each day* then she neatly signed her name at the bottom of the expense sheet.

She blew on the ink then handed the paper to Muriel.

"Thank you, Helen. How did your visit to the police station and newspaper go?"

"There were three men killed last August who weren't identified. They may or may not be David, but I'm going under the assumption that David is still alive."

Muriel nodded. "I've learned that it is best to have definite proof of death, philandering, or fraud for my clients."

"May I ask how long you've been in the detective business? It isn't something you think of a woman doing."

"It's not as unusual as you think. My great-aunt Maude was a lady detective for The Pinkerton Detective Agency for two years."

"I didn't know The Pinkertons hire women."

"They do. It started when a woman named Mrs. Kate Warne answered an advertisement for detectives placed by Mr. Pinkerton in a Chicago newspaper. When he met her, he argued it was no occupation for a woman. Mrs. Warne pointed out that as a woman, she could become friendly with the wives and lady friends of suspected criminals and learn their whereabouts. She said that men couldn't help bragging in front of an adoring woman and women were observant and noticed details.

"Mr. Pinkerton hired her, and in one case, she became the confidant of the wife of an expressman for the Adam's Express Company. He was the prime suspect in a $50,000.00 embezzlement of the company. Through Mrs. Warne's efforts, the expressman was convicted of the crime, and she was able to get the majority of the money back."

"She sounds impressive." Helen again thought about her childhood desire to be a detective. It was looking more and more as if it wasn't so unsuitable for a woman after all.

"Mr. Pinkerton thought so. He put her in charge of his newly founded Female Detective Bureau in 1860. That's where my great-aunt Maude worked. She would come here to visit and regale our family with her exploits. I was enthralled with her stories as a young girl and decided I wanted to be a lady detective. But there was no such thing here in Victoria, so I married and had Baxter. My husband had a hardware store, and when he died, I sold it. It took a year of indecision before I finally decided to open my agency. Great-aunt Maude even came for the grand opening."

"That's a wonderful story."

"Yes, most of it has been wonderful, but in the beginning, the sign read Davenport Detective Agency. Many men who came in walked back out again when they found out Davenport was a woman. Most of the women who wanted to hire me supported me. But to grow my business, I had to bring Baxter in as a partner and add Son to the sign."

"So that's why he has the bigger desk and sits in the front of the room."

"Yes. And so far, it's worked."

* * *

Helen was seated in one of the chairs in the lobby when Baxter entered the hotel the next morning. He was surprised to see the dignified woman of yesterday dressed in a beige jacket and brown bloomers gathered just below her knee. She had a brown hat tilted jauntily to one side of her head.

She noted the look on his face. "I'm not a representative of my father today. Today, I am a detective looking for clues as to where my brother is."

"This isn't a game to be played by amateurs," Baxter stated. "You don't seem to understand the danger that could be waiting for us when we get to Dawson. Maybe David killed someone and doesn't want to be found. Maybe someone killed David and won't take kindly to us asking questions about David. Some criminals have no problem eliminating anyone who tries to find them."

Helen stared at Baxter. He supposed she wasn't used to anyone talking to her in that tone of voice.

"I am not taking the search for David lightly," Helen said through clenched teeth. "Since I know my brother better than you I think me helping you will be invaluable."

"And it might be. But you have to understand our search isn't without peril. And you have to do as I say. I am the investigator."

Again, he wasn't sure how she would take that.

Rather than answer, Helen nodded curtly.

Baxter knew that was all he was going to get. He opened the hotel door for Helen to pass through. "Let's be going."

Baxter hailed a Hansom cab and assisted Helen up the low step into the seat. He walked around to the other side. "Take us to Mrs. Grimley's Boarding House," he ordered the driver perched on the high seat at the back above the cab.

"Yes, Sir."

Baxter glared at the smirking driver, then climbed the step and settled beside Helen on the two-passenger seat. Baxter was ashamed of what the driver assumed was their reason for going to the boarding house. It was well-known that Mrs. Grimley rented out rooms to prostitutes to entertain their gentlemen friends. Couldn't the man see that Miss Gastrell was a lady and he a gentleman? Then he grunted. The man probably couldn't think of any other reason for them to be going to the boarding house

They drove through some poor neighbourhoods, some accommodating Asian immigrants, others being all aboriginal. Finally, they reached the area that housed the unfortunate and destitute white citizens.

"Oh, poor David," Helen moaned.

"How much did your father send your brother each month?" Baxter asked, looking at the run-down wooden houses on the street.

"I don't know, but certainly more than it would take to live here."

"Do you know if your brother work?"

Helen shook her head.

The cab stopped in front of a large two-storey house in need of repairs and paint.

Baxter noticed the look of dismay on Helen's face at the sight of the sagging verandah and the boards covering one ground-floor window. "He may have had a gambling or drinking problem that took his money," Baxter said kindly. "You stay here while I go talk with Mrs. Grimley."

"No, I'll come too. She might be more co-operative if talking with a woman."

Baxter gritted his teeth. She hadn't heard a word he'd said in the hotel lobby. "Mrs. Grimley is not known for her honesty, so don't believe everything she tells you," Baxter said as he helped Helen down.

"How will we know what is true and what isn't?"

"That's something we'll have to judge on our own. If you think it sounds like something David would do, we could believe it. If it's out of character, we have to think it over."

Baxter told the driver to wait, and they walked to the house and up the steps. Baxter knocked on the door. When no one came, he knocked harder.

"All right, all right, hold your horses," a voice called as a lock clicked, and the door opened a few inches. A woman glowered from the small opening.

"What do yer want?"

"Mrs. Grimley. My name is Baxter Davenport, and this is Miss Gastrell," Baxter said quickly. "She is looking for her brother, David, who used to live here."

The woman stared from one to the other without saying anything.

Baxter took out the photograph and showed it to her. She squinted at it then nodded. "Ah, yes. He looks like a man who skipped out in the middle of the night. Have you come to pay up his last week's rent and collect his things? I'm not going to store them much longer."

Baxter looked at Helen. She nodded. "Yes. How much does he owe?"

At the knowledge that she would collect some money, Mrs. Grimley opened the door. "Come in."

Baxter let Helen in ahead of him. After Mrs. Grimley closed and relocked the door, they followed her into what at one time must have been a parlour. It had faded red velvet curtains closed over a large window, a worn Persian rug, and tattered furniture. A roll-top desk sat along one wall, and Mrs. Grimley went over to it. She pulled open a drawer and took out a ledger. Baxter could see the year 1897/1898 printed on the front.

Mrs. Grimley opened it and shuffled through the pages. She held it away so they couldn't see any of the writing.

"Here it is. He skipped out without paying his weekly rent of three dollars. And since I couldn't immediately rent out his room because of his clothes, you owe me six dollars."

Helen reached into her purse.

"And I've stored his clothes and other things all this time. That's another thirty dollars."

Baxter's lips twitched as he watched Helen take out two twenty-dollar bills from her purse. She handed them to Mrs. Grimley. Everyone had to make a living somehow.

"I don't have change," Mrs. Grimley grumbled.

"I don't need any. Where are his clothes?"

"Out back in the shed."

Mrs. Grimley turned and led them down a hallway to a back door. She opened it and pointed to a wooden shed with its door hanging open. "It's been broken into so many times that I don't know if there's anything left."

Baxter led the way to the shed and peered in. He heard rats scurrying for cover as he pushed the door further open.

"Baxter had a brown valise," Helen said.

Baxter stepped into the building and waited for his eyes to adjust to the dim light. Broken furniture, valises and suitcases, dirty clothes, and bedding were scattered about the floor.

"I don't think we'll find anything that belongs to him unless it has his name on it," Baxter said over his shoulder as he took out his handkerchief to cover his face. The smell of mouldy clothes, rat droppings, and old food was overwhelming.

Helen stepped in behind him. "Oh," she said, putting her hand to her nose and mouth. "His valise would have his initials, DMC, carved into the handle."

"What does the M stand for?" Baxter offered her his handkerchief.

She shook her head. "The M is for Mercy, my mother's maiden name. My grandfather Mercy had it made especially for David on his eighteenth birthday."

Baxter took two steps to the pile of suitcases and valises and sorted through them. They were mainly empty. He didn't find one with the initials DMC engraved on its handle. But he did find a brown valise with one handle missing. He held it up to Helen.

"Does this look like it could be his?"

She took it and opened it, examined the inside, then ran her hand through it before turning it upside down and shaking it. "If it is, it's not any help."

"Well, it was worth a try," Baxter said.

They stepped back into the sunlight and took deep breaths. Baxter wiped his hands on his handkerchief and offered it to Helen, who did the same. They walked up to Mrs. Grimley, who watched them closely.

"Do you know where Mr. Gastrell worked?" Baxter asked.

"He couldn't keep a job, always getting fired for something or other. He was lucky he had money coming from his family, or he would have starved."

"What about friends?"

"None that came around here. Wait a moment." Mrs. Grimley paused. "There was one chap who came by once looking for him. Said David owed him money. It was the week before he disappeared."

"Did he have a name?"

"None he told me."

"Did you tell Mr. Gastrell?" Baxter asked, wondering if this was a story she was making up.

"Um," again she hesitated. "Um, yes, I mentioned it to Mr. Gastrell when he came back, and he seemed scared of the man."

"Did he say why?"

"No, just turned a little pale, then went to his room. A while later, he left and was gone all night. I have a curfew, and if you're not back by then, you're locked out all night."

"Is there anything else you can tell us about him? Does he still look like his picture?"

"He had a large handlebar moustache when he lived here."

"Thank you for your time, Mrs. Grimley. You've been a big help."

Baxter took Helen's elbow and escorted her around the house to the waiting cab. "Take us back to the Colonial Hotel."

"Well, that didn't yield us much," Helen said.

"No, but I'm sure she was lying to us."

"David told Father he was staying there."

"And he may have, but we only have her word that he skipped out without paying his rent and that someone was looking for him."

"So, you think David may have paid his bill before leaving there, and she only said he had left without paying to get money from us?"

"It's a possibility." Baxter nodded.

"Then he may not have a moustache," Helen said sounding disappointed. "I thought it was a good sign when she said David wore a moustache. None of the three men who died last August had one."

"He may have shaved it off, or the police could have kept that quiet to make sure the person who came to identify the body had the right man. I'll go back to the police station and ask Constable Daffern."

"And we did learn he wasn't good at holding down a job. Which makes me wonder what he's been living on since last August."

"Maybe he struck it rich in the gold fields."

Chapter Five

Helen gave Baxter his steamer ticket and returned to the Colonial Hotel. She wasn't sure what to make of Baxter Davenport. He was stubborn and overbearing but he had a soft side to him. She'd noted the kindness in his voice when he mentioned that David may have had a drinking or gambling problem and that was why he'd lived in such a run-down place.

She knew he was right about the danger. After all, she lived in London and it was a hub for crime and murder. And she had to admit that David could be involved in some sort of crime and maybe even murder.

When Helen arrived at her room she found that Mattie had spread her purchases from yesterday on the bed. There was the new hat, the toiletries, the jacket that matched her mauve bloomers, and a pair of walking shoes. She doubted there was much in the way of transportation in the newly founded city. She would probably be doing a lot of walking, looking for her brother.

"I've packed everything except our clothes for tomorrow and your new things. I thought you'd want to decide what you need to keep out."

"Thank you, Mattie." Helen could almost hear Mattie sniffing in disapproval at what she'd bought. On several occasions, Mattie made it clear she thought Helen had brought too many clothes, shoes, toiletries, and other non-essentials. Mattie herself had one small trunk and occasionally commented on how easy it was for her to pack her things and be ready to go.

Mattie had been a fixture in the house since Helen was a little girl. Ten years older than Helen, she helped her father, the estate's gardener. Helen remembered Mattie playing with her when Mattie and her father had finished their work. Helen enjoyed those times and hadn't accepted that, when Mattie was fifteen, she'd been hired as a between maid. From there, she'd worked her way up to a position as Helen's grandmother's personal maid. Now the hired help, their status towards each other changed. Mattie became formal, addressing her as Miss and not having the time to play. Helen hadn't understood the difference and cried many a night at the loss of her friend.

Helen's grandmother died two years ago, and Mattie moved over to take care of Helen. At the start, she'd tried to curtail Helen's adventurous ways and fun-loving spirit by suggesting alternative activities more suitable for a young woman, but when she understood she couldn't, she got her message across by reproving her in small ways.

At first, Helen had taken exception to her bossy maid but then realized that Mattie only wanted the best for her and that Mattie, too, missed being friends.

"Have you ordered something to eat?" Helen asked. They'd taken all their meals in their room since arriving.

"It will be here at six o'clock."

Helen went to the desk and took out the hotel's stationery. She began to draft a telegram to send to her father. She didn't want to tell him that she'd learned David may have bolted without paying his rent and may have left his clothes behind in his hurry. It seemed that those clothes had been stolen. She didn't want to say she'd paid David's back rent or mention how upset Mr. Davenport had been about her and her maid going to Dawson with him. Her father had insisted his daughters get an education and wanted them to have the same advantages as his sons. Even if she told him that Mr. Davenport finally agreed, he wouldn't be happy to know the man he'd hired thought women had their place. She didn't want to mention that, of three men who died last August, one could be David.

Dearest Father. Tomorrow, Mr. Davenport, Mattie, and I leave for Dawson City. We talked with David's landlady, who told us he now sports a moustache. She recognized him from the photograph, so we should also be able to if we see him. Love to everyone. Helen.

She would give it and enough money to send it, plus a tip, to the concierge tomorrow morning when they left.

After their meal, Mattie drew a bath, and Helen soaked in the bubbles for half an hour before climbing out. Mattie handed her a towel and she dried herself then put on her nightgown. She sat in a comfortable chair while Mattie combed out her hair before tucking it under the silk nightcap that stopped it from tangling.

* * *

Baxter and Muriel closed and locked the agency doors and went to the bank to deposit the retainer. To celebrate, they headed to Levy's Restaurant for supper. Baxter's father, Barnabas, had met Henry Levy when they both took part in the Leech River gold rush west of Victoria in 1864. His father had talked about how Leechtown quickly sprang up with stores and hotels serving about twelve hundred miners. The rush had lasted less than two years, with both men finding enough to build homes in Victoria and set up businesses. Henry opened the Arcade Oyster Saloon, while Barnabus opened a hardware store. They each married and raised families and always remained friends. One of Baxter's friends was Henry's son, Arthur.

A few years ago, Henry renovated the saloon into the Levy Restaurant.

They were shown to a table and given menus. It wasn't until after they'd placed their order that they discussed their new client and her case.

"I think it will be a futile trip," Muriel said. "But Miss Gastrell is determined to go, and it will be a way for you to take part in the latest gold rush. I remember how excited your father was when he went to Leech River. Luckily for us, it wasn't very far from here, and he returned once a month to continue his courtship."

Baxter smiled. His parents had had a great marriage, and Muriel had been devastated when his father died. Baxter had worked part-time in the store and he and his mother shared equally in the inheritance of the store. They had tried hard to keep it open, but competition had been tough, and after many offers by a rival company, they'd eventually sold.

Baxter bought a house with most of his share and found another job. After a year of sitting at home, Muriel decided to open the agency and eventually cajoled him into joining her as a partner. While they had some lean times, they were making a name for themselves.

"So what do you think of Miss Gastrell?" Muriel asked.

Baxter grimaced. "I was right. She wants to be part of the investigation."

"He is her brother. And she doesn't' seem to be the type to sit and do nothing."

"No, she definitely isn't. I had to warn her today that our search could be dangerous. But, in spite of the Albatross around my neck, I'll do my best to find the missing David Gastrell."

"I know you will," Muriel laughed. "Just like you found Mr. Phillips last month after he left town with ten thousand dollars of his employer's money."

"This will be a little harder since I only have an old photograph and a sister who barely remembers him."

When their food came, they ate in comfortable silence. After Baxter paid the bill, he put his mother in a cab and headed to see Merrill at his saloon. Baxter occasionally brought clients or suspects to the saloon because he found they relaxed more after a drink or two. And if anyone in any of the saloons in the city knew of a man named David Gastrell, it would be Merrill.

"Evening, Baxter," Merrill said when Baxter walked up to the bar. "Not falling back on your old ways, are you?"

"No." Baxter hated to admit it but he hadn't handled his father's death very well. The two of them had been very close and while he helped his mother during the day in the store, as soon as it closed he headed to this saloon. He drank and gambled most of the night and then showed up at the store bleary eyed and unshaven the next morning. This had carried on until the store sold and Baxter realized he needed to sober up. He only drank now with clients or suspects. "I'm working on a case, and I'd like to ask you some questions." Baxter took the photograph of David Gastrell from his pocket. "Has this man ever been in here?"

Merrill took the photo and scanned it closely. "Looks like a younger version I knew as David. Used to come in here to play poker, even rented a table for a while. You should know him."

"I should?" Baxter asked.

"Yes. You tried to start a fight with him one night when you'd been drinking. Accused him of picking your pocket."

Baxter thought back to the year of his debauchery. He couldn't picture the face of David. "I don't remember."

Merrill grinned. "You could barely stand. When you took a swing at him, he just stepped back. You fell to the floor, and I had to help you up."

Baxter grimaced. There were many black spots in his memory from when he was drinking. But it stood to reason that he could have crossed paths with David. After all, it sounded like they may have lived the same lifestyle if only for a short time on his part. Would he one day remember their encounter? Might there have been more than one?

"Do you remember what night that was? Was there anything special about it? Like a holiday or something?"

"No," Merrill shook his head. "Just a usual Saturday night. Why are you looking for him?"

"He's supposed to have gone to the Klondike last summer, but no one has heard from him since. I'm trying to find someone who knew him while he lived here to see if he went north or somewhere else."

Merrill shrugged. "Sorry, I can't help you. I haven't seen him in here for a long time."

"Thanks, anyway," Baxter nodded and left the saloon. He stood on the sidewalk and looked up and down the street. The city was full of saloons. There was no way he could get to them all. He wished he had more time to seek out some of David's friends, visit a few gambling halls or try to find out more about him. As it was, the time was late, and he still had to pack for tomorrow.

Baxter tried to conjure up his meeting with David as he walked to his house on Yates Street. But nothing came. Should he tell Miss Gastrell that he'd had a confrontation with her brother? What good would it do? He didn't remember it, and it wasn't useful to their search. His house was a block from his mother's, close enough to be there if she needed him but far enough away to have his own life. Not that he had much of a life. He'd courted a few women over the years but hadn't found love yet. So he spent his days working at the office and his evenings studying the ways of the Pinkertons and learning new techniques in detective work.

Baxter entered his house and went to the basement, where he retrieved his suitcase and carried it upstairs. He surveyed the clothes in his closet and finally chose three pairs of trousers, four shirts, two waistcoats, and his tweed Norfolk jacket. He'd heard about the long list of clothing and supplies people heading to the Klondike were supposed to have. But since he would be returning to Victoria before the fall, he only required a few items. He was sure he could purchase more, if necessary, once there.

He also packed two books: *Fingerprints* and *Decipherment of Blurred Finger Prints*. Both were written by Francis Galton and detailed his belief that fingerprints could be used for individual identification. He also added a magazine titled *The Argosy,* a pulp fiction magazine. He'd been buying the magazine since he'd started working as a detective. He enjoyed reading the fictional detective stories and sometimes wondered if he should try fictionalizing some of the cases worked on by him and his mother. He wasn't sure if he could. The stories in the magazine were so much more action-packed and exciting than his detective job in real life.

* * *

The next morning Helen and Mattie ate an early breakfast, and Mattie sent for the bellhops. They arrived and carried Helen's three trunks and Mattie's one trunk down to the front door. A man waited with a wagon, and the bellhops loaded the trunks into the wagon bed. After giving the concierge the telegram message for her father, Helen and Mattie climbed into a Hansom cab, and the wagon driver followed them to the docks.

The docks were in organized chaos. Sizeable piles of freight were stacked along the wharves, waiting to be loaded onto two steamships by stevedores hurrying up and down the gangplanks. Plus, many passengers were carrying their baggage and supplies onto the ships. The wagon driver gestured to two men who were lounging on a bench. They jumped up and hurried over.

"These are the men I hired to load your trunks onto the boat," he told Helen. "They'll cost you two dollars each."

Helen thought it was a little costly but knew they were her only choice. She had no desire to drag the heavy trunks herself. "Fine. Take them onto the *Bristol*."

None of the men moved. Helen reached into her purse and removed two two-dollar bills, handing one to each man.

"And I'll take my payment now for my services," the wagon driver said.

Helen gave him two five-dollar bills, hoping none of the men would leave without fulfilling their side of the bargain. But she needn't have worried. They each grabbed one of Helen's trunks and hoisted it on their back. That just left Mattie's trunk. Rather than leave it behind, Helen took one handle, and Mattie took the other. They followed the three men.

They had to wait in line to climb the gangplank. The men dropped the trunks on the deck. "The purser will get them to your rooms," the wagon driver said. He touched the brim of his hat at Helen, and the three men left.

Helen showed their tickets to the sailor at the top of the gangplank, who directed them to their cabins on the middle deck.

Helen opened the door to her stateroom and gasped. It was much smaller than she'd expected. There was a single bed with a mattress, a desk and chair, and a closet, with barely enough room to hang her nightgown and housecoat, let alone any of her clothes. There was room under her bed for her shoes, but the big question was, where could she store her trunks? Even if she piled them in the corner....

A curtain hung over the small window looking out on the deck, the railing, and the water beyond. There was a knock at her door. She opened it and found the three trunks she'd just been thinking about lined up in the hallway. They were blocking the way of other passengers looking for their rooms, so she dragged them into her cabin. She thought about calling Mattie to help her but knew exactly what her reaction would be. She didn't need a lecture right now.

The connecting door between hers and Mattie's rooms opened, and Mattie stood in the doorway, a slight smile on her lips.

"Don't say anything."

"I wasn't."

Mattie's smile grew wider, and soon both women were laughing.

"So what am I going to do?" Helen asked. "I can't leave them in the middle of the room. I'd have to hop over them every time I want to get from one side to the other."

"First, I'll get your sheets out and make up your bed. Then we'll sort through them and take out the dresses and skirts you want to wear in the next couple of weeks. The rest we'll leave in them, and I'll move one into my room. We'll stack the other two out of the way."

"Thank you, Mattie. You always save the day."

"That's my job, Miss." Mattie opened one of the trunks.

* * *

Baxter stopped in to say goodbye to his mother before heading to the docks.

"Did you remember to take bedding for your bed?" she asked.

"Um, no," Baxter shook his head. "I completely forgot."

"I'll pack you some." Muriel hurried to her linen closet and took out two sheets, a blanket and a pillowcase. She stuffed them into a valise and handed it to him.

"Thank you, Mother." Baxter bent down and kissed her forehead. "I'll see you again in the fall."

Baxter walked downtown and then caught a Hansom cab to the docks, pushing his way through the crowd and carrying his suitcase and valise onto the *Bristol*. He showed his ticket and was given directions to his stateroom. As he passed what he figured was Helen's room, he heard women's laughter. Must be her and her maid, he thought, hoping they kept their sense of humour. From the stories he'd heard, it would be a long, tedious journey to Dawson City.

His stateroom was small, but he didn't need much. He unpacked his clothes, set his books on the desk, and put his toiletries on a shelf. He made his bed then pushed his suitcase and valise underneath.

Done. Now he had time on his hands. He could go out and tour the boat, but he would just be getting in the way of the stevedores doing their job. And tomorrow would be a better day to start asking questions about David. By then the crew should have settled into their jobs.

Baxter picked up *Finger Prints* and lay back on his bed. He would read until they were ready to set sail. Then he would go on deck and watch as they left the dock.

Chapter Six

Helen opened her top trunk and took out two decks of cards. She slipped them into her leather purse and attached the purse buckle to her belt. She knocked on the connecting door to Mattie's room. "I'm going up to the deck. Do you wish to come?" she said when Mattie opened it.

"I'll get my shawl."

They'd just stepped out into the hall when the door of the stateroom on the other side of Helen's opened.

"I thought I heard voices," Baxter said.

"The steamship should be leaving soon, so we're going up to watch. Would you care to join us?"

"Yes, thank you. I was getting restless in my cabin."

"And today is only the first day." Helen laughed. She introduced Baxter to Mattie, and they walked to the end of the hall and out the doors to the deck. Men and women crowded the railing, yelling and waving to the family and friends they were leaving behind.

Smoke bellowed from the smokestack, and the steamship slowly backed out of the docking berth. It turned and headed out of the harbour. The people moved to the stern and waved until their friends were just specks in the distance. Then with much laughter, they headed to their assigned rooms or places in steerage.

"I brought some decks of cards if we want to play bridge," Helen said. "I'm sure we can find a fourth."

They entered the social room with tables set up for card games, reading or visiting with fellow passengers. They found a table in the corner and sat. Helen took out her cards and set them on the table. She looked around the room. Next to them was a young man reading a newspaper.

"Would you care to join us in a game of bridge?"

The man looked up and smiled. He folded his newspaper, slipped it under his arm and moved to their table. "I'm afraid I'm not very good at the game," he said. "My name is Ronald Webster."

Helen introduced them, and they decided Ronald and Mattie would play against Helen and Baxter.

They cut for deal, and Baxter won. He shuffled the cards and dealt them each thirteen. They looked at their hands, and Baxter began the bidding.

Baxter and Helen won the first game, then Mattie and Ronald took the next two. They continued playing until the first supper sitting was announced, and Ronald left. The three returned to their rooms to freshen up for their meal. When it was their turn, they went to the dining room and enjoyed a hearty supper of roast beef, mashed potatoes, green beans, biscuits, and cake for dessert.

After eating, they joined others in taking a promenade around the deck. In the stern, an impromptu band of two men on violins and a woman on mandolin played music. A crowd gathered around them. Some were swaying to the music, and a couple were dancing.

"I will take my leave now to turn your bed down, Miss," Mattie said. "Good night, Sir."

"Good night," Baxter said.

Helen and Baxter watched the players for a few more minutes then continued their stroll.

"Your maid seems quite sociable," Baxter said.

"As in stepping out of her role as an employee and acting like an acquaintance?"

"Something like that."

"I've known her since I was a baby. Her father was my parents' gardener, and she played with me when she had time. When she was hired as a between maid in my father's household, our friendship ended. She went on to be my grandmother's maid and then two years ago, my lady's maid. So, when necessary, our relationship is formal, but when it's just the two of us, it's more casual."

"So she was obliged to come along as your maid and a companion."

"Oh, she wasn't obliged. When she heard that I was coming here to search for David, she insisted on accompanying me. She said she was the only one who could look after me properly. Plus, she is closer to David's age and knew him better than me."

"Why did your father pick you?"

"As in why did he choose a woman instead of a man?"

"Yes, I guess that's how I wanted to word it."

"Well, at least you're honest. My oldest brother is running the business, my other two brothers are in the military, and my two sisters are working. I was the only one available."

"So you were obliged to come," Baxter smiled.

"Again, not obliged. Insistent. Father was going to hire you by telegram, but I convinced him I should come along to bring the old photograph. And although it's been ten years since I've seen him, I still remember David's voice and laugh. I'm sure I'll recognize his smile. I finally wore my father down until he agreed."

"Yes, I've noticed you have a stubborn streak."

Helen wasn't sure how to take that, so she decided to turn in for the night. "I'm tired from this hectic day. I believe I'll go to my room."

"I'll escort you."

They walked in silence to Helen's stateroom, where Baxter said goodnight. Helen entered and closed the door. Mattie had lit an oil lamp and placed a bowl of water with a washcloth and towel on her desk. Helen washed and dried her face and hands.

Mattie opened the door between their two rooms and entered. "How was the rest of your evening, Miss," she asked as she helped Helen remove her dress.

"It was pleasant. Mr. Davenport and I walked and had a friendly chat," Helen said.

"Mr. Davenport is a handsome man."

"Are you trying to be a matchmaker?" Helen grinned.

"No, Miss, but he isn't married and neither are you." Mattie helped Helen put on her nightgown and cap.

"And I'm going to stay that way until after I've set up my practice," Helen said firmly, climbing into her bed. This trip was her last big adventure before she got down to the business of healing the sick and treating the injured. In spite of Baxter's warning that it could be dangerous, she knew there was nothing to fear from her brother.

"I'll take the bowl of water to the deck and throw it overboard," Mattie said.

When she returned a few moments later, she picked up the lamp and went to the connecting door.

"Goodnight, Miss."

"Goodnight, Mattie."

"And, Miss?"

"Yes?"

"Thank you for bringing me. You don't know what it means to me to have been able to come with you."

"You're welcome, Mattie," Helen said, glad that she appreciated the opportunity Helen had given her to see some of the world.

* * *

After breakfast the next morning, Baxter and Helen strolled the deck while Mattie chose to read in her cabin. Baxter wore his jacket buttoned to his neck. Over her long yellow dress, Helen had wrapped a beige shawl around her shoulders against the cool of the morning mist.

"Your mother said she's had her detective agency for about two years. How long have you been her partner?"

"For the past year." After a moment's deliberation, he decided to tell her what he'd learned from Merrill, the bartender. Baxter had thought about it ever since that night. By admitting he could easily fight when drunk, he knew he'd admit his life, for a while, had been just as wasteful as David's.

"I stopped in to see a friend of mine, Merrill, the night before we sailed. He owns a saloon, and I showed him David's picture. He recognized him."

Helen stopped and stared at him. "Did he say anything else about him? Did he know if David went to the gold fields?"

"He said he hadn't seen David in months, which suggests that David went somewhere." Baxter hesitated. "He also added that David and I had a fight in the bar one night."

"You knew David?" Helen gasped. "And you didn't tell me?"

"I don't remember the night. I was drunk at the time and not much of a fighter. Merrill did say that I accused David of trying to pick my pocket."

"That sounds like my brother," Helen said, sounding dejected.

"I don't know that for sure," Baxter said hastily. "I'm only telling you what Merrill said to me."

Helen continued walking. The steamship was close enough to shore that Baxter watched the scenery go by as he stayed at her side. He waited a few minutes before asking, "Is that why he's a remittance man? Because he's a thief?"

"One of the many reasons," Helen grimaced.

Baxter waited, but she didn't elaborate. She just walked in silence. Did she want to be alone? Baxter wondered. Should he stay with her or let her go?

"Whales!" Someone yelled. "Whales to the starboard side!"

Everyone on the deck headed to the starboard side, jostling each other as they tried getting a good view of the humps of the pod of humpback whales rising and falling in the ocean waters.

Baxter went and stood behind Helen, thankful he was tall enough to see over her head. The ship slowly pulled away from the pod, and some passengers went to the stern to watch them until they were out of sight.

"Wasn't that wonderful," Helen enthused, turning to him.

"Yes." Baxter was happy to see that she'd forgotten about his news. "I've only ever seen one other pod of whales in all the years I've lived in Victoria. A pod of Orcas came into the harbour when my parents and I were down at the beach. I think I was about nine years of age then."

"We saw some whales on our voyage from England, but they were further away from the ship."

Helen began to walk again, and Baxter continued beside her.

"Do you think you could have had other run-ins with David?" she asked. "Maybe you just don't recognize him in the picture?"

"I've tried to remember that night, and I can't. I probably did frequent the same saloons as he did, but I can't remember ever meeting him."

"Maybe something will jar your memory in the future."

"I'm hoping. And now it's time to get start my investigation. The men who work on this steamer have probably made many trips up and down this coast taking men and women north. I wonder if one of them might have met David."

"I like that idea. Let's start by asking the stewards on our deck."

Baxter smiled, tightly. Somehow he'd known that would be her reaction.

They went to their deck and walked along the hall until they found one of the stewards. Baxter took the photograph of David from his pocket.

"Excuse me, Sir. Have you ever seen this man as a passenger on one of your voyages up and down this coast? It would probably have been last summer or maybe early last fall."

The man looked at the photograph and, after a few moments, shook his head. "Do you know how many people we've transported to the Klondike since word of the gold discovery reached us last summer? Thousands and multiple that by the number of ships that sail from Victoria each week. I don't remember who sailed last voyage let alone someone from last year."

"Maybe you might have seen him while on one of your stopovers in Victoria," Helen suggested.

"Don't get much time to partake in any carousing in port. It's discharge the passengers as quickly as possible and get ready for the next ones to come aboard. Time wasted in port is money lost, according to the owners."

"Do you sail with the same crew each time?"

"No. Some only work until they have enough money to spend a week or so in port and then catch the next ship that's sailing. Others make two or three trips before quitting. It's a tough job, and not everyone is suited for it."

"Thank you," Baxter said.

"This could take us a long time if it's new crew members every trip," Helen said as they walked away. "And if the other crew members are like him, they're too busy to pay attention to any one passenger.

"Well, let's try a few more. We might get lucky."

They approached another steward, asked the same questions, and received the same answers. The third one stared at the picture for a long time.

"Why are you asking?"

"He's my brother, and the last we heard from him was that he was going to strike it rich in the Klondike gold fields."

"What colour hair does he have?"

"Light brown," Helen said. "And his eyes are blue. I remembering them sparkling when he laughed."

Baxter hoped for Helen's sake that the man would dredge up some memory. She seemed so hopeful, waiting for him to say something.

"He seems familiar. I think I saw him in Victoria at one of the saloons. He had a table and was dealing poker. I lost my whole pay to him."

"So you didn't see him on one of the steamships going north?" Helen asked, disappointment in her voice.

"No, but you could talk with the other crew members. Someone might have seen him."

Helen nodded and walked away.

"Thank you," Baxter said and hurried after her. "Do you want to come with me while speak with the rest of the crew?"

Helen shook her head. "That was too much of a letdown. I thought for sure he was going to say David had been on one of the steamers heading north. I'm going to my stateroom."

Baxter tried not to show his relief. He knew he had a couple of weeks to question the men on the steamer but he'd like to get it over with now. Work came first.

Chapter Seven

Mattie Lewis stood at the bow of the steamship, watching the water slide by. She enjoyed the feel of the wind on her face. So far, it had been an amazing trip from England. She'd seen places and things she never in her life expected to see. After all, she was a lady's maid, a servant expected to quietly and unobtrusively do her job and not have any life outside work. And she hated it. She'd wanted more since she was a child and went with her father when he worked on the Gastrell estate as their gardener.

She'd envied the Gastrell children, who always had enough to eat and servants to make their beds, clean up after their meals, and put their toys away after playtime. She envied them that they even had playtime. They had everything done for them. The only good part about it was that she had been able to play with Helen from when Helen was about a year old. The little girl had been so cute with her blonde curls and frilly dresses. She liked to run on her short legs and laughed a lot. They'd had fun together despite their nine-year age difference.

Then that all changed when she turned fifteen, and her father told her it was time she found a job. Because of his relationship with the family, she was hired on as a between maid in the Gastrell household. It was one of the inferior servant positions and meant that she went between helping in the kitchen and doing housework. The only positions lower in the female staff were the under nurses who helped look after the children, the undercooks apprenticed to the chef, the kitchen maids who kept the kitchen clean, the scullery maids who were the dishwashers, and the laundry maids.

But she was ambitious and worked her way up to a housemaid. Her duties along with the other housemaids were to open the shutters and drapes in all the rooms to let the morning sun in, clean the hearths and light a fire if it was cold, clean the carpets, and the bedrooms, which was the most important but also the most unpleasant. There were nasty smells to get rid of, chamber pots to empty, and mattresses to be cleaned or refilled with feathers, wool, or hair.

Then, at eighteen, she began working as the personal maid to Mrs. Gastrell, Helen's grandmother. But that old lady had been hard to work for. She'd expected so much. Mattie had to be up and waiting for when her mistress woke. She had to bring her breakfast in bed, haul hot water for her bath, help her dress, do her hair and make her presentable for her company, shopping, or visiting. Then while she was gone, Mattie had to open the window to air her room, hang her night clothes up, check for any tears in the clothes she'd worn the day before, and send dirty clothes to be laundered.

She'd helped the old lady downstairs that chilly, mid-November day David was sent away. Mattie remembered the family and the servants lined up to say goodbye to David as if he were going off to sea or on military training. His father made a big production of giving David money and making a speech about how he would enjoy his time in the new country.

Mattie and everyone else on the staff knew that in private, his father also told David he was never welcome back in the house and that none of the family ever wanted to see him again.

It was only because Mr. Gastrell was getting older and was in poor health that he'd sent Helen to find David. Not to bring him home but to make sure he was still alive and to resume his allowance. Mattie was sure that was Mr. Gastrell's way of relieving his conscience and saying goodbye at the same time.

The old lady finally died when Mattie was twenty-seven years old, well past marrying age and considered a spinster. Since she had no prospects of a suitor and Helen's maid had just married and moved away, she'd been hired as Helen's personal maid. By then, Helen was a young lady attending the London School of Medicine for Women.

Despite having a job, life had not been easy. The servant's quarters were cold and damp. She'd shared a small room with Clara Huxley, a pretty, young farm girl from northern England. They spend the evenings talking and telling each other about their lives. Mattie's had only been about growing up with her two siblings in a small house three blocks from the mansion and then being hired in the main house.

Clara's story had been about the tough life on a sheep and grain farm. She'd left as soon as she could and came to London. Her mother gave her some money but, desperate for a job, Clara was happy to hire on as a scullery maid. Mattie and Clara had the same afternoon off a week and spent it exploring the city. Mattie remembered Clara's excitement at seeing the shops, the lights, the Hansom cabs, and the tall buildings. Her bubbly laugh had floated in the air. At first, she'd been a little intimidated by all the people but had quickly embraced her new life.

Their friendship lasted for two years until Clara's death. Mattie had been heartbroken at losing her one and only real friend, and even today still teared up at the memory of Clara. It had been unfair that she had died so young.

Although she had a job, was fed, and had a roof over her head, Mattie wasn't satisfied with her life. Since she had nothing to spend her money on, she'd saved most of her paltry wages, starting at thirteen pounds per year as a between maid rising to the twenty-five pounds she now earned. She'd also saved the small bonuses she'd received at Christmas time. She had decided to one day use her savings to pay for an education or use it for rent until she found a job that didn't involve domestic service. She now had that money sewed into the hem of her petticoat. She just might need it here in Canada.

When it was decided that Helen would make this journey to find her brother, Mattie had insinuated her way into accompanying her, stating that she'd basically grown up with David and would be able to recognize him better than Helen or anyone else.

And that was truer than anyone knew. It was well known that the young female servants were supposed to be available to any of the males and their guests in many English households. Mr. Gastrell had been a perfect gentleman to all his female employees. Unfortunately, David hadn't.

* * *

Baxter picked up *The Argosy* magazine and went up on deck. He'd spent three days speaking with the crew members about David without success and now he was tired of walking around the ship, playing cards, and listening to music and needed something else to do. He avoided a few tables where gamblers drank and played poker. Being on the job, he needed to maintain his professionalism. He sat in a deck chair and read the table of contents in the pulp fiction magazine. Occasionally it included a short, true crime article. In this edition, he saw the story of Frank Novak, a murderer who had gone to the Klondike to hide and Detective C.C. Perrin, who followed him there. What a coincidence. He was on his way to find someone in the Klondike. He decided to start with that article and then read the fiction stories.

Frank Novak was a married businessman and the father of two sons in Walford, Ohio, in early 1897. He was the postmaster, owned the only bank, and ran a mercantile store. He was determined to be a rich man. However, he also had a gambling problem and was in debt. Deciding to get out of his situation, he took out a $30,000 life and accident insurance policy on himself. On February 7, 1897, he and a friend, Edward Murray, were drinking in his store. Frank hit Edward crushing his skull. He took his money and set the store on fire to hide the crime. He fled Walford.

The townspeople tried to put the fire out, but it was too intense, and they left the building to burn. When the fire was finally out, all that remained was the basement foundation and a brick wall. An inspection revealed a body burned beyond recognition. Also found were a penknife, a pair of pocket scissors, a metal identification tag and dental bridgework. Everyone thought the body belonged to Frank Novak, and his wife, Mary, filed an insurance claim.

However, Edward Murray, a good-natured, hard drinker, was also missing. The citizens of the town and surrounding area were divided as to whose body it was. One set believed Novak killed Murray, and the other thought it was the other way around. There was even speculation that burglars had killed them, robbed the store, and set the fire to hide their tracks. An inquest was held, and a dental assistant named Louis Hasek examined the skull and saw that the upper bicuspid and incisor were missing. He stated that Novak still had those teeth when he was examined a couple of weeks earlier.

The county attorney determined that Frank Novak had concocted a plan to get out of his debts by faking his death and ensuring that his wife would get the insurance money. The Travelers Insurance Company hired the Thiel Detective Agency to find Novak. The agency sent detectives to gather information. Over the next few months, they learned that a man matching Novak's description had travelled to Iowa City, Omaha, Nebraska, Portland, Oregon, and Vancouver, British Columbia. He was using the aliases of Frank Alfred and J.A. Smith. They found that he had booked passage on the Al-Ki steamer to Juneau, Alaska. The agents were called back, and a detective by the name of C.C. Perrin, known as 'Red' Perrin because of his auburn hair and thick red moustache, was put on Novak's trail. Perrin was described as part bloodhound and part rattlesnake.

Perrin went to Ottawa for extradition papers and headed to Vancouver, armed with a photograph and description of Novak's dental records. Novak had a six-week head start. Perrin went north on a steamer to Sitka. He hired a carpenter, and the two sailed to Dyea and hiked over the Chilkoot Pass. They set up camp at Lake Lindeman, and the carpenter built a boat. Five weeks and six hundred miles later, after battling rapids, mosquitoes, black flies, and headwinds, they arrived in Dawson City on the Yukon River.

Perrin began looking for Novak, ignoring the hustle and bustle of the gold rush town. He showed Novak's photograph to the store owners, gamblers, dance hall girls, greenhorns, and old prospectors. No one *had seen him. Then on July 12, Perrin spotted a man who he thought matched Novak's description. Even though the man claimed to be A.J. Smith, Perrin arrested him, read him the arrest warrant and then took him to the Northwest Mounted Police station. There, the post-physician compared the written description of Novak's teeth to the real ones and declared the man was Novak.*

It took another six weeks of travel for the two men to get back to Iowa. Novak was put on trial in November of 1897 and was found guilty of murder.

Baxter put the magazine on his lap and thought about what he'd read. Detective Perrin had shown Novak's photograph to and questioned everyone he could think of without finding anyone who knew Novak. And there weren't as many people in Dawson a year ago as there were now. Baxter had his work cut out for him, but he had little hope of succeeding in finding David. Deep down, he thought David was dead, possibly one of the three unidentified men they had read about in the newspaper.

* * *

Helen and Baxter sat side by side on deck chairs and watched the shore go by, an activity they'd started doing to keep the boredom away. So far on their journey, they'd seen glaciers that grew down the hillsides to the ocean, miles and miles of trees, and even a few grizzly bears that had come to the water to catch fish.

"I've heard the Gastrell name mentioned somewhere before," Baxter said. "It seems like it was something I learned in school."

"It might have been something you read about while studying William Shakespeare."

"Why Shakespeare?"

"According to the story, in 1597, William Shakespeare bought a timber and brick house called New Place in his hometown of Stratford-on-Avon. As was the custom, he planted a black mulberry tree in his garden. William Shakespeare died in 1616, and hundreds of tourists visited the mulberry tree every year after that. Sometime around 1700, Shakespeare's original house was replaced, but the tree continued to grow in the garden. An ancestor of mine, Reverend Francis Gastrell, eventually bought New Place in 1753 and after years of putting up with the tourists wanting to see the tree, he chopped it down in 1756. Supposedly, he sold the wood from the tree to make souvenirs, angering Shakespeare's followers as they considered it a shrine to the playwright."

"Why is this noteworthy?"

"There's more to the story." Helen smiled. "The Reverend got into an argument with the local council over taxes they felt he

95

owed, and he felt he didn't. He then knocked down the house that replaced Shakespeare's house on the New Place lot. There was nothing left of Shakespeare for people to visit anymore, which again angered and saddened his followers. But according to the story, a cutting of the original mulberry tree was supposed to have been planted in the garden to take the place of the original tree."

Baxter thought for a few minutes. "Yes, it seems to me that I heard that story when I studied Shakespeare in my drama class at school. How do people in England feel about your family now?"

"Apparently, all is forgiven because my father had no trouble building his textile business and its doing very well." Helen paused. "I have a question for you now."

Baxter nodded.

"Baxter is a most unusual name. Where does it come from?"

"Human beings haven't always had last names," Baxter began. "They were originally added in the Middle Ages to distinguish one person with the same name as another. For example: James the smith from James the fisherman. They were used, changed, or dropped at will, but over time, they became part of a family's name so that by the late 1500s, most people had last names. Then it became fashionable in this century for parents to give their child a last name as a first name. An example of this could be the mother's maiden name. Anderson originally meant the son of Andrew, so Andrew's son would be called Robert Anderson. Then in this century, it became a man's first name like Anderson Beck."

"So there was a Baxter years ago in your family."

"Well, I like to think that one of my ancestors was a baker and hence had the last name, Baker. For some reason, my parents named me Baxter, a popular Victorian name." Baxter paused and grinned.

"What?"

"I don't think they realized that Baxter is the name for a female baker."

Helen burst out laughing. "Now that is funny."

"I didn't think so when I found out, but now I'm used to it. And not many people know that story, so it seldom comes up."

They watched the scenery go by in silence.

"Why was David sent away?" Baxter suddenly asked.

Helen thought it over before answering. "I don't really know for sure. Being the youngest, I guess I was sheltered from the truth. From what I could gather, he got two women pregnant at the same time, and Father had to pay them off. Plus, he was a bit of a confidence man and was always trying to involve Father's friends in some scheme, much to Father's embarrassment." Helen paused. How much more should she tell him? Should she have told him and his mother more when she first met him?

"Is there something you're not telling me?" Baxter asked.

"First, let me say that I only overheard two servants speak about it just after he left, but David might have killed someone."

"What?" Baxter demanded. "Who?"

"I don't know. I questioned the two staff about it, but they told me I must have misunderstood what I'd heard and I shouldn't be eavesdropping anyway."

"Did your family say anything?"

"No."

"Did you ask?"

"I was only eleven years old at the time. I may have gotten the wrong idea of what was said like I was told."

"Why didn't you tell me this before?"

"Because I don't know if it's true or not."

"Well, I don't like the idea that the man I'm going to be asking about might be a killer. It could be putting my life in danger."

Chapter Eight

The man who now called himself Frederick Alden dressed in his finest trousers, shirt, and waistcoat and stuck his diamond pin in his tie. He admired himself in the mirror. He'd had his hair and beard trimmed and his moustache waxed this morning. If he did say so himself, he still cut a dashing figure, which was why he couldn't understand his lack of success when he tried courting Belinda Mulrooney.

When Freddie, as he liked to be called, first arrived in Dawson, he'd rented a cabin from Miss Mulrooney and found a job working for the Alaska Commercial Company Store. As soon as he realized how rich Miss Mulrooney was, he'd turned on his charm. Over the winter, he was friendly and helpful and complimentary with her. He said everything he'd learned women like to hear and done everything he'd learned women like a man to do. But she spent much of her time at her hotel in Grand Forks, at the confluence of Bonanza and Eldorado Creeks in the heart of the gold fields. When it looked like there would be a food shortage in the area, he'd sold her some of his ton of supplies to help feed her customers at the hotel. But none of it had worked. She spurned his advances, and he eventually started looking elsewhere.

Then she sold that hotel and moved back to Dawson. At first, he thought it was because she realized her mistake and missed him and his helpful, kind ways. But she hadn't. She had come to start construction on the biggest and best hotel in Dawson. He quit his job and started working on the building crew. He tried to make sure he met up with her in some way most days. But again, she rebuffed his advances. Since he found construction life too demanding, he quit and set up his table at a saloon, paying the owner a percentage of his earnings.

He then turned his charm to the dance hall girls. They took in a lot of money each night, and there was nothing for them to spend it on. He would take them flowers and tell them about the great deal he had to buy into a well-paying claim. He offered them the opportunity to buy a share and make their fortune. Unfortunately, there were too many men with gold dust in their pockets for the girls to pay attention to him. Plus, there were a lot of men who were using that same story. Some were honest and just trying to get ahead, while others were not.

Since he hadn't had any success with the women on this side of the Yukon River, he was going to see the two women who lived in a big white tent on the other side. They arrived near the end of July and caused quite a commotion when they hired four men to transport the tent across the river to West Dawson, as the small group of tents and cabins was called, and then paid many more men to set it up.

Freddie heard the stories that were circulating about the women. Mrs. Hitchcock was the widow of a Navy Admiral, while Miss Van Buren came from a well-off family. According to the *Klondike Nugget*, they spent their time travelling around the world. When they decided to go to the gold fields, they brought a portable bowling alley and an animatoscope to show movie films. They wanted to set them up as businesses for entertainment and to make money.

While the women arrived with a large amount of supplies on a barge towed by the riverboat, *Leah,* they had sent another ton of goods and other things they'd brought north with them from San Francisco on a separate riverboat called, *Rideout*. It was now the third week in August, and the *Rideout* still hadn't reached Dawson.

Freddie had an ace to play if he needed it: his friend Paul Gamon. Paul had a stellar reputation in the town. Everyone knew and trusted him. If he was part of the plan, Freddie was sure the women would agree to become involved.

Freddie met Paul last fall when he arrived in Dawson. He'd seen Paul deliver split firewood to the store for their stove. Everyone seemed to like him, so Freddie began chatting with Paul soon after that delivery. He wanted him as a friend, someone whose name Freddie could mention when talking with shop owners or miners, someone who would vouch for him. Freddie learned that Paul had been one of the first residents of Dawson. He saw that Paul worked hard, was honest, and had put away a tidy sum of money. He'd made sure to keep his not-so-stellar life away from Paul. Over the winter, he'd operated his own poker table in a couple of saloons in Dawson and run honest games. But honest games didn't pay him the money he wanted.

On the side, he'd worked a couple of scams with another man in Grand Forks, usually conning a miner out of some of his gold. He doubted the miners would brag about being so easily duped, so he wasn't worried about Paul hearing about it. But again, none of that paid in a big way. He needed a sizable score, which gave him enough money to catch one of the last riverboats out of here and arrive back in Victoria with a nice-sized nest egg. And he would use Paul's name today to make that happen.

Freddie walked down to the river and hired a man to row him over to West

Dawson. He knew men often approached the women, who turned down most of their propositions. He hoped his speech would win them over and called out to the ladies from the open flap at their tent. A gentleman didn't enter a woman's abode without her permission.

When he was asked to enter, he stepped in and introduced himself.

"Good afternoon, Ladies." He bowed slightly and smiled his best smile. "My name is Frederick Alden, and I have come to pay my respects."

"Welcome, Mr. Alden. My name is Mrs. Hitchcock, and this is Miss Van Buren. Do come in and tell us about yourself."

Freddie was led to an area with two deck chairs and some boxes to sit on.

"You have to excuse our accommodations," Mrs. Hitchcock said. "Much of what we purchased to bring with us has not arrived yet."

Freddie sat on one of the boxes while Mrs. Hitchcock sat in a chair. The tent had been set on the ground, and the wildflowers and grasses still grew inside it.

"Yes, the freight business is not what it should be here," Freddie said. He was suddenly nervous. These women came from rich and prominent high society families. The women he'd conned out of their money in the past had worked or were left a small insurance from a dead husband. They were happy for the attention of such a handsome man as he and fell in love quickly. But these two women had an air of self-sufficiency about them. They didn't look like they would be easily fooled. And they certainly didn't look like they needed a man around.

"Would you like a cup of coffee?" Miss Van Buren asked.

"Yes, please." Freddie had rehearsed his speech many times, but he wasn't sure how long he should chat with them before bringing up the reason for his visit.

Miss Van Buren went behind a screen and returned in a few minutes. "John will be out shortly with our coffee." She sat in the other chair.

Freddie decided to turn on his charm. He smiled his most winning smile. "I have to admire you, ladies, to have come all this way. According to the *Klondike Nugget*, you are quite an adventurous pair."

"We are trying to see as much of the world as we can," Mrs. Hitchcock said.

"This is quite the tent." Freddie looked around. A large bearskin rug and a few smaller ones lay on the ground. A shelf held magazines, books, and a graphophone. His eyes rested on the black Great Dane lying by Mrs. Hitchcock's feet. "How did you manage to get such a magnificent dog here?"

"He's a good traveller and listens well."

"And what about you, Mr. Alden?" Miss Van Buren asked. "Was it gold that brought you to Dawson?"

This was his opening.

"I came here from Victoria last fall," he began. "I have to confess that I knew nothing about prospecting when I arrived, so I hired on to work on a claim to learn. I was paid in gold dust and saved most of it, hoping to have a claim of my own one day. And now I have purchased a one-third share in a well-paying claim."

While none of it was true, Freddie was sure there was no way for the women to check his story. If they wanted to know who his partners were, he would give them fictitious names and say they had gone prospecting for other claims.

Before Freddie could go on with this story, a man appeared with a tray. He set it on one of the boxes and left. Mrs. Hitchcock handed Freddie a cup and saucer, then cut a piece off the cake and set it on a small plate. Freddie didn't want any cake since eating it would put a stop to his speech. But he felt it would be impolite to refuse, so he balanced the cup and saucer beside him on the box and took the plate. He held it in his hand while he continued.

"The claim I own the one-third share in is so profitable that we bring out a hundred dollars a day in gold. I am looking to purchase another third or even the full claim.

But to do that, I will need partners." Freddie took a bite of his cake and let the women think over what he'd said. In the past, he'd found that if he explained how lucrative his plan was, some women would offer to help finance it without him asking.

"That sounds like a fine opportunity for someone." Mrs. Hitchcock set her cup and saucer on the tray. "Unfortunately, you've come at a bad time. We have given many men money for their grubstake so they can go stake a claim or for part of a claim so they can work it, that we are worried we shan't have enough money to leave." She stood. "And now you'll have to excuse me. I have some writing to do."

Mrs. Hitchcock looked at Miss Van Buren. "Don't forget we have company this afternoon, and you need to make your biscuits."

"Yes," Miss Van Buren said. She turned to Freddie. "Thank you for coming to visit. It was nice meeting you."

It took some time for Freddie to realize he was being dismissed. And he hadn't even asked them for anything or been able to mention Paul's name. He'd been chatting about himself, as they had asked. But he wasn't going to let them know he was offended.

"Thank you for the coffee." He set his cup and saucer on the tray along with the remainder of his cake. "I hope we meet again."

He smiled and bowed slightly, then walked out of the tent.

"The gall of those women," he muttered as he walked to the river. "Refusing me while giving to many others."

* * *

It was evening when Baxter and Helen stood on the deck and watched the shore go by as they sailed up the Yukon River. They were close now, so close to the gold fields. Baxter could feel the excitement building in him.

A week ago, the *Bristol* had stopped at St. Michael, Alaska, and they and the other passengers had moved all their belongings to the riverboat, *Weare*, to make the journey to Dawson. Baxter has spent the week asking the crew of the *Weare* about David but again, with no success. Too many men of various heights, weights, hair colour, and eye colour had travelled this river in the past year.

Today, he'd made a list of possible people to question once in Dawson City: the police, the saloon owners, storekeepers, the miners themselves. While the crew on the ocean steamer and riverboat David had travelled on would only have known him a few short weeks, he was bound to have made acquaintances and friends in Dawson in the past year. Plus, he might have even made a few enemies.

Now, Baxter stood on the deck watching the activity on the river. He'd been surprised at the the number and sizes of the boats going in both directions. There were men in canoes or scows or on rafts. There were men with sails on their small crafts and men using poles to navigate the river.

They met many other riverboats heading down the river to St. Michael. All were filled with passengers and supplies. The passengers would wave and yell across the water. He wondered how many of them were taking gold out with them. Sometimes they passed a riverboat that was slower than them. Again there was yelling and waving, and occasionally a snide remark made about the passengers getting out and pulling the boat using a line on shore. It all seemed in good fun.

So far, the riverboat had stopped at every settlement along the way, dropping off passengers and supplies and picking up passengers. Sometimes it was a quick stay, while at other times, he and Helen had been able to get off and explore. There were few residents in most of the places. Most of them had heeded the call of gold and gone to Dawson.

The boat's whistle sounded just as Helen joined him on deck. They'd been told the riverboat was going to stop at Circle City this afternoon and they watched as the boat approached the town. The main street followed the curve of the river. There were many one and two storey high log buildings, their fronts facing the water. The street went into the distance to the right but to the left it curved out of sight.

The largest building had the name *McQuesten's Alaska Commercial Company* above its doorway. A tall flagpole, with a large US flag hanging limply in the still air, rose from the roof.

When the boat was secured to the dock, the gangplank was lowered and passengers surged off. Baxter and Helen waited until most of them had left before disembarking. They passed a pile of wood waiting on the bank of the river to be loaded for the steam engine's boiler.

The boat's crew began unloading the supplies, carrying sacks of flour down the plank, across the dock, up a slight hill and through the door into McQuesten's store.

"Let's start there," Baxter suggested.

A short, slender man with dark hair and a small moustache was checking the bags and boxes that the boat's crew had brought in. He looked up and smiled at them.

"May I help you?"

"Thank you but we're just looking around," Baxter said.

He nodded and went back to his work.

The shelves were full of winter clothing and boots, food stuff like sacks of oatmeal and bags of tea, and other sundry items like dog harnesses, fishing equipment, saws and axes, pots and pans, and fire pokers.

They stopped at the counter and Baxter bought them some butterscotch candy.

"Are you Mr. McQuesten?" Helen asked.

"Oh, no. He's a much larger man. I'm Otto. I'm looking after the store while he's in Dawson."

"It seems like many from along the river have gone to Dawson," Baxter said.

"Some places were like ghost towns for a while but people are slowly returning."

"Have you ever met a man named David Gastrell?" Helen pulled her brother's picture from her purse and showed it to him.

Otto studied it then shook his head. "Who is he?"

"My brother. We're looking for him."

"I've never heard of him nor met him."

Baxter had gotten used to receiving that answer from everyone they'd asked so far and decided to change the subject. "What is there to see here while we wait for the boat to sail again?"

"There's the opera house, a church, a library, and a couple of dancehalls," Otto said. "Not much happening in any of them right now but the doors might be unlocked so you might be able to look in."

They stepped outside and walked along the sidewalk and then went behind the front buildings to see the rest of the town. They passed the opera house, the bills describing the upcoming shows were old and faded. They could hear piano music coming from one of the dance halls but for most part the town was silent. Many of the log cabins along the short streets appeared empty.

When the boat whistle sounded they hurried back to the dock.

* * *

It was still light out a few days later when the *Weare* tied up at the bank for firewood. The captain had to stop often to replenish the wood supply 'to keep the ship steaming along' as he laughingly explained to everyone. Some of the crew went and checked the wood but quickly climbed on board again. They told the captain that it was all green. The boat continued up the river and stopped again about an hour later. This time the wood was stacked and ready to be loaded.

Baxter and Helen watched as crew members formed two lines to load wood onto the deck. The man closest to the woodpile picked up a block of wood and passed it to the man behind him. He, in turn, passed it back, and it continued until it landed near the engine room. Some men were serious and worked hard, while others turned and smiled at the women watching them. They would take a log and cradle it like a baby, while others would act like cats pouncing on the log. One man kept catching Helen's eye and smiling as he hefted the wood to the man behind him. Helen blushed a little and lowered her eyes.

Baxter and a few other men jumped off the boat and walked along the riverbank. The weather was warm, and the smell of the earth and trees was wonderful. But soon, all the wood had been loaded, and the whistle blew, 'All aboard.' Baxter hurried back and was the last one to leap on board.

The crew began moving the wood blocks down to the boiler room, while the captain steered the boat back into the river.

It was getting dark when they passed a boat stranded on a sandbar, the second one Baxter had seen. Some passengers had gotten off to lighten the load, and the crew was using poles to try and push the boat off the bar.

"Do you ever stop to help?" Baxter asked one of the crew.

"Only if it belongs to our firm. If it's from a rival firm, then we just wave and pass on by. It's our job to beat them to Dawson with our goods."

They usually tied up for the night but it was a full moon, so the captain decided to continue sailing up the river. While Helen and Mattie went to bed, Baxter stayed with some of the other passengers and experienced the night sailing. There hadn't been any problem with the steamship sailing on the ocean all night, but here the river alternated between deep and shallow.

They had gone a few miles when suddenly there was a crunching sound, and someone yelled, "Aground." The engines were put in reverse, but it did no good. The riverboat wouldn't move.

"Would the gentlemen kindly leave the ship to lighten it?" the captain yelled.

Baxter and nine other men walked down the lowered gangplank and stood to one side on the sandbar. Some crew members stabbed ends of poles into the sandbar and pushed while Baxter and the passengers heaved on the side of the boat. They could feel it moving, and someone yelled, "She's off." They scrambled up the gangplank again, and the ship continued sailing.

"Get out your pole and take soundings," the captain yelled at one of the crew.

The man put the pole in the water and called out depths. "Three feet. Four feet. Four foot six." The captain told him to bring the pole in when the number reached five feet.

Baxter finally went to bed. The excitement was over. They continued on their way but slower and were still sailing when Baxter woke up in the morning.

Chapter Nine

As Mattie walked the deck of the riverboat, her thoughts turned to Clara. How she would have loved to come on this trip. She was always up for any adventure. On one of their afternoon jaunts, they'd paid the price of admittance and entered the British Museum. They'd been scared to touch anything so just wandered the rooms under the watchful eye of a guard.

"Let's find the Reading Room," Mattie whispered.

"Why?" Clara asked. "I don't know how to read."

"Just come."

They walked into the Reading Room and looked way up in awe.

"Oh," Clara said, her mouth hanging open.

"This is the second largest dome in the world," Mattie said.

"How do you know?"

"I read it in a newspaper. And there are over a million books on the twenty-five miles of shelves."

"I wish I could read," Clara sighed.

"I can teach you."

"You would?" Clara asked in astonishment.

"Yes, then one day we can come here and read some of these books."

"Ahem," a voice said behind them.

The girls turned.

"The museum will be closing soon," the guard said. "It's time for you to leave."

"Yes, Sir," they both mumbled. They hurried out of the room and then out the museum.

"Well, at least he called us ladies," Mattie laughed as they walked away.

"Someday we'll come back all dressed up and show him we can be ladies," Clara declared.

It was a few months later when Clara had approached Mattie. "Let's go see where that man killed those women."

And that was how they'd started wandering the slums of Whitechapel during the reign of the man dubbed *Jack the Ripper*. They visited the sites of the first four attacks. Mattie remembered how they'd held hands in great fear and trepidation each time they walked down on of the streets and how they'd hurried home before dark.

"Who could be doing such an awful thing?" Clara asked after they'd visited the street where Catherine Eddowes was found.

"I don't know but I'm grateful that even though my life is one of a servant, I have a roof over my head and enough to eat."

116

"Yes, it would be terrible to have to work on the streets," Clara agreed. "I wonder how many of them started out like us but became pregnant with a child and were dismissed without any money. I've heard of that happening to many girls."

"Me, too, but Mr. Gastrell doesn't do that."

"How do you know?" Clara glanced at Mattie as they walked.

"Because his oldest son got one of the chambermaids pregnant and Mr. Gastrell gave her some money and sent her back to her family."

The ferociousness of the last murder on November 9th scared them enough to make them abandon their quest. In fact, they never went back to Whitechapel. Not that they'd had time anyway.

There had been a lot of upset in the household over the past two months. Mr. Gastrell and David were always fighting and everyone in the mansion, family and staff, hid from both of them. Then David was sent away in mid-November, and Clara died the first week of December.

* * *

It was August 24th when Helen stood on the deck with most of the other passengers and watched as the riverboat glided towards

Dawson City. In front of the city, three long docks were so crammed with people that she expected them to collapse under the weight. A huge white tent and a few smaller tents and shacks were on the opposite side of the river from Dawson.

On the shore above the docks, stores of all kinds, some no wider than ten feet, lined the main street in one and two-storey high log and lumber buildings. There were also other buildings in various stages of construction. The screeching of saw mills and the pounding of hammers filled the air. Hundreds of tents of all sizes sat on the hillside behind the city. To the north of them was a mountain with a massive silver-looking scar on its front from a landslide.

It had been a long voyage on the North Pacific Ocean to the town of St. Michael and a dreary trip up the Yukon River to Dawson. Helen was so happy when the Captain announced last night they would be arriving at Dawson City this afternoon.

"Is this what they term a city in the north?" she asked one of the crew on the deck.

"Yes, Ma'am. Dawson City isn't a city yet, but it is the official capital of the newly founded Yukon Territory. There are more people here than in Victoria, where you came from."

"But it looks like the majority live in tents."

"They do, but they're still considered citizens."

Most of the passengers hurried down to their cabins. It was time to get ready to unload. Helen continued watching as the boat docked and ropes were thrown out to men to secure it.

"Look at all the men," Helen said to Baxter.

"Yes, there's quite a crowd of them. Plus, there will be more in the buildings and tents and at the gold fields."

"It might be harder than we thought to find David." For the first time doubt that they would be able to find David crept into Helen's thoughts.

"Let's leave our luggage here until we find hotel rooms," Baxter said.

After telling Mattie their plan, they went out on deck again. The crew was busy unloading the freight, and the other passengers were eager to get off the boat. Helen and Baxter squeezed their way along the deck and down the gangplank to the dock.

"Oh, the smell," Helen said when they were up on the street above the dock. She wrinkled her nose at the odour of human waste, unwashed bodies, and garbage much like some older parts of London.

"That looks like a good hotel." Baxter pointed to the three-storey wooden building that towered over the other buildings on the street. It had the name *Fairview Hotel* across its front.

The street was a mass of men, some in jackets, some in shirtsleeves. Most wore a derby hat, a felt slouch hat, or a soft cap, and many had beards. Helen found herself studying their faces as they walked past. But the jostle and movement made it impossible to get a good look at any individual man.

"Do you think he would recognize you?" Baxter asked.

"I really don't know. I'm a lot younger than him, and he mainly ignored me when he lived at home."

They walked along the boardwalk on Front Street to where Front Street changed to 1st Avenue. On the corner stood the hotel. It was still in the finishing stages, with men building railings on the verandah and upper deck. They climbed the verandah and entered the lobby. A large chandelier hung over the centre of the room. The open door to the right led to a saloon and the one to the left to a hallway. They went to the counter.

"Good afternoon," the woman behind the counter said. "I'm Miss Belinda Mulrooney, proprietress of this hotel."

"I'm Miss Helen Gastrell, and this is Mr. Baxter Davenport. We want to book three large rooms."

"Oh. I'm afraid that's not possible. I do have two rooms with single beds available on the second floor. They weren't designed with women in mind. There is a common area with beds curtained off on the third floor."

Helen looked at Baxter. She didn't want Mattie accommodated on the third floor with just a curtain for a wall.

"I'll take the third floor," Baxter said. "But I'd like to be moved to the second floor as soon as there is an open room. We're going to be here for about two weeks, and I'd like privacy."

"There will be one available tomorrow." Miss Mulrooney turned the guest book towards Helen and Baxter. They each signed it, Helen putting down Mattie's name for the second room.

They went back onto the street and walked to the dock, where another riverboat had arrived. Its passengers eagerly carried their goods down the gangplank and onto the street.

"I think we need to hire some men to carry your trunks to the hotel," Baxter said.

Helen waited while Baxter went over to a group of four men. She watched him gesture at the ship as he spoke to them. They nodded and followed him back. Each man picked up a trunk at the staterooms, and Baxter carried his suitcase and valise. The group went down the gangplank and up onto the street. They walked to the Fairview Hotel.

"You have rooms twenty-one and twenty-two, Miss Gastrell. I apologize for the beds. Eventually, I want to have brass bedsteads. And we don't have the glass for the windows yet. That's on order, like a lot of things I need. Mr. Davenport, you have bed seventeen on the third floor."

The men carried the trunks up the stairs and deposited them in front of rooms twenty-one and twenty-two. Helen took four, one-dollar bills from her purse and handed them to the men.

"Thank you," they each said as they accepted their payment. They turned and went back downstairs.

Mattie opened her door and dragged her trunk into her room. Helen went to her room and peered inside. It was slightly larger than the cabins on the steamships. It had a single, primitive, wooden bedstead with a mattress, sheets, and a blanket. There was a small washstand with a tin basin but no pitcher, although there was a slop bucket for used water. Beside the basin was a flat piece of wood with three long nails pounded in a circle. Inside the circle was a candle.

There wasn't a closet or wardrobe, just a few pegs on the wall for hanging clothes. But, as Miss Mulrooney said, the rooms were designed for men who probably didn't have much in the way of clothes and really didn't care where they hung them up at night.

At odds with the spare accommodations, though, was the brightly flowered Brussels carpet on the floor. It would have been expensive to buy and transport all this way. However, it did brighten the room.

Helen went to look out the window. Pushing aside the cheesecloth covering, she peered through the opening at a view over the roofs of buildings beside the hotel. She wouldn't mind being cramped in this room as much as she had the cabins onboard the boats coming here. She had a city to explore and a brother to find. She wondered if there was a place where she could store two of her trunks and the clothes in them that she wasn't using. She hoped she wouldn't have to stack them in this cramped space, and Mattie wouldn't have to take one into her room.

This time Mattie didn't laugh at Helen's predicament with her trunks when she came out of her room.

"There's enough space to keep the one with my toiletries and the clothes I need. I'll ask Miss Mulrooney where I can store the other two," Helen said as Mattie opened one of the trunks.

"The weather is warm here, so you need to keep out your light walking skirts, shirtwaists, and bloomers," Mattie said.

Helen stood so Mattie could open the other two trunks. She sorted through Helen's clothes, organizing the ones she thought

Helen would need into one trunk and hanging some on the pegs inside the room.

Baxter came down the stairs and over to them. He carried his suitcase and valise.

"Something wrong?" Helen asked.

"A hanging blanket is not a very strong deterrent to a thief," Baxter said. "May I leave these in your room while we are gone?"

"Yes," Helen nodded. "I have to go speak with Miss Mulrooney about storing two of my trunks, and then I will be ready to start looking for my brother."

"I'll come with you. She can be the first person we question."

Helen and Baxter walked down to the ground floor and to the desk. Belinda Mulrooney smiled at them. "Everything fine?"

"Yes, thank you," Helen said. "Do you have a room where I can store two of my trunks?"

"Most certainly. There's a corner in my office where you can put them. They'll be safe there."

"Thank you. Could you send a porter to bring them down in about an hour? My maid is rearranging my clothes for me now."

"And have you ever seen this man?" Baxter produced the photograph of David.

"He's my brother; his hair is light brown, and his eyes are blue," Helen explained. "He might still have a British accent."

Belinda studied it and then shook her head. "I don't think so. Does he have any scars or other distinguishing marks?"

"He might have a moustache."

"Most men here have moustaches or beards. Why are you looking for him?"

"He's been missing for a year. The last my father heard from him was that he was headed here."

"Well, I've been here since the spring of 1897, and I don't believe I've ever met him."

"That picture is ten years old. He may have changed a lot in that time."

Belinda scrutinized the photograph. "No. He doesn't seem familiar at all."

"Where is the police station?" Baxter asked.

"The Northwest Mounted Police barracks are just a short walk from here. Follow Front Street around the curve at the mouth of the Klondike River," Belinda handed the photo back. "They keep on top of what's happening here."

"Is there a post office here?" Helen asked.

"Yes. Are you expecting mail?"

"My father mailed a letter to my brother. I'm just wondering if he picked it up."

"It's on King Street." Belinda described how to get to it.

"I think we should talk with the police first," Helen said, as they crossed the lobby. "If David's being his normal self, they may have had to arrest him for drunkenness or attempted robbery or some sort of scam."

"No," Baxter said abruptly. "You should get something to eat while I go to the police barracks."

Helen stopped and looked at him. "What do you mean? I'm coming with you."

Baxter shook his head. "Now that we are in Dawson it's time for me to get serious about my investigation."

"I thought we were doing this together."

"Well, we're not. I've told you before that this could be dangerous and I would appreciate it if you did some sightseeing or stayed in your room."

Helen was speechless. She had thought he'd realized she would be an asset to his search for David. But her first instincts had been right. He thought a woman's place was out of the way in the home. She was seething.

"I'm paying your wages, so I have a say in that decision."

"Technically, your father is paying my wages," Baxter pointed out. "And in this frontier town of mainly men, having a woman with me will stop some men from talking."

Helen knew he was right, but she had been looking forward to seeing how a real detective worked. Plus, she wanted to test her mind with whatever clues they may find. It would be a welcome change from the serious studies she'd been doing for years.

"I think the police will talk to both of us especially since David is my brother and I came all the way from England to find him. We can decide what we do after that."

Helen watched as Baxter gained control of his anger.

"That's fine with me," he said, tightly then turned on his heel and left the hotel.

Helen hurried after him. They stepped out into the sunshine and headed south on the boardwalk in the direction of the Klondike River. The sidewalk and street teemed with men walking in both directions. Helen was surprised at how sad most of them looked. Certainly not the happy, excited men she thought she would see when they arrived. These men had a look of despair on their faces as they moved listlessly in pairs or groups along the street. Some were dressed in stained white shirts with suspenders holding up patched trousers. Others wore dirty, faded jackets over their shirts. Most had beards of various lengths, and their faces above the beards looked worn and lined. They were still polite, moving aside so Helen and Baxter could walk past.

Along the waterfront, boats of every style lined the banks. Some looked as if they were used as places to live by their owners.

Helen and Baxter came to a stockade of ten-foot upright poles set in the ground as a boundary marker. There was a sign at the gate with the name Northwest Mounted

Police on it. They walked through the gate into a yard with one completed, single-storey log building and two more under construction. They continued to the completed building and entered. A man behind a counter wore a scarlet Norfolk jacket, blue breeches, and a brown leather belt with a revolver holster.

"Good afternoon," he said.

"Good afternoon, constable. My name is Mr. Baxter Davenport, and this is Miss Helen Gastrell. I'm a private detective from Victoria, hired by Miss Gastrell to come here and find her brother, David Gastrell." Baxter produced the photograph. "He's supposed to have come here last fall, but their father hasn't heard from him since then. I'm wondering if you may have seen him."

The constable took the picture and looked at it. He shook his head. "Since gold was discovered here in the fall of 1896, thousands of men and some women have come and gone from here. Right now, there is an estimated 25,000 to 30,000 men and women in the Klondike area, which stretches from here to Grand Forks on Bonanza Creek where the gold was initially discovered."

"So he hasn't been arrested for fighting or operating a dishonest game of poker?" Helen asked.

"Not that I know of, but I've only been here for two months. You'd have to ask one of the senior constables." He turned and went to a back room and returned with an older man.

"This is Mr. Davenport and Miss Gastrell. They are looking for a David Gastrell, Miss Gastrell's brother." He picked up the photograph from the counter. "Have you heard of him or seen him?"

"David Gastrell," the older man said. "The name is familiar. Just a moment." He left and returned in a few moments, a piece of paper and an envelope in his hand. "This is the letter your Father sent us. The mail service is quite sporadic, and we just received it three weeks ago. I asked some of the saloon owners, and none of them had hired a man with the last name Gastrell. I was getting ready to send your father a reply, explaining that while we were still asking about your brother, with the number of men wandering the streets here and living along the creeks and rivers, it would be an impossible task to find him."

"He might have kept the name David and changed his last name," Helen said. "or changed both. He isn't the most honest man."

"If he is a poker player, I suggest you visit the saloons in town. You could start by asking Tom Chisholm at the Aurora Saloon. He might recognize the picture."

"Where is that?" Baxter asked.

"It's one of the many saloons on Front Street. It's a lively place, so it might be too busy and noisy for you to talk with him."

"Thank you." Baxter picked up the photograph and put it in his pocket.

"That went well," Helen said as they left the barracks. "And it proves that you need me to explain that the man we are looking for is my brother."

Baxter didn't answer.

"Since I'm not interested in going to the saloon with all its smoke and men drinking and gambling, you go while I head to the *Klondike Nugget.*"

"Why there?"

"My father sent them an advertisement to publish in their paper asking David to write home."

"And why didn't you tell me this before?"

"It wouldn't have done any good until we got here." Teach him to get all superior with her.

They walked back along Front Street until they found the newspaper office. They entered and went to the counter.

"May I help you?" the man sitting at the desk asked.

"I'm Miss Helen Gastrell, and this is Mr. Baxter Davenport. Mr. Davenport is a private detective. My father, Mr. Algernon Gastrell, sent you a letter asking you to place an advertisement in your newspaper."

"Ah, yes. I received that letter and payment and placed the notice in my newspaper as requested." He went to a table behind his desk and sorted through stacks of newspapers. He found one and brought it back. "Here it is." He opened the newspaper to the *Personals* and showed it to Helen.

"Mr. David Gastrell is requested to write home for allowance. Family would like to hear from you," Helen read. At least they knew that if David had bought a newspaper and read it, he would know their father wanted to contact him.

"Thank you," Helen said.

The man nodded and took the newspaper back to the table.

"May I buy a copy of the past three newspaper editions?" Helen asked. She took some money out of her purse.

The man bent down and drew some papers from under the counter. Helen paid for them and carried them out of the building. She'd read them later. Maybe there was something in them that might help their investigation.

"Now, let's go see if David has picked up his mail at the post office," Baxter said in an authoritative voice when they were on the street again.

They followed Miss Mulrooney's directions to King Street and found a large crowd of men standing outside the building.

"Are you waiting to go in for your mail?" Baxter asked one of them.

"Yes, but the post office has closed for the day. We have to come back tomorrow."

Chapter Ten

It was late afternoon, but Freddie Alden was already at his table in the Northern Saloon. Usually, he didn't arrive until after eight when all the night's activities began, but he'd decided to come early. He was having supper with Paul later.

He dealt out five cards to each of the men across from him. His actions were automatic: exchanging cards when requested, checking his hand to see if he had a winning combination, and watching for someone cheating.

He had a lot on his mind. First, he was beginning to wonder if he was losing his touch with women. He'd wooed them in the past and even wed a couple when necessary. They usually were lonely women who wanted a man to make them feel safe, protected and loved. He'd been able to get them to agree to finance his schemes before running off with their money.

He'd been angry when the two women in the big white tent rebuffed him. He hadn't expected them to fall for his smooth talking on their first meeting, but he'd at least expected them to listen to his plan. They were always helping others, giving to the needy, looking after anyone who was sick in West Dawson, and allowing church services to be held in their tent. But they'd certainly been less than polite with him.

Since he'd visited them, he heard they'd gone and staked their own claims on Bear Creek. If he had known that was what they wanted to do, he could have offered to do it for them or to accompany them. That might have given him a better chance of them being friendlier towards him.

Ever since he'd arrived, he'd kept an eye on where the gold from the claims on Bonanza and Eldorado Creeks was stored. At first, the prospectors kept their gold in tobacco cans and boxes in their cabins. Then some enterprising men set up a transport system. They would take supplies in wagons to Grand Forks and return with sacks, cans, and boxes of gold dust and nuggets in their wagons. The drivers would take the gold to the Alaska Commercial Company Store, where was stored in their vault. The vault was fourteen feet by twelve feet by nine feet high and made of steel. The AC Company, as it was called, also had an assay office behind the store and was able to melt the gold dust it received as payment for goods into bricks for transportation out on their riverboats.

When the Bank of British North America and the Bank of Commerce opened in May and June, miners, town merchants, and government agents moved their businesses to the banks. Freddie heard that when the Bank of Commerce opened, they had a million dollars in bank notes. They exchanged the money for gold dust and nuggets and were able to ship out $750,000 worth of gold two weeks later.

He'd robbed banks in the past, but while the ones here had cash, they mainly held gold which would be too heavy to carry. And if he insisted on taking paper money, the only way in and out of Dawson was by the river. He couldn't make a quick getaway with his loot. The Northwest Mounted Police kept a strict eye on everything, and they would be hard to evade.

But now fall was coming, and he wanted to leave Dawson with money, a lot of money, enough money to set him up in the luxurious lifestyle he craved. No more relying on the trivial savings of the women he'd courted and convinced to give him. No more of the petty amounts he'd gotten from his cons. He wanted one last big scheme that would set him up for life.

His dishonesty and underhanded ways didn't bother Freddie. Those qualities had gotten him this far in life. And he planned to use those qualities to help him leave Dawson with enough gold to set him up for life.

* * *

Mattie followed the porters carrying the trunks down the stairs to Miss Mulrooney's office.

The door was open. Mattie knocked on it.

"Come in," Miss Mulrooney looked up from her paperwork and smiled.

"Thank you for letting us keep them here, Miss Mulrooney," Mattie said as they entered. She watched the men safely stack the trunks in the corner.

"The least I can do for making you lodge in the small rooms. I hadn't expected ladies from England to stay in my establishment so soon."

Mattie smiled at being called a lady. She liked Miss Mulrooney.

There was a quiet knock behind her. She turned to see a woman in a long black dress and white apron standing in the doorway, holding a tray with a teapot, teacup, sugar and cream, and a plate of small cakes.

"Please bring it in, Catherine," Miss Mulrooney said. She looked at Mattie. "Would you like to have tea with me?"

"Oh, ah, yes, ah, I'd like that, Miss," Mattie stuttered, shocked at being asked to stay and have tea with this prominent hotel owner. After all, she was a servant with no right to speak with a woman of Miss

Mulrooney's stature. She took a deep breath. "Thank you, Miss."

"Could you bring another cup and saucer, Catherine?"

Catherine set the tray on the table, nodded, and left the room.

"Sit down, Mattie." Miss Mulrooney indicated the chair in front of the desk. "And call me Belinda."

"Yes, Miss, um, Belinda." Mattie slid into the chair.

"Have you worked for the Gastrell family long?" Belinda asked.

"Since I was fifteen, Miss. Fourteen years."

"That's a long time."

"Too long," Mattie said before she could stop herself. She blushed at her blunder. She'd never told anyone about her dissatisfaction with her job.

Belinda inclined her head to one side. "Is it time for a change?"

Mattie hesitated, then said, "Yes." But before she could say anymore, Catherine returned with her cup and saucer.

Belinda poured the tea into each of the cups and passed one to Mattie. "Help yourself to the cream and sugar and a cake."

Mattie poured a little cream into her cup and picked up a spoon to stir it. This was the first time someone poured her a cup of tea and offered her cakes. She was so used to doing it for others.

"Do you have anything special in mind?" Belinda asked.

Mattie hesitated. "I've heard the dance hall girls here make a good living."

"Yes, they do, but it's a lot of work. They are on their feet from when the band starts at around eight at night until eight in the next morning. Their only day off is from midnight Saturday night until two am Monday morning."

"Why that time?" Mattie sipped her tea.

"The Northwest Mounted Police close down all the saloons, dance halls, and theatres for Sunday. In fact, most of the town is closed down. No one is supposed to do anything in the way of work on penalty of a fine or a day chopping wood."

"What other type of work is there here?" Mattie asked.

"Oh, there's a lot for women. You could work for me in the kitchen, cleaning, or as a waitress. You could get hired in a woman's dress shop or a bakery."

"Those aren't much different from what I do now," Mattie said, slightly dejected. "What about setting up a business? I do have some savings."

"What type of business are you looking at?"

"I don't know. I hadn't thought much about it until now."

"I'm afraid there are enough stores and cafes and hotels. There are newspapers, dentists, doctors, pharmacies, and every business type found in the southern cities."

"What about buying into a gold claim?"

"The good-paying ones are selling for fifty thousand dollars and up, and the worthless ones are selling for whatever the seller can get."

Mattie couldn't hide her disappointment. She had thought she could come here, get a job, work for a while to see what was needed in the town, then supply that need.

"How did you start out?" She wondered if she was being presumptuous to be asking.

"It's a long story. I set up a sandwich stand at the 1893 Chicago Exposition and made enough money to move to San Francisco, where I opened an ice cream parlour. The next-door neighbour decided to burn his building down for the insurance, and mine burned, also. I left there and worked on a steamship plying the waters between California and Alaska. When gold was discovered in Juneau, I moved there and then came here in 1897. I brought silk underwear, bolts of material, and rubber hot water bottles. I sold them at a profit, built cabins for miners to rent, and bought a diner. When I heard about a small settlement forming at the junction of the Bonanza and Eldorado creeks, I decided to build a roadhouse there. I immediately sold it and began construction on this one."

Mattie was amazed at this woman. She'd had the most exciting life Mattie ever heard of. She didn't let misfortune stop her.

"Can you suggest anything for me to do?" Mattie hoped for some suggestions from this woman with so much experience.

"I'm afraid not," Belinda said sadly. "But my offer of employment in my hotel is open."

Mattie nodded and stood. She set her cup and saucer beside Belinda's on the tray. "I'll take this back to the kitchen for you."

Chapter Eleven

It was early evening when Freddie leaned against the saloon wall and took from his jacket pocket his tin of pre-rolled cigarettes. He removed one of his last five, stuck it in his mouth and put the tin back. He found his matchbox in his other pocket, struck a match on the edge and lit the cigarette. He inhaled deeply, needing that. It had been a long, tiring day.

But all his thinking had paid off. He'd come up with the perfect plan to make his fortune and leave Dawson without getting caught. He had to decide how to mention it to Paul and ask for his help. This new plan was risky, and he needed assistance to pull it off.

He was now waiting for Paul to meet him here to go for supper. Freddie felt good again. Last week Paul had bought a wagon and began hauling supplies to Grand Forks and bringing back gold from the mines. He hoped their friendship would compel Paul to help him to carry out his plan.

"Ready?" Paul stepped up beside Freddie.

"Yes." Freddie thoroughly stubbed out his cigarette on the street. All the buildings in the town were wood, and anyone putting their cigarette out on the boardwalk risked a beating by the business owners and townspeople. No one wanted to have to fight a fire. "Where are we going?"

"I thought we'd eat at the Fairview Hotel dining room."

Freddie hesitated. He knew Paul only wanted to go there to spend time with Pearl Owens, who worked as a waitress. Paul was in love with Pearl and had been as long as Freddie knew him. Paul had been distraught when Pearl only wanted him as a friend. And then he'd been stricken when she'd become engaged to a doctor who arrived in Dawson this past spring. Freddie didn't know why Paul would want to distress himself by seeing her.

"That's fine with me," Freddie said. At least he'd be there to distract Paul.

It had been years since Freddie had had a friend, in fact, not since he'd met Wilbur in Ontario. They'd headed west across the country, supporting themselves by stealing from stores, rolling drunks, and begging farmers for food in exchange for some work. Usually, they'd show up in the late afternoon, promise a day's work for a meal, eat a good supper with the family and then sneak away in the middle of the night. Once they reached a cow town named Calgary, they'd honed

142

their pickpocketing skills and lived on what they managed to find in wallets.

Freddie and Wilbur had hung around in small gangs, and sometimes the gang would roll a drunk coming out of a saloon. But the gang members would turn on each other in a heartbeat if one did something another didn't like. Freddie and Wilbur preferred to run on their own.

Their favourite scam was where Freddie dressed up as a priest, and Wilbur would be his assistant. They would go to a catholic church where Freddie introduced himself as Father Coudrin from some far-off city. He would present the appropriate documentation to the priest and be given the hospitalities of his residence. On a day when the priest was away, Father Coudrin and his assistant would visit a jewellery store to purchase a gift for a cardinal in his home city. He would pick out some high-quality pieces and arrange to have them sent to the priest's residence. When the jewellery store owner arrived, Wilbur would meet him at the door and invite him in. He would take him into a room where Father Coudrin waited. Father Coudrin then explained that he wanted to show the jewellery to another priest and would leave the room. He and Wilbur would slip out the back door.

Sometimes the trick worked mainly because the jeweller was excited about selling such expensive items and trusted a priest to be honest. Sometimes it didn't work because the store owner didn't totally trust a priest to be honest.

Then Wilbur took sick and died.

Freddie had gotten drunk and ended up in jail for a few days. There he'd met a man who taught him how to shuffle and deal cards so that he could distribute any hand he wanted. Freddie found a saloon that allowed him to run his own poker table for a percentage of Freddie's take. That worked for a while, and then he'd met Christine while checking out her father's shop for a possible robbery. When he realized she had an inheritance from her grandfather, he wooed and courted her and proposed in three months. She accepted. While discussing wedding plans, he convinced her to lend him the money he needed to buy some diamonds that a friend was selling at a discount.

"He wants money quickly," Freddie said. "We can double our investment."

Once he'd cashed her cheque, he'd walked away from the relationship. And that was the first of many women he'd swindled in Calgary. One had insisted on marriage before handing her money to him, and he'd agreed. After all, he didn't care if he had a wife. He never intended to be a husband.

After taking her money, he left Calgary and continued west to Victoria on Vancouver Island. There he married his second wife,

Brenda, to get the money she'd saved from her teaching job. He'd liked Victoria, and instead of leaving as he should have, he found another woman desperate for a man in her life. He married her and was just about to invest her money in the restaurant when Brenda showed up and spoiled everything.

When Freddie arrived in Dawson, he'd heard that the mounted police were tough on criminals. In some cases, they kicked the man right out of the city. So since coming to Dawson, Freddie had tried working at an honest job. He'd really tried, but it went against his nature to pass up an opportunity to relieve someone of their money or anything else they might have that he could see a use for. After all, they would be more careful if they really wanted to keep it.

So far, he'd only been caught once and had spent an afternoon chopping wood as punishment. He'd been afraid that Paul would end their friendship, but instead, it had grown over the past few months.

Freddie wasn't sure why, but he was grateful and afraid. Afraid that he was getting soft, that he was letting his feelings get in the way of his plans. What would happen if he had to make a choice?

Freddie and Paul walked to the Fairview Hotel and entered the lobby. The band was there playing like it was every evening. Through the doorway, they could see the gamblers at the tables in the saloon. They went in the opposite direction to the dining room.

Pearl's face lit up when she saw them. Freddie had spoken with her a few times, and he could understand why Paul fell in love with her. She always had a smile on her face, was kind and thoughtful, smart and beautiful. She wrote articles for one of the newspapers here in town and one back in her hometown of Halifax.

Paul told him the story of their first winter in Dawson, how she and her cousin, Emma, supported themselves by baking sourdough bread and selling the loaves to the men in town. Paul set up a business of splitting wood to sell to the town's stores, companies, and individuals. He'd also worked in a saw mill and occasionally as a bartender. Paul had fallen in love with Pearl, but she'd loved another man named Joseph. When Joseph left town, Paul thought he'd be able to win her affection, but she only wanted friendship. So now Paul was her friend.

"Good evening, gentlemen," Pearl said formally. "Follow me to a table."

Freddie knew she'd been told to address all men that way who came to eat in the restaurant, but he liked the way she called him a gentleman. If she knew his background, though, she probably wouldn't even talk to him.

"It's nice to see you, Paul," Pearl said as she led them through the full dining room to a table in the far corner. There was conversation, laughter, and the clinking of silverware on china. Belinda had definitely outdone herself on this room. "And you, too, Freddie."

When they'd sat down, Pearl handed them each a menu. "I'll give you a few minutes to decide."

Sometimes Pearl could spend some time visiting with them, but this evening she was busy, only taking their order and then delivering their plates of food before rushing off to another table. Freddie could see that Paul was disappointed. He tried to keep the conversation going as they ate.

"Let's go have a game of checkers," Freddie suggested at the end of the meal. Paul was an avid checker player and had taught Freddie the game. Now they had a friendly rivalry going. He would bring up his idea over a game.

"Yes, let's."

They stood, and Freddie paid for their meal. Paul lingered until he caught Pearl's eye and waved. She smiled and waved back.

Chapter Twelve

"You and Mattie have supper while I go and talk with this Tom Chisholm before the saloon gets too busy," Baxter said as they walked through the ever-moving crowd of men to the Fairview Hotel.

"When will you eat?" Helen asked.

"Later." Baxter held the door open for Helen. "And don't go asking any questions of anyone."

Helen entered the lobby. A band played softly beside the counter. She stopped and listened, then climbed the steps to the second floor. The trunks were gone from the hallway. She opened her door and saw that Mattie had pushed the one trunk she kept into the far corner against the foot of the bed. Baxter's suitcase sat on top. She set her newspapers beside it.

Helen went to Mattie's room and knocked.

"Would you like to go down to the restaurant for supper?" Helen asked.

"I am getting hungry," Mattie said.

The two women went down the stairs and through the door into the dining room. A waitress dressed in a long black skirt and white shirtwaist came up to them. They were shown to a table for two in the corner and given menus. A linen cloth covered the table, and there were matching napkins. Each place setting had sterling silver cutlery, crystal drinking glasses, bone china teacups and saucers.

"This is quite the hotel," Helen said as she looked around the room. A crystal chandelier was suspended in the centre. Paintings hung on two walls, gilded mirrors were on a third and lace curtains covered the cheesecloth over the open windows on the fourth.

"Yes, Belinda said she is trying to bring some sophistication to this rugged town."

"You were talking with her?"

"When I supervised storing the trunks, she asked if everything was to our liking. I mentioned how splendid this hotel was, and she told me it had been her dream since coming here in the spring of 1897. She'd brought some rubber hot water bottles, silk underwear, and bolts of material with her. She sold all of them and used that money to open a restaurant and build some cabins to rent. Since the gold was discovered on the Bonanza and Eldorado creeks, she constructed a two-storey log roadhouse at their confluence. She then sold that and built this hotel. It had its grand opening at the end of July."

"She accomplished all that in a year and a half," Helen said with admiration. "Ambitious woman. We need more women like her to prove that we are as intelligent and strong as men."

Helen scanned the menu and was surprised at the offering.

The waitress came over to take their orders. She looked at Helen.

"I'll have the tomato soup, the chicken en casserole, boiled potatoes, lettuce salad, and a peach tart for dessert. And a cup of tea."

"And I'll have the tomato soup, chops and mushrooms, green peas, and preserved pears." Mattie handed her menu to the waitress. "And tea, also."

"Did you have any luck with the mounted police?" Mattie asked after the waitress left.

"A constable told Baxter to go to the Aurora Saloon and talk with one of the owners. He's there now. But I've decided I'm not going to wait for him to do all the work. Maybe I can't go in the saloons that David is most likely to frequent, but he does have to eat, so I thought I would ask the staff here if they know or have heard of him." She shook her head. "It's too bad that I didn't bring two photographs of David. Describing someone does not give as clear a picture of that person as a photograph does, even if it's ten years old."

When the waitress returned with their soup, Helen stopped her from leaving. "My brother David Gastrell came to Dawson last fall, and since then, my family hadn't heard from him. Have you ever heard that name?"

"No, Ma'am, I haven't. What does he look like? Do you have a photograph?"

"Not with me. He's about five foot ten inches, slim build. He has light brown hair and lovely blue eyes. He might still have a slight British accent."

"A lot of men here have British accents. Anything else?"

"He has been known to grow a moustache."

"And he also has a scar on the palm of his right hand," Mattie added.

"He does?" Helen asked. "I didn't know that."

"You would be too small to remember. He said he cut it with an axe trying to chop kindling to start an outdoor fire with his friends. It bled a lot but wasn't very serious."

Helen shook her head. "I haven't been telling anyone that. I'll have to in the future."

"It's been a lot of years. It's probably faded by now and not even noticeable."

"Sorry, but I'm still unable to help you." The waitress shook her head. "And I'll leave you to your soup."

When the two women finished their meal, Helen said. "The evening is warm, and it's still very light out. Would you care to go for a stroll?"

"And we can watch for David?" Mattie smiled.

"I doubt that we would be so lucky."

They stepped out onto the sidewalk. The sun was still bright on the horizon even though it was after nine o'clock.

"The land of the midnight sun," Helen said.

"It must be amazing to see on the summer solstice when the sun sets and rises at the same time."

They began walking along the sidewalk.

"That looks like a bazaar." Helen pointed across the street. "I noticed it earlier when Baxter and I went to the police barracks. Let's go see what they have for sale."

They crossed the street and came to an array of goods being sold out of water-stained tents, scows, and what looked like hastily assembled shacks. They found food, clothes, some of which was badly worn, games, jewellery, and much more.

"Why are you selling all this?" Helen asked one man who had rows of canned milk for sale. "Don't you need it to live here?"

"I'm leaving this hellhole, pardon the language, as soon as I have my passage home."

"But aren't you here to find gold?"

"There ain't no more gold claims to be had. All the claims were staked last year, but no one told us," he said bitterly. "They just sold us all the supplies and gear we were told we needed and sent us on our way. We spent months fighting our way through the deep snow of the Chikoot Trail to the Chilkoot Pass where we had to make about a hundred trips up the Golden Staircase cut in the snow to the top of the Pass. After we got to Bennett Lake we built boats for our supplies and sailed down the Yukon River only to find nothing here for us." He gestured at the other Klondikers with their goods. "Now, most of us just want to get back home."

The man in the next stall selling bags of flour leaned over. "And more men are coming every day. It's lucky that the steam companies offer cheap passage for those who want to leave."

So that was why all the men looked so dejected, Helen thought as she led the way back to the sidewalk. She looked at the men wandering the sidewalks. There was nothing here for them. All their dreams were dashed as soon as they arrived. She suddenly felt distressed. Had their trip been for naught, also?

"What if David decided to leave here?" she said to Mattie. "What if he was on one of the boats we met as we came up the river?" This was something she hadn't thought about.

"I don't suppose there is any way we can find out except locate someone who knew him. Maybe Mr. Davenport is doing that right now."

"Yes, maybe." Helen nodded. "I hope he learns something."

"Do you wish to continue your walk?"

"No. I think I'll retire for the evening. It's been a long day."

"I'll go turn down your bed. Would you like a cup of tea?"

"Yes, that would be nice."

Mattie hurried ahead of Helen into the hotel. Helen stopped and listened to the band for a few minutes, then went and stood at the door into the saloon. Did any of the men in there know David? Would they answer her if she walked in and asked, or would they insist she be removed?

She turned and climbed the stairs, and went to her bedroom. Mattie had lit the candle on the washstand. She'd also found a pitcher of water which was set beside the basin. There was a towel on the bed. Baxter's suitcase and valise were now beside her open trunk, taking up more of the little space she had.

Helen looked at herself in the hand mirror Mattie had tied to one of the hooks. Her hair needed a good brushing, and her face had a streak of dirt on it. She looked tired; she was tired. It had been a long day and they'd learned nothing. She washed her face and hands.

Mattie returned with a tray. She set it on the bed and Helen gratefully picked up one of the cups of tea. Helen sipped her tea and then tried one of the scones. Not as good as those at home, but at least it was a scone. And she'd been subjected to a variety of different types and flavours since leaving England.

Mattie remained standing as she drank her tea. "What do you wish me to do with Mr. Davenport's luggage, Miss?"

"Well, I certainly don't want him entering my room in the middle of the night looking for it."

"We can't leave it out in the hall either," Mattie said. "And he won't know to knock on my door if we put it in my room."

"I'll put it beside my door. That way, he can reach in and grab it if he so desires."

"He's a gentleman. I doubt he will do that. I'll take it down to the front counter. They can give it to him when he comes in."

The women placed their teacups on the tray. Mattie picked up the valise in one hand and balanced the tray on her forearm. She opened the door then picked up the suitcase in her other hand. "Good night, Miss," she said, carrying them out the door.

"Good night, Mattie." Helen closed the door.

Helen took the newspapers she'd bought and looked at the front pages. It appeared they were published every three or four days. She chose the one with today's date and scanned the front page looking for any headline that might be of significance. There were none, but on the next page one grabbed her eye.

Look Out For Gold-Dust Swindlers.

Promising Looking Sacks Turn Out To Be Bogus.

Helen read the article with interest. Apparently, some men who wanted to gamble put gold dust in a sack and took it to a gambling hall. They gave the poke to the dealer and asked for a stack of chips. The dealer put the sack in a drawer in his table. The men then played poker, faro, or whatever game they choose, and their losses were recorded on paper and set beside their poke. If they had winnings and decided to leave the game, they traded their chips in for more gold dust and were given their poke back without it being checked. If they lost, their losses were taken out of the gold dust in their sack, and the remainder was returned to the player.

Some men filled the sack with shot instead of gold and handed it to the dealer. If they continually lost, they then left the table on some pretext and never we back. The poke was opened to reveal the shot. However, if the dealer was observant, he

156

would notice that the shot bag rolled instead of sitting flat, and was able to stop the gambler from playing. Some men even took it further by filling the sack with black sand so that it was close to the same weight as gold and sat like gold dust.

Helen looked out the window. This could be one of David's tricks. She would have to show the article to Baxter.

Helen read another article about the formal opening of the Church of the Immaculate Conception by Rev. Father Judge the past Sunday.

There were advertisements for the businesses in the town. One was for the Fairview Hotel, described as Dawson's Finest Hotel. European and American Plan. Fine Cuisine. Elegantly Furnished Rooms. Every Modern Improvement. Miss B.A. Mulrooney, Proprietress.

A headline on another page read: **Attempted Murder and Robbery**. The full details of the attempted murder and hold-up of a man on Bonanza Creek will be given in a future issue.

Again, something David might do if desperate, Helen thought. And without his remittance from their father, he might just be that desperate.

Chapter Thirteen

Baxter pushed his way through the hundreds of men who milled along Front Street. They were looking for entertainment and there were plenty of saloons, dance halls, and theatres on this street, as well as side streets, to satisfy them.

He reached the Aurora Saloon on the corner of Front and Queen Streets, one block from the hotel. There was constant movement as men jostled their way in and out of the building. Some were in good spirits, others looked discouraged and disheartened. He remembered each of those moods well: the elation of coming away with more money than you started with and the misery of losing all your money and sometimes your watch or a ring. Once he'd sat on a straight in a poker game, and come close to throwing his house title into the pot. But a little voice told him to bow out when the bidding was more than he had in chips. And he'd been so happy he'd listened to that little voice. The winning hand had been a flush.

Baxter walked through the open door and entered the hazy room. A long bar ran along the right wall where patrons lined up three deep. The bartenders hustled up and down the bar pouring drinks for those who held up their glasses. There were a few tables, and men sat around them talking.

The only time Baxter had been inside a saloon since he'd quit drinking was when he was there to ask questions. The agency's clients had to trust them to be discreet when they did their job and getting drunk wasn't one of the ways.

But now, he knew that ordering a drink would be a good opening to ask where Tom Chisholm was. And Chisholm would be more open to answering Baxter's questions if he was supporting his establishment by drinking.

Baxter worked his way through the crowd. When he reached the bar, he asked for a double whiskey. That way, he wouldn't have to come back.

"Where is Mr. Chisholm?" Baxter asked when he paid the bartender.

"What?" The bartender leaned closer.

"Where is Tom Chisholm?" Baxter yelled louder.

"Back room."

Baxter nodded, picked up his glass, and fought through the throng of men. He took a sip of his drink and felt it burn as it went down. He went through the doorway into the back room. It was large, and there was a flurry of gambling activity. Behind the gambling room was the dance hall. Baxter could hear the music and the stomping of feet as the dancers hopped around the room.

Baxter didn't know what Tom Chisholm looked like. He expected the owner would be dressed in a fancy suit, maybe smoking a cigar, and walking around the room slapping gamblers on the back, laughing at their jokes, encouraging them to have a good time.

He didn't see anyone who matched that description. So he looked for someone slinking around, watching for cheats using slight-of-hand at cards or the roulette wheel to beat the dealers. He'd seen owners of the saloons he worked at doing that. They not only watched for cheaters amongst their customers, but also for anyone of their staff who might be skimming money. And he spotted him.

Baxter sipped his drink as he moved between the tables to the corner where a short man with dark curly hair and dressed in a less than clean jacket wound his way through the crowd, his eyes darting back and forth.

"Mr. Chisholm?"

Tom Chisholm stopped and looked at him. "What do you want?"

"I'm looking for a man named David Gastrell. The constable down at the police barracks said you may know him."

"David is a fairly common name and I've hired a few, but I don't recognize the last name."

Baxter reached into his pocket for the photograph. "This picture is ten years old. Do you know him?"

Tom looked at the photograph. "He does look like the man named David I hired earlier this summer. I kicked him out of here in June and told him never to come back."

"Do you remember his last name?"

"I have so many men come for work and then leave after their first pay. I don't keep track of all their names. I only remember that David because he cheated the customers and stole money."

"You said he worked for you for about a month. Do you know where he went after that?"

"No, and I don't care. Worst mistake I ever made." Tom Chisholm handed the picture back and walked away.

Baxter looked around the room. There seemed to be two different types of men in the room: those with money sitting at the tables with a drink beside them and a stack of chips in front; and then those who wandered the room, hanging on the edges of the games. They cheered when someone won and made sorrowful noises when someone lost. At first, Baxter thought maybe they were in partnership with one of the players, but after watching for a few minutes, he realized they had little money and watching the men playing was a form of entertainment for them.

Baxter looked for an empty seat. If he played a few games he'd get to ask some questions. Should he play draw poker, roulette, blackjack or faro? He slid into a chair at a poker table and bought some white and red chips from the dealer. He lined them up in front of him. The ante was one dollar, and Baxter pushed his white chip into the pile. The dealer shuffled the cards.

Baxter signalled to one of the waiters and asked for another double. He'd decided he might have a better reception to his questions if he appeared to be a drinker like everyone else.

Baxter picked his cards up: two fours, a seven, and two eights. He had two pairs, but they were small. He could trade the seven and hope for a four or eight to make a full house. Or he could get rid of the two fours and seven and hope for something higher. One of the players raised two dollars. Did he want to continue? Maybe one more round.

Baxter threw in two white chips and placed the seven face down on the table. He picked up the new card. A nine. The stakes were raised another two dollars. It would be foolish to continue with the round. He should quit now. Instead, he placed his bet, took the nine and two fours and laid them face down on the table.

The next three cards were a three, another nine, and a queen. Baxter folded his hand on the table. He'd lost. He took a small sip of his whiskey.

When the hand was over, Baxter put in his one-dollar ante and waited for his cards.

"That must have been a huge landslide to leave such a scar on the hillside," Baxter said to start a conversation.

"The native Han peoples had a fishing camp at the mouth of the Klondike River According to their legend, whenever a member of their tribe went missing, it was the work of another tribe in the area. One day, when members of the Han tribe were at the top of the hill, they spotted the other tribe at the bottom. They began fighting, and one of the Hans cut down a tree. This supposedly started the rockslide and wiped out the other tribe."

"How did you learn that?"

"I'm a newspaper reporter and historian. I asked questions."

The dealer dealt the next round of five cards.

"How long have you been here?" Baxter asked, looking at his hand of two kings and three smaller cards. He laid these on the table, and the dealer gave him three more. Checking at them, Baxter saw a full house of three kings and two sevens. He kept a straight face as he met the bet of the man before him. He refused more cards and waited while the other men finished adding to their hands.

"Since the spring. I hiked the Chilkoot Trail and over the Chilkoot Pass with thousands of other hopeful prospectors."

He met the bets and raised them, never going too high. He wanted to sucker the others into continuing the play.

The dealer and four of the other players eventually bowed out. Finally, it was just him and the historian. The historian called and laid down his hand of a flush. Baxter smiled as he laid out his full house.

He pulled the chips toward him. He'd won and won big. He stacked the chips. He couldn't go back to the hotel now. It was bad manners for a winner to take the money he had just won and leave, especially if it was during the first couple of hands. The other players wanted a chance to win their money back.

The man beside him gathered up the few chips he had and left the table. Someone quickly took his spot.

"Nice win," the new man said.

Baxter grinned at him. "Lucky." A winner didn't brag. He didn't need to. The pile of chips in front of him said it all.

"I may have to take some of those chips from you," the man said.

"You may try." Baxter placed his ante on the table with the other dollar chips.

The man handed a sack to the dealer. "I'd like fifty reds and fifty whites." The dealer put the sack in a drawer and counted out the white and red chips.

Baxter watched the exchange, wondering what it was about. He thought about asking, but no one else seemed interested.

The dealer dealt the five cards. Baxter looked at his. Not as good as the last hand.

"Have you heard of a man named David Gastrell?" Baxter looked at the historian, hoping the others would hear.

"Who's asking?" one of the men asked.

"I'm a friend of his. I was supposed to meet him in Dawson last month but I didn't make it and now I can't find him." No need to say he was a detective or to mention Helen or even show the photograph. Someone looking for a friend was a believable story but showing a picture seemed like something a police officer would do. Plus, they were in the middle of a game. No one wanted to be interrupted by looking at a picture.

"I haven't," the man said.

"Neither have I." The historian slid a two-dollar chip into the centre and traded in one card.

Baxter stared at his hand of a two, six, seven, jack, and king. There was nothing he could do with them. He dropped them in front of him. None of the other men said anything about David.

One of the men left the table, and his place was quickly filled. Again the new man handed the dealer a sack and received fifty white chips and twenty reds. Baxter couldn't hide his curiosity any longer.

"I've played lots of poker hands where money has been exchanged for chips, but I've never seen someone give a sack to the dealer and receive chips. What's in the sack?"

"Gold dust," the new man said. "It's the most widely used form of currency in town. Most stores and shops have scales, and they weigh the gold dust out of a man's poke to pay for his purchases."

Baxter's luck went back and forth over the night. He'd win two hands and then lose three, then win one. He was enjoying himself even if he hadn't found anything out about David. When he finally looked at his pocket watch, he saw it was after one in the morning. He couldn't believe he'd played poker that long. He'd better go back to the hotel and get some sleep. He had a job to do tomorrow.

Baxter traded in his chips for money but instead of leaving he wandered the smoke filled room. He stood beside one man and pretended to watch the spin of the roulette wheel.

"Never was too successful at that game," he commented.

The man looked at him and Baxter smiled.

"Not my game either."

"My friend David was always lucky at it," Baxter paused. "You haven't heard of a man named David Gastrell?" he asked casually. "I was supposed to meet him here a month ago and I'm late."

Again, the man peered at him then shook his head. He turned his attention to the wheel again.

Baxter tried that approach with a few more men in the room but received a no reply or a shake of the head each time. Finally he left the saloon.

Men still packed the streets, some in various degrees of drunkenness. There were no streetlights to light his way. The brightness of the half-moon let him see the sidewalk, and he stepped carefully as he walked. Light from lanterns spilled out the doors and windows of the dance halls and saloons he passed. He could hear bands playing and people dancing inside. Quite a lively place, this Dawson City.

But not everyone was having fun. He passed many men lying on the benches in front of the businesses along the street. Their clothes were dirty, and some appeared to be underfed. Baxter wondered if they were homeless. Had they sold their supplies and then, instead of using the money to buy a ticket home, had spent it here?

He shook his head as he walked. What would he be doing now if he had come here last year as he intended? Would he be one of the more successful men, or would he be sleeping on a bench? As he neared the hotel, he thought about his luggage. Where would it be? Had they kept it in Helen's room or set it out in the hallway for him to pick up?

Baxter entered the hotel and was relieved to see his suitcase sitting beside the desk, with the valise on top. He picked them up and went to the bed hidden by curtains on the third floor.

Chapter Fourteen

The light was coming in brightly through the cheesecloth covering the window opening when Baxter opened his eyes the next morning. At first he thought he'd over slept then he remembered where he was. He reached over to where his jacket lay on his suitcase and took out his pocket watch. Seven forty-five.

He could hear movement in the beds around him: men groaning, the shuffle of feet, the closing of the washroom door at the end of the room. He stood and stretched then pulled on his shirt and trousers. This morning he would escort Helen to the post office to get her mail and then make sure she was settled somewhere before he went out. He might learn more from the men who cleaned the saloons then from the ones who worked at night or who played the games.

Baxter waited his turn in the washroom. He took his shaving kit with him and looked at himself in the mirror. His eyes were a bit red from lack of sleep. He poured water into the basin and washed his face then made quick work of lathering his face up with soap and scraping off his beard. The straight razor pulled a bit. Tomorrow he'd have to take the time to sharpen it on his strop.

When he got back to his bed, he decided to take the chance and leave his suitcase. He'd move it after breakfast. He went down one flight of stairs and knocked on Helen's door. There was no answer.

He tried Mattie's with the same result. He hurried down to the dining room door, opened it and stepped in. At first, he thought Helen and Mattie weren't there, but then he saw them at a table for two by a window. They were deep in discussion. He walked over to them.

"Good morning, Ladies."

"Mr. Davenport," Mattie said.

Baxter reached for a chair from another table.

"Take mine," Mattie said, standing. "I was just leaving."

Baxter moved out of her way and then sat in her chair. A waitress came over with a menu. He was hungry, having not eaten the night before. "I'll have fried bacon, eggs, griddle cakes, and coffee."

He handed the menu back to the waitress and faced Helen.

"Do you want to hear about my visit to the saloon last night?" Baxter asked.

"Yes, please." Helen took a sip of her tea.

"I found Tom Chisholm and asked him about your brother. He said he'd hired a man named David last June, but he doesn't remember his last name. When I showed him the photograph, he said he isn't sure if your brother is the man who worked for him."

"You told him the picture was old."

"Yes, and he agreed that could make a difference."

"Does he still work there?" Helen asked.

Baxter hesitated. How did he answer her? With the truth. After all, she knew her brother. "No. Chisholm fired him after a month. Said hiring him was the worst mistake he'd made. He claimed that David cheated the customers and stole money."

"Does he know where David went after that?"

"No, and he didn't care."

The waitress came with Baxter's food. She set the plate and a cup of coffee in front of him. He downed the coffee and asked for another.

"So we don't know for sure that the man named David he hired is my brother," Helen said.

"No." Baxter buttered his griddle cakes. "He could be going under a different last name or a totally different name. And he might not even be your brother. I also asked some of the patrons but none of them had heard of David."

"Mattie said that David cut his right palm with an axe many years ago and that it left a

171

slight scar. She thinks it's probably faded by now."

"Nothing was mentioned about a scar on any of the men who died in Victoria."

"Yes, another reason to think he is alive and could be living here," Helen said. "I spoke with Miss Mulrooney this morning. She suggested we speak with Father Judge, a priest who runs the St. Mary's Hospital here. Apparently, we've arrived during a typhoid fever outbreak which isn't surprising. So far, I haven't seen any garbage disposal, and from the smell, there isn't much in the way of sanitation."

Baxter was about the jump into his speech about her staying out of his investigation but decided against it for now. He knew that if he told her he had other plans, she would go ahead and visit the priest without him.

"Where is this Father Judge?"

"He's at the hospital administering to the sick men. Belinda said he has buried many of those who have died from the disease."

Baxter paused in his eating and looked at her.

"Yes," she nodded. "We may find out that David died here."

* * *

172

Helen had wanted to see the priest since Belinda told her about him. She wanted to talk with him but had decided to wait for Baxter. After all, as he kept pointing out, it was his investigation. Now she impatiently watched him eat his breakfast.

Baxter finished his meal and an extra cup of coffee. Helen had given Belinda a bank note that would cover a week of their meals and rooms, so they stood and walked out of the dining room. Baxter went to the desk and asked about his room.

"Yes, Sir. You are in number twenty-eight."

"I'll be right back."

Helen watched Baxter dash up the stairs. He must have quickly grabbed his suitcase and valise and set them in his room because he soon returned to the lobby.

"Did Miss Mulrooney mention where the hospital was?" Baxter asked as they left the hotel.

"She said it's at the north end of the city."

They headed along Front Street in the direction she'd seen Baxter take the night before. As they moved in and out of the crowd of men avoiding those who were staggering from their morning libations, Helen explained what she'd read about the gold dust pokes that were sometimes filled with shot or black sand.

"Yes, I saw some men using their gold poke to play last night. If the dealer was busy and didn't check what was inside, I could see the scam happening."

They passed the Aurora Saloon and paused when they reached the Northern Saloon. They could hear someone inside yelling out numbers.

"What's happening in there?" Baxter asked a man beside them.

"It's an auction for the men who are selling their outfits and heading home."

"I thought they were selling them at the bazaar," Helen said.

"There, too," the man nodded. "They're trying any way they can to get some of their money back before going home. They don't want to go back totally empty-handed."

"Isn't it a saloon?"

"There's not much happening during the day, so the owners have turned it into an auction house. They do that two days a week."

"Let's go in," Helen said. "Maybe David is in there selling his goods so he can go back to Victoria." They pushed their way through the door and to one side. It was noisy inside, with men talking and discussing what was heaped on the floor.

"What am I bid for this tent with stove pipe, stove, and two sacks of flour?" The man running the auction yelled.

"Five dollars!"

"Seven!

The auctioneer looked around. No one upped the bid. "Sold!" He then pointed to another pile. "We have several winter shirts and trousers, a pair of boots, and a warm jacket."

"Two dollars!"

"Five!"

"Six!"

When no one bid higher, he yelled. "Sold!"

Helen tried to see over the heads of the men in front of her. She looked at Baxter, who shook his head. "There are a lot of men about the same height and with the same hair colour as your brother, but with their beards, I can't say for sure."

Helen nodded, and they left. "That's so different from how the auction house, Christie's, operates their auctions in London. It's more dignified and restrained, with the auctioneer speaking in a normal voice and the bidders raising cards to bid."

"Yes, I've been to an auction in Victoria, and it was much quieter."

"Dawson City definitely isn't the exciting place depicted in all the newspapers and advertisements I saw in England."

"It does seem to have been glorified beyond its actual potential and prospects," Baxter agreed.

They continued walking, and Baxter pointed to the huge scar on the mountainside ahead of them.

"I learned last night that's known as the Moosehide Slide," Baxter said. "It's the result of a massive slide centuries ago."

"Interesting name. Do you know where it came from?"

"Before Dawson was established, this was the fishing grounds of the native Han peoples. They called it *weathered moosehide hanging*."

They walked a few more streets and came to a log building that looked to be about forty feet by twenty feet situated with the slide as background. There was a newly built church and another building that might be the priest's residence.

They walked in the door of the hospital. There was a hallway to the right with doors along it. They could hear moans coming from the rooms. Helen's instincts and training made her want to go and help the patients. But it was not her place. There were probably doctors attending to the sick and for her to step in and try to help without their permission or knowledge would upset them. Especially since she was a woman.

The London School of Medicine for Women had been formed in 1874 because women were not permitted to attend British medical schools to train as doctors. Even after graduating, they weren't allowed to obtain their degrees as doctors. Why, even last year, a proposal was put in front of Cambridge University's Senate to grant full degrees to female graduates. The male students responded with indignation and anger by hanging an effigy of a woman on a bicycle, the bicycle representing the new woman, outside the Senate's window. Because of the protests, the proposal was defeated.

Some women resorted to going to Europe or the United States to study since they were way ahead of England in admitting women to any university or college. Helen thought it was sad that she was fighting so hard to get her doctorate degree while David, who had gained admittance into Cambridge with no problem and studied to be a doctor for two years, left before completing his studies.

But women in England were slowly forging ahead in gaining more rights. The big movement now was to obtain the vote, which Helen was going to join when she returned to England.

A small, tired-looking man came out of one of the rooms. He had on a black cassock with a white collar. He stopped when he saw them.

"May I help you?" He took off his steel-rimmed spectacles and cleaned them on his cassock.

Since she was the one who had learned about the priest, Helen jumped in first. "My name is Helen Gastrell, and this is Mr. Baxter Davenport. We've come to Dawson

City to find my brother David. Miss Mulrooney suggested we speak with you since you've been administering to the men sick with typhoid fever."

"Yes."

"Do you remember if you had a patient named David Gastrell?" Helen handed him the photograph. "Or even a parishioner?" She knew that was far-fetched, but maybe David had changed. "He might also have a moustache."

Father Judge put his spectacles back on and took the picture. He studied it a moment then gave it back. "I'm afraid I don't recognize him. Many men in the city are sick, and we don't have enough room for all of them here. Some have to remain in their tents. Some can give their names when they come in, and some can't. Most are brought in by their friends and left. We aren't worried about who they are, just that they get better."

"But you can't say you had a patient named David Gastrell who looked like that?" Baxter asked. "Maybe gave him last rites."

"No, I'm sorry, I can't. The ones who died were a lot alike: thin, sickly, coughing, and pale. I gave them the best burial I could, but I didn't always know their names. You could check with some of the doctors in Dawson. One who worked especially hard with the typhoid patients here in the hospital and in their tents was Dr. Andrew Beckwith. But he's now on his claim in the gold fields."

"How bad is the outbreak?" Helen asked. She remembered learning about all the epidemics of various diseases that had scourged London, mainly in the slums. Like here, they spread rapidly because of overcrowding and lack of sanitation.

"Hundreds of men have died so far. It won't get better until everyone boils their water and a sanitation system is set up."

"Do you have help here?" Helen thought she might lend a hand for an afternoon if the frail–looking priest needed it. Give him a chance to rest.

"Yes, three Sisters of St. Anne arrived this summer to work in the hospital." Father Judge paused. "When did your brother come here?"

"He left Victoria late last summer. Why?"

"I expected the Sisters last fall, but the ice on the Yukon River prevented the riverboat from bringing them. They stayed at a mission near St. Michael for the winter while the others on the boat spent the winter in St. Michael. Maybe the same thing happened to your brother."

"So they may know him. Is one of them here so we may ask her?" Baxter said.

"Sister Mary Zephrin Sanders is in the kitchen. Come with me."

Helen and Baxter followed the priest into the kitchen, where a nun was cutting vegetables.

"Sister Mary, this is Miss Gastrell and Mr. Davenport. They are looking for Miss Gastrell's brother, David."

Helen held out the photograph for her to look at. "He's now ten years older than he was in this picture and could have a moustache."

Sister Mary stopped her chopping and took the photograph.

"He was supposed to have come here last fall," Helen continued. "Father Judge told us you were delayed arriving until this spring because of the ice. We're wondering if maybe he was too and spent the winter in St. Michael."

"I'm sorry. I don't remember meeting anyone with that name who looks like him." Sister Mary gave the picture back.

"Thank you for your time, Sister," Helen said.

They left the kitchen.

"We're staying at the Fairview Hotel if he happens to come into the hospital, Father," Baxter said as they bid the priest goodbye at the hospital door.

"If he comes, I'll tell him to contact you there."

Chapter Fifteen

Mattie put on one of the dresses handed down to her by Helen. Yes, it was out of style in England, but no one would notice here. It was yellow with a tight bodice and leg o'mutton sleeves. Its wide skirt just skimmed the ground. Nowadays, most women wore shirtwaists with bloomers or walking skirts reaching above their ankles. But Mattie didn't mind being out of fashion. She always wore a uniform of a full-length black dress covered by a long white apron, so she was never in society's fashion; she was in servitude fashion, a fashion that never changed.

She wrapped a white shawl over her shoulders and clipped her cotton purse to her belt. She had a few Canadian dollars that she'd changed from her British pounds in Victoria. Helen hadn't given her any spending money, not that she'd expected any. After all, this was a working, not pleasure, trip and Helen covered all of Mattie's expenses. She didn't need to buy anything for herself.

Mattie wove her way through the crowd strolling on the boardwalk along Front Street.

She was surprised at the number of men who tipped their hats in respect as she walked by. She'd never had that happen before. Usually, she was the unseen help, ignored by anyone who came to visit Mr. or Mrs. Gastrell. Here she was seen as a woman, a lady even. Maybe the stories she'd heard about men offering women gold to marry them were true. After all, there were very few women to the number of men.

Again, Mattie wished Clara was here to enjoy it with her. Just think, the two lowly maids of the Gastrell household being treated like ladies. She smiled at the thought of the two of them having fun together, maybe getting jobs in a dancehall, or even marrying one of the miners. Then she sobered. How would Clara's life have gone if she hadn't died? Would she still be a maid like Mattie? Would she have found someone to marry?

Oh, if only Clara hadn't died. Mattie dug in her purse and drew out a handkerchief. She dabbed her eyes. As she had so many times in the past, Mattie concentrated on pushing the thoughts of Clara from her mind. It was no use speculating. Clara was dead and nothing would bring her back.

Mattie put the handkerchief away and turned back to finding David. She thought about going to every business and asking the owners if they knew him. But she was afraid Helen and Baxter would do the same and be suspicious if they were told that a woman answering her description had been asking the same questions. She didn't want them to find out she was looking for him. So, on the first day here, she'd spent her time walking up and down Front Street trying to see if she could spot him. She soon realized it was impossible with all the men on the sidewalk and in the street. And at each corner, Mattie looked down the side streets where there were hundreds more men in front of the cafés, saloons, and dance halls.

So now, she found a bench in front of a store and sat. This way, she could watch the men walking by. She definitely couldn't scan all of them, but she thought she had a better chance of spotting him.

As she watched, she thought about her conversation with Belinda. Should she try for a job in a dance hall? As much as she would like to have her own business like Belinda, she doubted she would be good at it since she had no training. Maybe she should take Belinda up on her offer to work as a waitress in her dining room. She smiled ruefully. She did have a lot of training in serving people.

Mattie knew she had to find something while here because she'd decided she wasn't returning to England after she, Helen or Baxter found David. Whether she stayed here or in Victoria, she wasn't sure.

Mattie got up and started walking. Sitting was something she'd never gotten used to.

Only the rich had the luxury of sitting. Those who worked for them had to keep moving.

She walked past a jewellery store and stopped. Was that David's tie pin in the window? Mattie entered the jewellery store. She'd only been in one before, and that had been with Clara on one of their afternoons off. Jewellery stores contained merchandise she and Clara would never be able to afford, but they decided to go in and look at all the pretty pieces. They'd walked slowly past the display counters, pointing at a ring or a brooch and whispering about to which grand ball they would wear it if they were rich. The snooty store owner finally came over and asked them to leave.

After that, she and Clara's exploring of the city mainly concentrated on the fairs, parks, and gardens and they'd never entered a jewellery store again. Their favourite place had been Covent Garden Market. There they'd been entertained by watching the colourful costermongers who walked the area hawking their fruits, vegetables, and cooked foods. They were assisted by a barra boy who pushed a wheelbarrow full of goods behind them.

Remembering the way the snobby owner of the jewellery store in London had treated her and Clara made Mattie hesitate to enter this store. She didn't want to be so embarrassed again. But she had to see if the pin was David's. She took a deep breath and opened the door. The room was small and square, with a counter on one side, shelves on the other, and a back wall. Mattie walked the square, amazed at the displays of necklaces, rings, bracelets, and brooches for women and tie pins, shirt studs, and cufflinks for men. It had much the same merchandise as the store in London, only on a smaller scale.

"May I help you, Miss?" the man behind the counter asked.

"I'd like to see that tie pin in your window." Mattie liked how the man addressed her as Miss with respect in his voice. He didn't know she was a lowly servant in a rich household in England and was wearing her mistress's hand-me-down dress.

"It's a lovely pin." The man reached into the window display and pulled it out. "A diamond set in real gold made by a gem smith at the beginning of the century. Used to keep the silk and lace cravats of its owner in place. One of a kind, not like the lower quality, mass-produced tie pins of today with bugs, animal heads, or flowers on them."

He handed it to Mattie. She looked at it carefully. It was similar to the one David owned, but it wasn't the one. There had been a circle of pearls around the diamond on David's.

"Thank you." Mattie handed it back.

"I could give you a good deal on it. Your husband would be so proud wearing that in his ascot."

Mattie smiled. He even thought she was capable of capturing a husband. "It's not the one I was looking for."

"And what one would that be? I have more in the back room."

She hadn't thought about the idea that David might have pawned his pin for money. "It's a diamond like that one, only with a circle of small pearls around the diamond."

"I don't think I have one like that, but I'll take a look." He pushed aside the curtain behind the counter. He returned a few minutes later. "I have these two." He laid them on the counter for her to look at.

One was just pearls without a diamond, and the other was a diamond surrounded by small blue sapphires.

"No, neither is the one I'm looking for." Mattie smiled and left the store. She should get back to the hotel before Helen and Baxter. She didn't want them to ask her any questions.

There was a loud whistle down at the dock. "Steamboooat!" someone yelled. Hundreds of men surged towards the docks. She remembered the huge crowd on the riverbank when they'd arrived. This seemed to be part of the daily entertainment. She watched as passengers leaned on the railing, looking over the horde as if searching for someone they knew. There was the same look on many of the men's faces on the street.

* * *

"Well, that wasn't very productive," Baxter said as they left the hospital grounds.

"But we know that David might not have gotten ill or died here." Helen thought that was a good thing.

"Except Father Judge said he couldn't remember everyone he'd given last rites to."

They walked in silence for a few minutes.

"What do you suggest we do now?" Helen asked. He was the detective. He should know the next step in an investigation.

"*We* aren't doing anything," Baxter said. "I will walk you back to the hotel and then I will carry on with my search for your brother."

"I found Father Judge," Helen sputtered. "We can basically rule out David died of typhoid here. I think that shows I am capable of helping you."

"No, it shows that you are taking me away from my investigation. If David is true to form, he will be found working in the saloons or gambling halls. That is where I am going to concentrate my efforts for now."

"And what am I supposed to do?"

187

"You could walk the streets hoping to spot him. You could go into every shop, store, and café and ask if anyone has seen him. Or you could go back and have another nice visit with Miss Mulrooney. And there is always having tea and scones with Mattie." They had reached the hotel and Baxter held the door open for her.

"I don't like your attitude," Helen fumed. "I knew I should have found a different detective after our first meeting."

"Well, you didn't and as for my attitude, I'm only thinking of your safety."

"Humph." Helen stormed past Baxter into the lobby her temper boiling. What an insufferable man. She should have gone with her first instincts and looked for someone else to find her brother. Maybe she should have insisted on Mrs. Davenport coming. At least she would have been shown some respect by her.

There was a man was behind the desk.

"Is Miss Mulrooney in the hotel?" Helen asked.

"She's in her office."

"May I go see her?"

"I'll find out if she's busy," the man said. "Whom should I say is asking for her?"

"Miss Gastrell."

The man went out the door to the hallway. He returned quickly, leaving the door open. "You may go."

Helen went through the door and down the hall. She saw Belinda Mulrooney through an open door at the end, sitting at a desk looking at papers.

"Come in," she said when Helen knocked gently on the door. "Sit down. What can I do for you?"

"Mr. Davenport," Helen had a hard time saying his name. "and I talked with Father Judge, but he couldn't tell us if he'd ever met David either at the hospital or elsewhere."

"That man has been so busy looking after the sick and raising money to reconstruct his church that burned last May. He's not in the best of health, either. So he probably wouldn't remember individual men who came to him out of the hundreds he's treated."

"That's basically what he told us. I'm wondering if there is someone else in Dawson that I could speak with. Father Judge mentioned a Dr. Andrew Beckwith."

"Ah, yes. Dr. Beckwith and his sister, Florence, arrived early in June after travelling over the Chilkoot Trail and Pass. He set up an office in a tent on the hillside when he heard all the claims were taken. David may have gone to him for some reason."

"Father Judge said he shut down his practice and now has a gold claim."

"It's a long story," Belinda smiled. "Andrew's sister, Florence, fell in love and married a man named Eugene, who worked on a claim owned by Sam Owens. When Sam Owens's partner, Donald, decided not to return to the two gold claims they had staked together, he offered to sell his share to Sam. Sam, in turn, sold it to Eugene and Florence, who included Andrew in the sale. A little convoluted, but that's the reason Dr. Beckwith is no longer here." She paused. "But his fiancée, Pearl Owens, who is Sam's cousin, is still in town. She's been in Dawson since the beginning of the gold rush. She's a newspaper reporter, so knows a lot of what has happened here. She may have crossed paths with David. Also, right now, she rents a cabin from me and works here in the hotel. Once she and Dr. Beckwith are married, she's moving to his claim on Bonanza Creek."

"Can I speak with Miss Owens?"

"She starts work at three this afternoon. The cabin she's renting is on 2nd Avenue, but she might not be there. She's working on a newspaper article and interviewing some men who came here but didn't find the riches they hoped for."

"Thank you," Helen said. Then she switched subjects. "Could you tell me about that big white tent across the river? It's been fascinating me since we arrived."

"Mrs. Mary Hitchcock and Miss Edith Van Buren own it. Mary is the widow of a United States Navy commander, and Edith

190

is related to former United States president Maarten Van Buren. They came on a riverboat with a dog, a parrot, a canary, and a number of pigeons."

"Birds?" Helen asked. "Dogs, I can understand, but why did they bring birds?"

"Apparently, they didn't want to leave them at home."

"How long have they been here?"

"They arrived on the same day as my grand opening: July 27th. They're wealthy and are world travellers. They receive visitors for lunch or a chat every day. You could go visit them. You'll have to hire a canoe or raft to take you across. They probably won't have met David, but they are fascinating to talk with. They also hold church services each Sunday."

"It would be interesting to meet them. I wonder if they've been to London in their travels."

"I read an article about them in the Seattle newspaper when I was there purchasing some things for this hotel. According to it, they travelled across the United States by train last spring and at every stop, reporters asked them if they realized the hardships they faced if they went to the gold fields. Even their friends didn't believe they would actually go. I guess that big tent is proof they made it."

"They're rich women," Helen mused. "They might be an easy mark for a smooth talking man."

"Do you think David would have gone over there?" Belinda asked.

"I wouldn't put anything past him. It won't hurt to ask them if they've seen him."

"You'll have to hire a man with a boat to take you across."

"Thank you." Helen stood. "I'll come back after three to see Miss Owens."

"If you decide to go and see Dr. Beckwith, you should also speak with Sam Owens since he's been in the area for years," Belinda said.

Helen nodded and left the room. She walked to the post office but saw there was a big crowd outside the door. Maybe she should get Mattie to wait in line then decided against it. She would check again after her visit with the two women.

Chapter Sixteen

Baxter stomped down the street from the hotel. He had never been so angry in his life. Who did she think she was trying to tell him how to run his investigation? He knew it was a mistake to have let her come with him. He should have insisted she remain in Victoria or at least stay out of his way here. He should have made that part of the deal. Life would be so much easier for him now.

He stopped outside the Aurora Saloon. It looked so different in the daylight than it did at night. The false front was painted white with blue trim around the windows and doors. It was quiet inside, none of the loud conversation or the piano playing if the night before.

Baxter stepped inside. A man behind the bar was washing glasses and setting them upside down to dry. Another swept the floor, while a third restocked the liquor bottles. There were a couple of customers sitting at one of the tables, each with a glass of whisky in front of him. They all looked at him when he entered then went back to what they were doing.

Baxter walked to the bar and leaned on it. It felt sticky to the touch and he straightened up. He reached in his pocket then realized Helen hadn't given him the photo of David. He cursed under his breath.

"Can I help you?" the man behind the bar asked.

"My name is Baxter Davenport. I'm looking for a friend of mine, David Gastrell. I spoke with Mr. Chisholm last night and he said he'd hired a man named David in May but couldn't remember his last name. Do you remember the man and maybe his last name?"

The man looked at the others then back at Baxter. "Why are you looking for him?"

"We lost touch. I was supposed to meet him last month but I was delayed getting here. I can't find where he went."

"What does he look like?"

"He's about my height, slender, with light brown hair and blue eyes. He may have a moustache."

The man laughed. "Have you looked at the men in town? Half of them match that description. Anything else?"

"He has a scar on his right palm."

"Anyone here recognize him?" the bartender asked the other men.

"No," they mumbled.

Baxter wasn't very disappointed. He hadn't thought he'd be lucky but it was worth a try. After all, he had so little to go on. A description that basically was useless, a scar on his right hand, and sparkling blue eyes that could mean anything. Even the photograph was too old to be of any use today.

As he walked along the boardwalk, Baxter wondered what his hero John Wilson Murray would do in this situation. John Murray was a detective hired by the attorney general in Ontario in 1875 and had been Ontario's only full-time detective until 1884. He solved many cases of larceny, arson, counterfeiting, and murder over the years and was so popular that he worked throughout most of Ontario. His exploits were noted in the newspapers across the country and he was a minor celebrity.

Baxter read every one of the articles he found on Murray and hoped to emulate the man by being just as good a detective. But here he was on his first international case that could make Davenport & Son a household name and he had nothing.

Murray claimed his job was: *to follow criminals to any place and run them down*. Baxter wasn't sure if David was a criminal but he was hired to run him down. He thought back to the article he'd read on Murray tracking Edwin Johnson, then known as the greatest counterfeiter of his day. Murray spent months travelling across the northern United States and southern Ontario until he finally spotted him. He began to trail him gathering evidence against him.

Johnson would go to taverns in the evening and start out paying for his drinks with real Canadian money. Then eventually he'd switch to his counterfeit stash. Finally, after months of trailing him, Murray arrested the seventy-five-year-old Johnson in Toronto.

Baxter stopped at the next saloon and entered. He tried the same story on the bartender and patrons there and received the same answers. He stepped out into the sunshine and looked up and down the street. There were over twenty saloons with dancehalls and gambling establishments in this town. He would have to visit each one of them every hour in order to speak with the men who would filter in and out during the day and night. But if he did a few more, maybe word would get to David that someone was looking for him and he would come forward. Or, the opposite might be true and he would disappear further.

Baxter tried three more establishments before deciding it was time for lunch. He wondered if Helen had cooled down so he could give her a report on his actions. He'd noticed she'd written it on the contract before signing her name. Another part of this case that irked him; he didn't like the idea of having to report to a woman.

* * *

Helen looked in her purse to make sure she had a calling card. Back home in London, it was an obligation for an upper-class woman to carry a calling card to present when she arrived at a friend's house. If the time was right and the circumstances favorable, she would then be invited in to visit. But there didn't seem to be such etiquette or standards here. Belinda said that anyone who wanted to just dropped in to see Mrs. Hitchcock and Miss Van Buren. She hoped the time was right and the circumstances favourable when they went over.

She walked down the river and saw several men sitting and talking near the dock.

"Anyone able to take me across to the other side?" Helen asked.

Two men jumped up.

"I can go it for six dollars."

"I'll take you for five dollars."

Helen chose the cheapest man, who led them over to his skiff, parked partially on the sand.

"Name's Jim," he said as he helped Helen into the boat.

"Miss Gastrell."

When she was seated, Jim pushed the boat further into the water. He climbed in and, picking up one oar, deftly turned the boat around until the bow faced the other side of the river. Then he sat backward in the front seat and began rowing. However, they were going in the wrong direction. Helen wondered if Jim had misunderstood where she wanted to go.

As if reading her mind, Jim said. "I have to go with the current to work our way out into the centre of the river. Then once I am close to the other side where the current is less, I can row back up the river to the bank."

"Do you know a man named David?" Helen asked.

"First or last name?"

"First. David Gastrell. He's my brother. He may have worked at the Aurora Saloon a few weeks ago."

"Can't say I've made his acquaintance." Jim shook his head. "Why are you looking for him?"

"My family hasn't heard from him in almost a year."

On the other side of the river, Jim rowed until the bow hit the sand. He jumped out and dragged the boat further up on shore. He helped Helen our and she gave him a five-dollar bill.

"Would you like me to wait?" Jim asked.

"Yes," Helen said. "We shouldn't be too long." At home, a typical visit usually lasted less than an hour.

Jim sat on the river bank then stretched out in the sun.

Helen started up the bank to the huge, rectangle-shaped tent. A flap was open, and since there was no place to knock, Helen stuck her head in and called. "Hello!"

"Come in," a woman said. "Come in."

Helen stepped in and gaped at the inside, surprised to see the pigeons flying freely and a canary singing in its cage. A parrot was in another cage and just stared out at her. With the wild flowers growing the tent had the look and feel of a conservatory.

"I'm Miss Helen Gastrell."

"I'm Miss Edith Van Buren," said a tall, beautiful woman in her early forties. "And this is my friend Mrs. Mary Hitchcock. Do come in and sit down."

"I'm afraid there are only a bench and two chairs," Mrs. Hitchcock said. She indicated for Helen to sit in one of the steamer chairs that could be stretched out into loungers. She was shorter and heavier set than her friend.

Helen sat on one of the chairs, and Mrs. Hitchcock took the other.

"Would you like a refreshment?" Miss Van Buren asked. "We don't have much to offer. Most of our supplies were shipped separately on the riverboat *Rideout.* We were assured they would be here at the same time or even before us, but they haven't arrived. We brought enough provisions and delicacies to last us a few weeks. Right now, we are paying the exorbitant prices demanded here in Dawson for the same tins of food we paid half the price for in Seattle. We do, though, have a powder that, when mixed with water, makes a delicious cider."

"Thank you, that would be nice," Helen said.

"I'll tell John, our cook, to make some up." Miss Van Buren went around a screen, and they heard voices. She soon returned.

Helen decided to get right to the reason for their visit. "My brother, David Gastrell, was supposed to have come to Dawson last fall. However, our family hasn't heard from him since his telegraph message telling us he was leaving Victoria."

"And you've come looking for him," Mrs. Hitchcock said.

"Yes." Helen wasn't sure if she should give the reason why she had come to see the two wealthy women.

"Are you from England?" Miss Van Buren asked, returning to sit on the bench.

"Yes, London."

"And your brother is a remittance man?"

"How did you know?"

"I've met many a remittance man in my travels through the United States. Most managed to purchase land and build a life, but some never seem to lose their philandering, wasteful, gambling ways." Miss Van Buren smiled. "Some have actually thought I should marry them."

Helen sensed Miss Van Buren knew why she there. She took David's picture from her purse. She was glad Baxter hadn't asked for it. "This is ten years old. He has a scar on his right palm and may have a moustache. Has he approached you?"

Miss Van Buren took the photograph and looked at it. "I don't think he has, do you, Mary?" She handed the picture to Mrs. Hitchcock.

"He does look something like one of the men who came wanting us to finance him in buying a claim. He'd work it and pay us back. I don't remember his name, though."

Helen felt a jolt of excitement. David may have been here. "When did he come?"

"It would be about three weeks ago."

Helen felt a pang of disappointment. He could be anywhere now.

"I'm assuming you didn't take him up on his offer."

"No, we staked our own."

"You have gold claims?" Helen asked.

"We just came back a few days ago," Mrs. Hitchcock said. "I recorded my claim today. Miss Van Buren is doing hers tomorrow. They aren't on Bonanza or Eldorado Creeks. We're further away on Bear Creek."

"And it was quite a feat tramping through the bush and along the creek until we found a place not staked," Miss Van Buren said.

"Our poor feet did suffer so, and we are still taking care of them."

A man came around the screen with a tray. On it were glasses, a pitcher, small plates, forks, a plate of crackers and one of tinned, smoked oysters. He set the tray on the table and poured the cider into the glasses.

"Thank you, John," Miss Van Buren said. She handed the glasses to everyone and a plate and napkin. "Help yourselves to the oysters and crackers."

"Have you seen that man since?" Helen asked, placing a cracker and oyster onto a plate.

"No." Both women shook their heads. "But we've had many more offers like that," Miss Van Buren said.

"Oh?" Helen inclined her head.

"We've had lots of men who think we're millionaires come and offer us a wonderful deal. All they needed was one hundred dollars or more to put towards a grubstake, so they had food and shelter to keep them going while they searched for a claim to stake. Once they returned to Dawson, we would pay to have their claims recorded. Then while they were working their claims, we would buy all their supplies. When their mines were producing, they would give us half of the gold they recovered."

"And that's not a good plan?" Helen asked.

"For us, it isn't," Mrs. Hitchcock laughed. "They could skip out with our money; they could go through the whole process and not find anything while continuing to ask us to pay for their food; or they could withhold how much gold they actually found and only give us a pittance of what the claim was worth."

"We did have a couple of men who had already staked their claims ask us to pay for their recording and then support them while they worked them," Miss Van Buren said. "They'd already found the claims, so we asked Mr. Alex McDonald about them. He went over the maps with us and gave us a lesson about geological formation from all his years of prospecting in the north. According to him, those claims were useless. Because of where they were situated, there wouldn't be any gold on them."

"Who is Mr. Alex McDonald?" Helen asked. "I've heard his name mentioned a few times."

"He's known as the 'King of the Klondike,'" Miss Van Buren answered. "He's a big man from Nova Scotia who'd been in the north for years before gold was discovered here. When he heard of the gold strike, he came to Dawson with the idea of owning as many full or partial claims as possible. He bought his first claim for a bag of groceries. But he didn't want to do any work to recover the gold, so he hired two men to work it for him. With the gold from that claim, he bought shares in other claims and kept using the money from them to acquire more. Right now, he's not even sure how many he owns or partially owns."

"I wonder if he would know David," Helen mused.

"Have you thought about going to the recorder's office to check the claims and see if David recorded one?" Mrs. Hitchcock asked.

"No, I haven't," Helen said thoughtfully. "It never crossed my mind that David would want to work that hard. But it is a good idea. Where is it?"

"It's on Front Street. And being a woman, you shouldn't have to wait."

"Oh?"

"When I went to record my claim, I was admitted into the private office ahead of the long line of men. I felt a little guilty, but my feet were still hurting from our long trek to find our claim, so I went in. I hurried through my registration as quickly as possible so as not to delay the line very long."

"Are you ladies spending the winter here in this tent?"

"Oh, no," Miss Van Buren said. "We're making plans to build a log cabin next to the tent to store our goods over the winter, if they ever arrive. We'll be taking a riverboat to Lake Bennett around the middle of

September and hiking over the Chilkoot Trail."

"I've heard it's a tough trail."

"After our trek through the woods in search of our claims, we can handle anything," Mrs. Hitchcock laughed.

"I'm staying at the Fairview Hotel," Helen said. "If that man comes back with another proposal, could you let me know?"

"Yes, we will."

After thanking her hostesses for their hospitality and saying goodbye, Helen went down to the river where Jim still waited. He rowed her back across and she paid him, giving him a tip for waiting.

* * *

When Helen got back to the hotel she found Baxter waiting in one of the chairs in the lobby. He looked to be in a better mood. He stood as she walked up to him.

"Where have you been?" Baxter demanded.

Well, maybe not in a better mood. "Let's get something to eat and I'll tell you."

They entered the restaurant and found a table. Once they'd ordered Helen told Baxter about her morning.

"I went to visit the ladies who live in the big white tent across the river. They said a man who looked a little like David had approached them with a scheme to stake a claim. They would pay for everything and he would do the work."

"Did they get a name?"

"They couldn't remember it. They have so many men approaching them for money. They did say I should check the recording office to see if David staked a claim."

"Did you?"

"Not yet. Did you learn anything in the saloons?"

Baxter shook his head. "David's description is too vague."

Helen nodded. He could match most of the men she saw on the streets. She took a chance on Baxter losing his temper again and asked. "What are your plans for this evening?"

"Same as last night. I'll check out another saloon or two. Maybe if I keep asking word will get to David and he'll contact me."

Helen nodded, not taking the bait that he used 'I' and 'me' instead of 'we' and 'us'. She wasn't going to have that argument again. He could do his investigation and she would do hers.

Their food came and after they'd eaten, Helen stood.

"I'm going to the recording office and then the post office," she said.

"I'll join you," Baxter said.

Helen paused in surprise then led the way out of the hotel. They walked to the recording office where there was a short line of men. They listened to some of the conversations as they waited their turn.

"I'm selling my share in a claim on Hunker Creek to this man," one prospector said, pointing to a man beside him. "Then I'm heading home."

"I'm trading my share in a claim for a ticket on the next steamer out," said another.

"I'm selling my half to my partner and buying a saloon. There's more money in liquor than there is in gold."

"Excuse me, Ma'am," A man came up to them. "Would you and your gentleman friend like to come into my office?"

Helen stood. Mrs. Hitchcock had been right. Like Mrs. Hitchcock, Helen wasn't sure about going ahead of the men who had been there first, but the man was holding the door open for her.

When they were settled in the office, Helen spoke first and explained that they were looking for a claim that could have been registered under the name David Gastrell.

"What creek is the claim on?"

"We don't actually know if he has one." Helen told the man about their quest to find her brother and that someone suggested they see if he'd staked a claim.

"Do you know anything about the procedure of gold claim recording?"

Helen and Baxter shook their heads.

The man looked at his watch then explained. "A miner has to have a Free Miner's Certificate number, which he obtains for five dollars. Then he goes to a creek and pans the gravel along it, looking for flakes or nuggets of gold. If he finds some, he measures off five hundred feet of the creek and pounds posts into the ground at each end which marks the boundaries of his claim. He puts his name and certificate number on the posts and then comes here to fill out an application form with his name, address, Free Miner's Certificate number, where the claim is situated and its size. Every application is given a consecutive number.

"The records are kept in chronological order for each creek in the territory, and a note is made every time one of those claims changes ownership. That is why we need the name of the creek first."

Helen and Baxter looked at each other. Helen sighed. Another disappointment.

"Thank you," Helen said.

"Good luck finding your brother," the man said as they left the room.

Chapter Seventeen

They walked to the post office and it seemed as if the same crowd of eager-looking men was still standing outside. One man came out of the door with three letters in his hand while two others tried to push their way in.

"I've been here over an hour now," a man beside them said. "The boat came in two days ago with sacks full of letters, packages, and newspapers. It takes them a long time to sort through everything, but we line up here anyway. We all want to hear from home."

"We could wait here the rest of the day and still not get in," Baxter said.

The man nodded. "The crowd will be lesser tomorrow but grow again when another steamer arrives with more mail. There is a lady's entrance on the side, though." He pointed to where a woman in a long pink dress and carrying a parasol came out.

"I'll be right back," Helen said to Baxter

Helen walked to the entrance and opened the door. She went up to the wicket and was immediately served.

"Is there a letter for a man named David Gastrell? It may have been here for a few months."

"Why are you asking for it?"

"David is my brother. I'm Miss Helen Gastrell. My father sent it to David, care of Dawson City, because this is the last place we knew he was."

The postmaster nodded. "That name does ring a bell." He went to the back of the room and looked in some pigeonholes. He grabbed two envelopes and came back.

"This one arrived a month ago." He held one up for her to read the name.

"That's my father's writing," Helen said. "But he mailed it last winter."

"The mail service here isn't very reliable." The postmaster slipped it under the wicket to her. "And this one came just last week. It's addressed to you." He pushed the second letter to her.

Helen reached to pick it up. It wasn't from her father. This one was in her mother's handwriting. "Thank you," Helen said.

Helen walked slowly out of the room. Baxter waited outside the door. She showed him both the letters.

"This is the one my father mailed last winter. And this one arrived for me last week. It's from my mother."

"Oh," Baxter said.

Helen stared at the envelope addressed to her in care of Dawson City. If it wasn't from her father, then that could mean only one thing, for she could think of no other reason for her mother to write to her.

Helen started towards their hotel. She didn't know what to do. She knew what message the letter to David contained. It was reading the letter from her mother that she dreaded.

Helen and Baxter entered the restaurant at the hotel and found a table. Helen set the envelopes in the centre of the table while she ordered tea and scones, and Baxter asked for coffee and a piece of apple pie.

She didn't touch the letters until after the waitress returned with their food and then she just stared at them while she took a sip of tea. In London, mail delivery began at seven-thirty in the morning and the last delivery was at seven-thirty in the evening. Mail was delivered twelve times a day, although there was talk of reducing it to six times. A person could mail a letter and expect a reply in a few hours. And some complained when they didn't get it.

Here it didn't matter when a letter was mailed. It could be received at any time, from a few months to even a year later.

Helen set her cup down and picked up her father's letter. She opened the flap and took out the sheet of paper. It was good to see her father's handwriting. Even though she hadn't felt homesick so far on this trip, it brought back the feeling of home. She read it out loud.

My son David.

I hope you are in fine health and enjoying your time in the gold fields. Because I haven't heard from you since you left Victoria I have sent Helen to contact you in Dawson to make sure you are alive and well. She will be arriving the latter part of August.

This is not a request for you to come home, nor is it a letter of forgiveness. You still are not welcome here.

Your Father
Algernon

Helen looked up at Baxter and nodded. "That's what Father told me he had written."

"It sounds like he didn't need to send you all this way. If nothing has changed, he could just have forgotten that he has a son named David."

"He could, but my father does not believe in male line primogeniture."

"Primogeniture?"

"The custom of passing on your entire estate to the first-born son and leaving the rest of your children to make their own way."

"Oh." Baxter nodded.

"It's done to keep an estate, usually farmland, intact instead of it being divided into smaller pieces that can't support

212

farming. It not only preserves the size of the property, but also the supremacy and status of the aristocracy, which is based on ownership of land."

"So your father is dividing his estate among all his children."

"Yes, however, not equally. He's giving my oldest brother, Peter, the business because he wants it to continue unblemished by arguments among us siblings over how it should be improved, changed, or even sold. He's leaving the house and enough money to run it to my mother until her death. And he's allocating his real estate holdings to the rest of us children. His money will be divided equally among all of us. Father was going to change his will if I found out David was dead."

"So your father wasn't mad enough at David to cut him out of his will all together."

"He was, but his solicitor explained that David could come back, demand a share, and hold everything up in court for years. Father figured it would be easier to give David ten thousand pounds than make the rest of us suffer."

Helen put down the first letter and ran her hand over the second one. She was sure she knew what was in it. She picked it up and slowly opened it. She read it silently, her eyes filling with tears. It was true. Her father was dead.

"Bad news?" Baxter asked.

Helen was unable to speak. She handed the letter to Baxter and picked up her napkin to wipe her eyes.

"I'm so very sorry." Baxter laid the letter down after reading it.

Helen nodded. "I think I will go to my room and lie down."

Baxter jumped up and held out his hand to help her stand. He picked up both letters and offered her his elbow. She slipped her hand in and allowed him to lead her up the stairs to her room.

"I'll summon Mattie," Baxter said when they reached her door.

Helen nodded and entered her room. She had just removed her hat when Mattie knocked and entered, the letters in her hand.

"Mr. Davenport told me the news, Miss." Mattie set the letters on the trunk and then lit the candle. "I'm very sorry to hear it. Mr. Gastrell was a wonderful man."

"Yes," Helen said quietly.

"You have had quite a shock, Miss. Let me help you to lie down."

Helen climbed onto the bed and turned to the wall.

* * *

Freddie knew he had to kill Paul. That was his only choice if he wanted to end up with enough money to leave Dawson. He had come to the conclusion that stealing gold was the way for him to go back to Victoria or some other place and live the life he wanted. While they were playing checkers a few nights ago, he'd brought up the subject of the possibility of someone stealing gold from one of the wagons coming back from the gold fields. He claimed he wanted to know if Paul was worried about that.

They'd discussed it, and Paul said that it was unlikely anyone would try because there was so much wagon, cart and foot traffic on the road, and they would be seen.

"What if they waited until the wagon was in town? Freddie asked. "Could they jump the driver and steal it?"

"I guess they could," Paul said thoughtfully. "But what would they do with the driver, and where would they take the wagon so no one would see them? And then how would they get the gold on a riverboat?"

Freddie agreed that it was an impossible task alone. "What if the driver was in on it?"

"You mean they drive the wagon to the docks and load the gold on the boat?"

"Not quite. I'm thinking one of them lives in a cabin. They go there and transfer as much gold as they can into suitcases or trunks and then take them to the boat as if they are filled with clothes. They board the boat just as it sails away."

"What do they do with the horse, wagon and remaining gold?"

"They cover the boxes and leave the wagon parked somewhere. There are enough horses and wagons in town that it could be a couple of days before anyone checks it."

"You've done some thinking on this, haven't you?" Paul asked.

"I'm sure I'm not the only one."

"Well, I don't know any drivers who would go along with the plan. I know I wouldn't."

Freddie wasn't sure if Paul had just been making a statement or if that was his way of saying don't ask me to help. Freddie had grinned and slapped Paul on the back. "It's nice to have such an honest friend."

Since Paul made it plain that he wouldn't go along with that plan, Freddie had adjusted it. He could offer to go with Paul on one of his trips and, on the way back, kill him and conceal his body. If Freddie hid it well enough, he would have time to escape by riverboat. He would have to calculate it perfectly because sometimes the riverboats didn't leave on schedule. He would also have to make sure no one saw him. And that was a tricky part since, as Paul pointed out, that road was well travelled by both miners and carts and wagons.

There was one place, though, where he could hide a body. The road went by a thick grove of trees. If Freddie could convince Paul to stop there so he could relieve himself, Freddie could hit him over the head and drag him into the bush just as he had done before.

* * *

It was early evening when Helen stirred. She hadn't slept; her mind remembered her father and ran through her life with him from her earliest memories of him walking her to school, to how proud he'd looked at her graduation from the London School of Medicine for Women. She hadn't thought that, when she said goodbye to him at the docks in London, it would be the last time she saw him.

According to her mother's letter, he had died a week before Helen reached Victoria. Her father was dead long before she sent him the telegram saying she was on her way north. He was in his grave, and her family had been mourning him for almost two months. She found it hard to come to terms with the time frame.

Her mother had written the letter immediately after his death but, not knowing where to send it at the time, had taken the chance and addressed it to Dawson. The postmaster had said the mail wasn't very reliable. It also seemed that it wasn't very predictable. Her mother's letter arrived in Dawson before she had, and it had been sent from London. It must all depend on which company worked the fastest to get their boats and passengers here with the least amount of problems.

Helen needed something to keep herself occupied, something to take her mind off her father's death. She needed to find David, and lying here wasn't doing that.

Helen sat up and saw that Mattie was sitting on her trunk. It brought back memories of when she was a child and would wake from her afternoon nap to find Mattie waiting for her.

"How are you feeling, Miss?"

"Sad, but more determined than ever to find David for my father. I can grieve for him when I get home." Helen stood. "Let's find Mr. Davenport and have supper."

"I'll go knock on his door." Mattie hurried out of the room.

They ate quietly, Helen not in the mood for talking and the other two not sure what to say.

"I'll shave and change, then try another saloon or two tonight," Baxter said when they'd finished their dessert.

"And I'll talk with Pearl Owens."

"Do you feel up to it?" Baxter asked. "I know what it's like to lose a parent. It catches you off guard and upsets your mind and body."

"I have to do something. And it's more important than ever that I find David. It's the last thing I can do for my father."

"I understand," Baxter nodded.

"And I'd like David's photograph."

Baxter took the picture from his pocket and handed it to her. He left, and Mattie stood.

"I'll be in my room," Mattie said.

Helen nodded absently. Belinda had told her that Pearl started work at three but didn't have a set job. She went wherever she was needed at the time. Helen would try the kitchen first. She wasn't sure if she should knock on the kitchen door or just walk in. She decided to walk in. The room was full of men and women working various jobs. Some were at a long table cutting vegetables. Others were at the stove cooking. Three were washing dishes.

Belinda had said Pearl had blonde hair and liked to hide her figure under bloomers and a shirtwaist. There were four women wearing bloomers.

"May I help you?" a man at the stove asked.

"I'm looking for Miss Pearl Owens. Miss Mulrooney said she might be here."

"I'm Pearl Owens." A young woman about Helen's age put her knife down and stepped away from the cutting table.

"May I speak with you for a few minutes?"

Pearl looked at the man at the stove. He nodded.

"Come back out to the dining room," Pearl said. "I need some tea."

"I've just finished eating," Helen said. "But you go ahead."

They sat at a table in the corner, and Pearl ordered tea and a muffin for herself.

"What do you wish to speak with me about?"

Helen took the photograph out of her purse and handed it to her. "I'm looking for my brother David Gastrell. He was supposed to have come here last summer. Belinda said you've been here for two years and may have met or heard of him."

Pearl took the picture and looked at it. "I've never heard the name David Gastrell, and I don't recognize him, either." She slid it across the table back to Helen.

Helen had a hard time hiding her disappointment.

"You might ask a man named Paul Gamon. He's been here since gold was discovered in 1896. He works in one of the saw mills, delivers wood, and occasionally is a bartender in Dominion Saloon. He might have heard of David."

"Thank you." A least they had another name.

"Where in England did you come from?"

"London. David sent my father a telegram last summer stating he was coming here, and we haven't heard from him since.

"Did you come all this way yourself?" Pearl asked, admiration in her voice.

"No," Helen smiled. "I travelled from London to Victoria with my maid and then came north with her and a private detective named Baxter Davenport, who I hired to help me find David."

The waitress came with Pearl's tea and muffin. She set them in front of her.

"Your story is similar to Anna Degraf's story," Pearl said, breaking her muffin in two.

"Who's that?"

"A woman I interviewed and wrote an article about. She lived with her 23-year-old son, George, in Seattle. George yearned for adventure, and one day in July of 1892, he told her he was going on an excursion and would be back in two weeks. He never returned.

"When she heard that he had been seen in Juneau, Alaska, she sold her business and headed north, taking her feather bed, sewing machine, and other necessary possessions. When she arrived in Juneau, she found a wild frontier town with a dance hall, some stores, and a few saloons. She went to the mining camps looking for her son or information about him. She made a living by mending clothes and making new outfits for two years without finding her son.

"In 1894, Anna met Joseph Ladue, who founded Dawson City in 1896. He told her he remembered someone by the name of Degraf stopping at his trading post at Ogilvie, where the Sixtymile River entered the Yukon River. In July, she left Juneau with a married couple and two single men, taking her feather bed, her sewing machine, and the clothes on her back. They sailed to Dyea and hiked the Chilkoot Trail over the pass. Anna, who by then was fifty-five years old, had broken her leg years before and needed a crutch to help her along the trail. They built a boat and sailed across Bennett Lake and down the Yukon River to Ogilvie. There, another person confirmed that he'd met a man named Degraf a year before.

"She continued down the river to the town of Fortymile but didn't find George. In October, she reached another town named Circle City, Alaska, where she set up her sewing business. For the next two years, she kept asking about her son. In 1896, she returned south, going to her daughter's place in San Francisco.

"But in 1897, she was on her way north again with a new sewing machine and bolts of cloth. She arrived here in Dawson and set up her business making tents, clothing, and fancy costumes for the dance hall girls."

"Has she found him?" Helen asked.

"Not so far, but she says she's not giving up."

"Well, I don't plan on giving up until the day we have to leave Dawson." Helen wasn't sure how she felt about hearing that another woman like her was also looking for a family member. It was disheartening to know that even after six years, Anna Degraf hadn't found her son. And most of that search was before so many men were in the north. But she might be someone to talk with. Maybe she had met David while asking about her son.

Helen decided to change the subject. "I hear you're getting married soon."

"Yes," Pearl beamed. "In three weeks."

"Congratulations. Is it true he's a doctor who had a practice here in Dawson?"

"Yes, until he bought the claim. Why do you ask?"

"I'm just wondering if he may have treated David."

"He could have," Pearl admitted, finishing the last of her muffin. "There were a lot of sick men while he was here, and he was very busy."

"Where's his claim? Would Mr. Davenport and I be able to go talk with him?"

"It's a day's walk from here, but you could try hiring a wagon and make it in a few hours. Paul Gamon would be the man to talk with about that. He just bought a horse and wagon to use for hauling his wood and to take supplies to the stores in Grand Forks."

"That's the town that grew up at the gold fields."

"Yes. Andrew's claim is not far from there. You could stay overnight at the Grand Forks Hotel."

"I'll discuss that with Mr. Davenport."

"If you go, would I be able to hitch a ride? I haven't seen Andrew for over a week. Plus, my bridesmaid is out there, and I want to take her the dress I found for her to wear."

"By all means. It will be good to have someone along who knows the directions."

After saying goodbye, Helen hurried to Baxter's room, hoping he hadn't left yet. She had to tell him about Paul Gamon and was glad when he answered her knock.

"Pearl Owens gave me the name of another person we could speak with. His name is Paul Gamon, and he sometimes works as a bartender in the Dominion Saloon. He also delivers wood and works in a saw mill. And if we want to go and speak with Dr. Beckwith, Paul Gamon could take us there in his wagon."

"Hmm, maybe I'll visit the Dominion Saloon and see if he's working tonight."

"Here's David's picture. Hopefully, it will help."

Chapter Eighteen

Baxter left the hotel and walked down Front Street, looking for the Dominion Saloon. He marvelled at Helen's fortitude. Reading the letter of her father's death and burial had shaken her but, instead of using it as an excuse to climb into bed and hide, she was putting more effort into fulfilling his last request. And he would encourage her to do so. Who was in charge wasn't important now. They were both working towards the same result.

He'd spent the afternoon going to the doctor and dentist offices asking if David had been to visit them for an ailment or toothache. None of them remembered him and all pointed out that hundreds of men visited them each week. Most came one time only.

Baxter wondered at the feasibility of them going to the gold fields to see Dr. Beckwith. The downside of going was that Beckwith would probably give the same answer as the doctors here in town. The upside would be that he and Helen would get to see creek where the gold had been discovered, something he wanted and, he suspected, she was just as excited about seeing.

He reached the row of saloons, dance halls, and theatres. Callers, holding megaphones, stood in front of each one, yelling out the value of visiting their business establishment. Some were accompanied by fiddlers who scraped out a song.

All the gambling, dancing, and shows inside were in full force. Men swarmed on the streets in front of the saloons and gambling-places, some trying to push their way into the already full establishments. There were so many places where David could be, and they were open around the clock. Men could have a drink and play poker morning, noon or night except on Sundays. They could watch a floor show then dance all night with the ladies if they had the stamina. Plus, there was Paradise Alley, where ladies of the evening were available.

Baxter entered the Dominion. As in the other saloons, it was hazy with cigar and cigarette smoke, noisy, and packed with men. Dark wallpaper splashed with gold colouring covered the walls of the Dominion. Three long mirrors were behind the painted and varnished bar. The gambling hall was in the back, and a broad stairway led up to billiards and poker rooms.

He worked his way across the patterned oilcloth floor to the bar, where three bartenders were kept busy pouring drinks.

As the night before he would only buy one or two whiskies and play poker. He'd ask questions when the opportunity arose.

"What will it be?" one of the three bartenders asked.

"Double whiskey." He figured he'd get more information if he ordered a large drink. That way he wasn't wasting the bartender's time.

The bartender set a glass on the bar and poured a hefty amount of whiskey in it.

"Paul Gamon working this evening?"

"Who wants to know?"

Baxter hadn't expected that. "Um…I was told by a friend he delivers wood, and I would like to talk with him about ordering some."

"No, he's not on tonight. You could go to the police barracks tomorrow. He usually delivers wood there twice a week."

Baxter touched the photograph in his pocket then decided against showing it. The bartender was too busy to take the time to look at it. "Has David Gastrell ever been in here?"

"Again who's asking?"

"My name is Baxter Davenport. David is a friend of mine and we were supposed to meet in Dawson last month. He made it and I didn't until this week. I'm trying to find him."

"Don't know anyone by that name."

Baxter nodded and backed away from the bar. His spot was quickly filled. What did he do now? Should he try the billiards and poker rooms or the gambling hall? He opted for the gambling hall. The room was stuffy and hazy from cigarette smoke. It was lit by kerosene lamps hanging from the ceiling. They did little to light the tables.

Baxter wandered around the room, sipping his drink. There was roulette, baccarat, and Monte, but the most popular game was faro. Baxter studied the patrons of the hall. With their beards, hats shading their faces, the dim light, and the smoke, it was hard to make out facial features. He was able to check the ones standing by height and eliminate many that way. Most were shorter than David was.

Baxter climbed the stairs to the poker room. He went and bought some chips. He carried them in his hand while looking for anyone who might resemble David. As he strolled, he made sure he didn't stop behind any gamblers. They might think he was working with the dealer or another player and looking at their hand.

There was an empty seat at one of the tables. Baxter sat and placed his chips in front of him. A waiter came and asked him if he wanted another drink.

"A double," he said, setting his empty glass on the tray.

The first round he was dealt four small cards and a king. He traded in the four cards and received four more of basically the same value. He folded, placing his cards face down on the table, and watched the others play. The man beside him eventually folded his cards. He was short and heavy set with a large moustache.

"I'm looking for a man named David Gastrell," Baxter said, quietly so as not to disturb the others playing.

"Never heard of him," the man said gruffly.

Baxter brought out the picture and showed it to him. The man shook his head. Baxter stuck the photo back in his pocket.

The dealer dealt the next round, and Baxter's prospects were better. He had a jack, a queen, a seven, a six, and a three. Four of the five were hearts. He threw the six of clubs on the table and picked up the card the dealer gave him. It was the five of hearts. He had a flush. He kept anteing with the others, and finally, it was time to raise the bets. He added a five-dollar chip to the pile and waited. The others did also, and one of them raised it to ten dollars. Three of the men folded. Baxter and the other man kept raising until Baxter was almost out of chips. He finally called.

The man laid down a straight in diamonds. Baxter smiled as he put down his flush. He pulled the chips towards him and stacked them in piles while the dealer dealt the next hand. Two of the men left, one of them being the guy next to him. Two more joined them.

Baxter anted and waited while the dealer shuffled, then dealt a fresh round of cards. He picked up his cards: two jacks, two eights, and a four. He had the potential for a full house.

"I hear you're looking for a man named David Gastrell." The man beside him traded in two cards.

"Do you know him?" Could he find David on their second night here? He tried to keep calm as he threw down the four.

"I had a couple of run-ins with a man named David over his dealing when he worked at the Aurora Saloon."

Baxter tossed in a dollar chip and this time received a king. He still had two pair, about the lowest hand there was. He decided to stay in for another round. He had the money, and it would make the others feel better if they could get some of their money back from him. He threw away his king. He noticed that the man didn't trade any more cards.

"Was his last name Gastrell?" Baxter asked.

"Don't know."

"Do you know where he is now?"

"Last I heard, he was heading to Atlin, British Columbia. Gold was discovered there this summer and he wanted to stake a claim."

Baxter lifted his glass and looked at the man over the rim. He had a close-cropped brown beard and moustache. His eyes were blue, and his hair a dark blond. He didn't look like the photograph he had of David, but again, ten years could make a difference in someone's appearance.

Baxter set his glass down and pushed a five-dollar chip into the pile. Should he believe this man? Would David have left here to stake a claim in northern British Columbia? Baxter doubted it. David was a remittance man. Usually, the sons were an embarrassment to their families either by being a drunk, a scoundrel, or a thief. They avoided hard work, wanting to enjoy the good life.

He had heard of some of the men using their money to buy farms or ranches and starting a new life here. But he had also heard of men who paid their month's lodging and then drank or gambled their money away in the first few days they had it. From then until their next allowance arrived, they begged or stole food or money to stay alive.

Baxter picked up a jack. He now had two pairs, jack high. He doubted that would be enough to win. He folded and finished his whiskey.

"Tough luck," the man said. He went on to raise the pot twice and then laid down his straight flush in diamonds. Like Baxter had done the round before, he pulled the chips towards himself.

231

While the next hand was being dealt, Baxter showed the man David's photograph. "This is ten years old, but is he the man you're talking about?"

"Could be." The man picked up the hand he had been dealt.

Baxter waited for more, but the man concentrated on his cards. Baxter gathered up his hand and stared at them. He felt buoyed that he had found a second person who knew a man named David who had worked at the Aurora saloon. Both men said he could resemble the man in the picture. And it was only his second day of searching.

* * *

Freddie Alden stood in the shadows created by the lanterns outside the Dominion Saloon and watched Baxter Davenport saunter out the door. He'd heard through idle chat that a detective, calling himself a friend, had come from Victoria looking for David Gastrell. It took him a while to come up with a story to tell Baxter. He thought of saying David had died, but then Davenport would have gone to the police for proof. He thought about saying David had returned to Victoria, but then he might have asked for the passenger lists of the riverboats. He'd finally decided to say that David had gone to Atlin. He didn't give a last name, so it couldn't be confirmed one way or the other. Davenport would have to leave town and go to Atlin to check the story. And that would take the pressure off Freddie. For he didn't need anyone asking questions about David Gastrell.

He wasn't sure if he convinced Davenport of that, though. It sounded like a good story to Freddie. Men were always coming from and going to other towns and gold rushes in the north. And, if they believed David had come here to find gold, it stood to reason that if he couldn't get a claim in this area, he'd try somewhere else.

"Step right up and guess where the pea is hiding," the thimblerigger called out to the men walking past him on their way into the saloon or leaving it.

Freddie saw Baxter spy the little man standing behind a small, folding table. He walked over to the table. Freddie grinned. It was a fool who was taken in by a thimblerigger. He watched as the con man or 'sharp' as he was known, held up the pea for Baxter to see then slipped it under one of the three thimbles on the table. The sharp placed a dollar bill on the table.

"Put your dollar down and guess which thimble the pea is under," the sharp said as he slowly shifted the thimbles around the table. "If you guess right, the money is yours."

Sometimes the con man had a 'shill' or accomplice who would win a few times to entice the 'flats or victims to play. The thimblerigger didn't need a shill with Baxter. He seemed eager to try his luck just as he'd been eager to lose his money at the poker table. He slapped a dollar down. When the thimblerigger stopped shuffling the thimbles, Baxter picked one. The conman lifted the thimble.

"And we have a winner," he called out. He pushed the two dollars to Baxter. "Take your money, Sir."

Baxter grinned and shoved the two dollars back at the con man. This time the thimblerigger deftly scooted the thimbles around at a faster pace. When he stopped, Baxter picked one.

"Not a winner this time." The man lifted the thimble showing nothing underneath. He pocketed Baxter's dollar and placed his on the table again. He lifted the other two thimbles and showed Baxter the pea. He covered it again and rearranged the thimbles.

Freddie, who had his own set of thimbles and pea, caught the slight movement as the thimblerigger lifted one of the thimbles just enough to pick up the pea in his fingers. He continued rearranging the thimbles until Baxter put another dollar down. He stopped and let Baxter choose one.

"Bad luck." The thimblerigger again pocketed the money.

"Let me try," a drunk pushed Baxter aside. He put a two dollar bill on the table.

The con man went through the motions and lifted the thimble the drunk picked. "A winner!"

The drunk's chest puffed out. He threw a five dollar bill next to his winnings.

This time he picked the wrong thimble. "Let me see under the other two," he yelled when told the bad news.

Freddie saw the con man drop the pea under one of the thimbles when he picked it up.

"I hope you're not calling me a cheat," the man said, sounding disappointed.

"I know how the game is played, and I know you had the pea in your hand. I want my money back."

"You lost fair and square." The thimblerigger stacked his thimbles and put them and the pea in his pocket.

"You can't leave with my money." The drunk took a shaky step towards him.

The man pushed him back and continued to take his table apart.

Freddie saw Baxter attempt to calm the drunk down but the drunk refused to be stopped. In a rage, he dashed at the man, knocking him to the ground. He sat on him and lifted his arm, smashing his fist into the man's face. Baxter grabbed the drunk's arm and pulled him off the con man. The drunk swung at Baxter but Baxter easily stepped out of the way.

Suddenly two police constables appeared and grabbed the drunk. "That's enough," one of them said.

Freddie faded into the darkness. He didn't need any run-ins with the law.

Chapter Nineteen

Baxter walked slowly back to the hotel ignoring the noise and activity around him. The police constables had listened to his story about the fight between the drunk and the thimblerigger. They'd let the con man go with a warning and took the drunk to the jail cells.

But what bothered Baxter about the night was that he had seen a man standing in the shadows when he'd come out of the saloon. At first he thought it was the man who had told him about David going to Atlin. Then he thought it might be someone wanting to talk with him about David.

So he'd paused at the thimblerigger to play a couple of games. He'd hoped he might be able to get a better look at the man but the drunk had stepped in and blocked his view. When he started fighting, Baxter had stopped him but by the time the police had stepped in and Baxter had answered their questions, the man was gone. Baxter wondered if the man would try again.

The next morning Baxter told Helen about his evening while they ate breakfast. She seemed a little pale but was doing better than he'd expected. She was a tough woman.

"I talked with a man last night who told me your brother may have left here to go to the gold rush at Atlin, British Columbia.

"David's gone?" Helen looked stricken.

"We only have that man's word for it," Baxter said hastily. "And he didn't specifically say David Gastrell. He just said David."

"Who was he? Can we find out more?" Helen took a sip of her tea.

Baxter had been trying to remember if he'd even heard the man's name. "He didn't say. We were playing poker, and there wasn't time for a long chat." He didn't tell her about the man in the shadows.

"But it does prove that David did come here, that he's not one of the men who died in Victoria." Helen smiled in relief.

"It does, if we can believe him." Baxter wiped up his plate with a piece of toast.

"I did meet a man yesterday evening who said that many of the men who made the long trip here are trying to sell their goods for enough money to get back home. Maybe David did that also, only instead of going back to Victoria, he went to Atlin."

"Do you think your brother would have the ambition to work a gold claim?"

"David didn't have the ambition to even deliver newspapers. He had the job for a week when he was fifteen but got fired because he threw the papers in the bins instead of delivering them. Why do you ask?"

"Remittance men aren't known for their determination or their honesty." Baxter chose his words carefully. "I think he would rather have stayed here and run a con game instead of getting a claim and working it at Atlin."

"Maybe he had to leave here; maybe he was kicked out of town and decided to go there to fleece prospectors."

"Yes, that could be. But I'm sure the constables would have told us."

"What are we going to do?" Helen asked.

"Well, for sure we're not taking that man's word about David leaving Dawson," Baxter said. "I'll check with some outfitters if he bought supplies to go overland. And we'll keep asking questions."

"If we can find Paul Gamon today and he'll take us to Dr. Beckwith, Miss Owens would like to go along and see her fiancé. We can stay at the Grand Forks Hotel while we are there."

"I was told he might be delivering wood to the police barracks today, so I will go there later."

"And I'll talk with Anna Degraf about her hunt for her son and find out if she has any tips for our search."

* * *

Baxter walked the boardwalk to the police barracks. He could hear the whacking of axe on wood behind the building. He entered and asked if Paul Gamon would be delivering wood that day.

"Yes, he should be here soon. You can wait for him outside."

Baxter headed around the side of the building to find out what the whacking noise was about. He found huge piles of various lengths of logs and three men chopping blocks of wood into quarters. A constable sat in the shade of the building and watched them.

All three had taken off their shirts and were sweating in the warm sun. He recognized the drunk from last night. This must be part of his punishment for hitting the thimblerigger.

Baxter watched as he selected a block of wood, set it upright on the splitting log, raised the axe over his head and smacked it into the wood. The piece broke in two and they fell to the ground. He picked up one and repeated the process. He did the same with the other one and threw the four pieces on the split pile.

Baxter looked over at the two other men. What had they done that they were sentenced to wood chopping? Should he ask if they knew David? If they'd committed some sort of crime, they would be the type of men David might hang around with. From the way they picked up their axes and struck them into the upturned wood, they had done this before. Was it from being sentenced here a lot or from their upbringing?

One of the men stopped to wipe his face.

"Get to work," a constable yelled. "Idleness will only increase your time."

"Is there any water?" one of the men asked the constable.

"Over there." The constable pointed to a bucket and dipper in the shade of one of the buildings. "Be quick about it."

The man hurried over to the bucket. He plunged the dipper into the water and brought it out dripping. He took a long drink then poured the rest on his head rubbing the water over his face.

As he watched the man go back to where his axe awaited him, Baxter heard the plodding gait of a horse and the squeak of wheels. He turned to see a man leading a horse pulling a wagon full of long logs. More wood to be cut and split for the stoves.

Baxter went over to where the horse had stopped. "Baxter Davenport," he held out his hand. "Are you Paul Gamon?"

"Yes." Paul shook his hand.

"I'd like to talk with you."

"I'll take this end, and you grab that one," Paul said pointing to the top log on the wagon.

Baxter nodded. He picked up his end, and they carried the log to the nearest pile. They hefted it on top and went back for the next one.

"Do you know a man named David Gastrell?" Baxter asked.

"Why do you want to know?"

Baxter had expected that, and as they unloaded another log, he launched into David's history, his supposed coming to Dawson, and his believed disappearance. "I'm a detective from Victoria, and I've been hired to find him."

"The name is familiar. What does he look like?"

"He's thirty-one years of age and about five foot ten inches. He has light brown hair and maybe a moustache. His eyes are bright blue."

"That could describe any number of men here. Do you have a photograph?"

"Yes. I can show you after we're finished."

They were silent as they unloaded the rest of the logs.

When they dropped the last one on the pile, Baxter reached into his pocket and pulled out the photograph. "This is David ten years ago. He has a scar on his right palm and like I said might have a moustache."

Paul shook his head. "I don't think I've met him."

Baxter hid his disappointment as he put the photograph back in his pocket. "I've heard you have a wagon for hire to take people to Grand Forks."

"Well, it's mainly to run supplies from here to Grand Forks and bring back gold but I also take passengers if there is room. Why?"

"David's sister and her maid are with me, and we would like to go visit a Dr. Beckwith and see if he may have treated David for typhoid or some other reason."

"I'm taking a load of supplies there tomorrow. You three can ride with me if you wish."

"There will be one more passenger. A Miss Pearl Owens also wants to go to see Dr. Beckwith. They're engaged."

"Yes, I know." Paul suddenly looked downcast.

Baxter wondered why but didn't have time to ask. Paul was climbing onto his wagon seat.

"I can only take three passengers," Paul continued. "More puts too much of a strain on my horse. The maid will have to stay here."

Baxter nodded. "What time are you leaving tomorrow?"

"Seven."

"We'll be there." He didn't want to take the time to ask Helen and then get back to Paul. "Where do you live?"

"I have a cabin up on the hill," Paul said. "Just follow Harper Street. You'll see my horse and wagon in the yard."

Baxter watched Paul leave and then headed out onto the boardwalk. On his way back to the hotel, he tried to bring up an image of his fight with David in Victoria. He'd spent a lot of time thinking about it since leaving Victoria but try as he might, he couldn't remember it. Even staring at David's picture didn't jog any memory.

Chapter Twenty

Freddie watched through a space in the pole fence of the police barracks as Baxter Davenport helped Paul unload the wagon. They seemed to chat a lot. Baxter was probably asking about David, but what else would they have to say that took that long?

When the wagon was empty, Paul left the yard. Freddie watched him come through the gates and head towards the main street. Freddie followed at a distance. He didn't want Paul to know he was spying. When Paul reached Queen Street, Freddie thought it was safe to approach him.

"Good morning, Paul," Freddie said, jumping up on the seat beside him. "I'm glad I found you."

"Hello, Freddie."

"When are you going to Grand Forks again? I need to see someone there."

"I'm going tomorrow, but I'm taking some passengers."

"Oh," Freddie tried to hide his disappointment. He had already found out that the next riverboat was leaving Dawson the day after tomorrow. He had reserved a cabin on it under a different name but hadn't paid, first wanting to find out when Paul was making a trip to Grand Forks.

"Yes, it's quite a story. I met a man this morning who is a detective from Victoria. He'd looking for a man named David Gastrell and wants to talk with Andrew Beckwith to see if this David was his patient."

"Sounds intriguing." Freddie did his best to hide his anger. That damned Davenport hadn't believed his story about David going to Atlin. He was still asking questions. "Why is he looking for this David Gastrell?"

"Seems he's missing, and his family in England wants to find him."

"Well, since you're busy, I guess I'll have to find another way." Freddie jumped off the slow-moving wagon.

Freddie walked towards his cabin. Baxter Davenport had to be stopped. This evening. Freddie needed to go with Paul tomorrow. It was time to put his plan into action. He would have a rest and then wait outside Baxter's hotel. When he came out this evening, he would follow him and when the opportunity arose, Freddie would strike.

* * *

Baxter had the feeling someone was watching him. He looked around the theatre in the Horseshoe Saloon, checking for the man who had been hiding in the shadows the previous evening. But he didn't see him and all the men's eyes in the room were on the petite Oatley Sisters singing and dancing on the stage. Tonight was his third evening of searching for David and he'd decided to check out the dance halls. Maybe David liked to dance with the ladies.

Baxter had been in the Horseshoe Saloon on Front Street for an hour, watching the performance of the sisters, Polly and Lottie, as they executed the buck and wing tap dance. Their shoes clicked furiously on the floor as they twirled and dipped in front of their audience. Then they quit dancing and began singing, their clear voices resounding around the large room in two-part harmony. A hush fell on the men as they sang *A Bird in a Gilded Cage* and then *Break the News to Mother*. Baxter looked at the men around him. Some were listening with their eyes closed, others had tears in their eyes. The songs brought back memories of home.

When they finished singing, the band struck up a lively two-step, and men surged forward with their dollar in hand, wanting their turn at dancing with the sisters or one of the other women waiting in the wings. All the women wore high-necked shirtwaists with sleeves to their wrists. Their long skirts swished along the floor.

Baxter paid his dollar for a dance with Lottie, but the noise of the band and stomping feet made it impossible to ask her any questions. He watched as the girls were guided around the floor for twenty minutes. Then they started their performance all over again. It must be exhausting to do this every night, all night, Baxter thought. They sure must look forward to the Sunday closures when they could recuperate.

Baxter sipped his whiskey while thinking about going to another saloon or dance hall, but was beginning to think it a futile venture. He could be standing two men over from David and not know it.

It was getting dusk outside. He returned the glass to the bar and left the building. He didn't feel like playing cards or hanging around a bar listening to conversations while looking for David. He decided to stroll along the boardwalk, watching the men as he passed them. Not that he expected to find David; that would be too much to ask for.

Baxter turned down York Street. Like every side street, it had its saloons and dance halls and was just as busy as Front Street. He stepped into one dance hall and saw that a magician was on the stage.

The magician stood behind a small table performing card tricks. When he'd picked the card the audience member had chosen, he received a round of applause. He held up his hands and when the clapping stopped he showed them that he had a small ball in each of his hands. He stretched his arms out to the sides, palms up with the balls showing.

"Pick one of my hands and I will move the ball from it to the other hand without them coming close to each other."

"The left! The left!"

"The left one it is." The magician stood still and scrunched up his face in concentration. Nothing happened.

Keeping his hands out from his body, he took a couple of steps to the right and dropped the ball from his left hand onto the table. He grinned at the audience as he stepped to the left, bent his knees, and picked it up with his right. The audience was silent for a few seconds then burst out laughing at having been so easily taken in. They clapped again as the magician left the stage.

The band quickly set up while the chairs were moved aside. They began playing and soon the floor was full of dancers waltzing around the room.

Baxter continued his walk down York Street and stopped when he reached Paradise Alley. Here there was no light from lanterns or candles. And the sun had set, so what light there was came from the moon. Maybe David had visited the ladies here, but how to ask? He started along the narrow street between rows of identical shacks, each with one window. They were called *cribs,* and each one had a woman's name

249

painted on the door. Women of various sizes and ages leaned in doorways and called to the men who walked by.

Baxter went up to one woman who gave him a big grin. When he was close enough, she grabbed his arm. He yanked it back. "I'm not here for business," he said quickly. "I want to ask you a question."

"Ask someone else. You're costing me money."

"I'll pay you." Baxter dug in his pocket and came up with a five-dollar bill.

She grabbed it. "For that amount, you've got three minutes."

"Has this man ever been to visit you?" Baxter showed her the photograph. "His name is David Gastrell."

She didn't bother to look at it. "I don't ask their names and I don't look at their faces," she said. "Now move along."

Baxter decided not to go any further up the alley. It would cost too much to pay each lady to look at the picture and get the same reaction.

He turned and started back to York Street. He had almost reached the corner when he heard a noise behind him. He started to turn, thinking maybe the woman had remembered something, when he was hit over his head. He staggered and was hit again. This time he fell to the ground.

"Hey!" he heard someone yell. "Leave that man alone!"

"Get out of here and go back to Victoria!" A voice grated in his ear before his attacker ran back along Paradise Alley.

The man who had yelled hurried up to Baxter. He knelt and assisted Baxter into a sitting position.

"Are you hurt?"

"No, I think I'm fine," Baxter said although his head throbbed. He reached up with his left hand and felt something sticky. He must be bleeding.

"Let me help you stand."

Baxter got to his feet and swayed a bit.

"I think you need a doctor and the police."

"My friend is a doctor," Baxter said. "I'll go see her."

"What about the police?"

"I didn't see who hit me, so I wouldn't be able to give a description. Did you get a look at him?"

"Unfortunately, no. He was too far away. Would you like me to walk with you?"

"Thank you, but I'll be fine, Mr...?"

"Edmund Davies."

"I'm Baxter Davenport," Baxter held out his right hand. "I thank you for your help, Mr. Davies. I'll just go back to my hotel."

* * *

Helen was pulled up from a deep sleep by someone tapping on her door. Who was it at this hour? And where was Mattie? Couldn't she hear the noise and come to see who it was?

"Miss," Mattie whispered from the other side of the door. "Miss. Mr. Davenport is injured and needs you."

Helen threw back the covers and opened her door. Mattie was holding a candle, and Baxter leaned against the wall. Helen could see blood in his hair.

"Come in," she beckoned, heedless of protocol. "Sit on my trunk."

Mattie held the candle so Helen could examine Baxter's head. "What happened?"

"I was walking along the street when someone came up behind and hit me."

"You have two wounds here."

"Yes. I stumbled with the first and fell with the second."

"Mattie, get me some water and clean rags. I need to wash the blood off."

Mattie lit Helen's candle and then left with her own.

Helen carefully moved Baxter's hair around, checking the injury.

"Ouch," Baxter said and tilted his head away from her.

"Stay still." She pulled his head back. "I have to see how bad it is."

Mattie returned with a pitcher of water and poured it into the basin. She handed Helen a piece of cloth and a towel.

"Who did this?" Helen asked as she dipped the cloth in the water and gently dabbed at the wound.

"I don't know. I didn't see him."

"Did he rob you?"

"No. A man named Edmund Davies came to my rescue and chased him off." Baxter hesitated.

"What?" There was something he wasn't telling her.

"Before the attacker ran away, he told me to leave Dawson and go back to Victoria."

Helen gasped. "You mean this has something to do with us looking for David?"

"It seems like it."

Helen examined the gashes once the blood had been washed away. "They aren't very deep and don't require stitches. But your head is going to hurt for a few days."

"Thank you for looking at them for me," Baxter said, standing. "I'll go to my room now. We have to get up early to go to Grand Forks."

"Do you still feel like going? This could be the danger you warned me about."

"Yes. This has made me all the more determined than ever to find your brother. There is more to this than just a missing man."

Chapter Twenty-One

"Come in," Helen answered the knock on her door. Was it morning already? It seemed she had just gotten back to sleep after cleaning Baxter's head wounds.

"Good morning, Miss," Mattie said, entering with a pitcher of water and a towel. "It's time to get ready to go to Grand Forks." She set the pitcher on the washstand. "I'll be outside the door."

Helen washed and called for Mattie to come back in. Mattie opened Helen's trunk and removed the clothes she'd placed on top and then helped Helen into her combination and held up a dark blue, split riding skirt. Helen stepped into it, and Maddie pulled it up. The skirt legs reached Helen's calves, and each leg had a row of buttons down the front. These were to hold the modesty panel that could be attached to the skirt. Helen did up the top three buttons on the left to close the skirt but declined to wear the panel. Mattie helped Helen put on a matching blue, hip-length jacket and did up the buttons.

Helen sat on the bed while Mattie pushed on her light blue stockings and her garters to hold them up.

Mattie did Helen's hair in a bun at the nape of her neck. "Your hat will sit nicely if you need to wear it," she said. "You go and meet Mr. Davenport while I clean up here. I'll bring your valise down when I'm finished."

Helen nodded and picked up her wide-brimmed hat. As she walked past Baxter's door, she wondered how he was feeling and if he was even up. He had a nasty head wound and his head must be sore. She thought about knocking just to make sure, then decided against it. She headed down to her table in the dining room.

She was surprised to see Baxter sitting with a cup of coffee in front of him.

"Good morning," Baxter smiled.

"You're looking chipper this morning," Helen said as she sat down. "How is your head?"

"Much better, but I still have a headache."

"Do you think it's wise that we continue looking for David?" Helen asked. She didn't want anyone else to get hurt.

"I believe so. We are going to be away for a couple of days. Whoever it was might think we've quit asking questions."

"Did you find out anything last night?"

"No. I asked a few of the ladies at a couple of dance halls, and they don't remember dancing with him. I even checked along Paradise Alley, but the one woman I spoke with was uncooperative, so I didn't try any others. So far, our only lead is that he may have gone to the gold rush at Atlin."

"And there is no way we can confirm that because I'm certainly not going there."

"Maybe Dr. Beckwith will have some information to help us. How was your visit with Mrs. Degraf?"

"We had a long chat, but she hasn't met anyone named David Gastrell in her search for her son."

The waitress came over and took their order.

They'd just finished their breakfast when Mattie came into the dining room, Helen's valise in her hand.

"It's all packed," Mattie said, setting it on the floor.

Helen didn't like the idea of not having her maid with her. Mattie did so much for her and now she'd have to do it herself. She shrugged. She guessed she'd manage.

* * *

Baxter and Helen walked up Harper Street, Baxter carrying Helen's valise. On the way, they discussed who they had angered by asking questions about David and, more importantly, why was the attacker angry.

"It couldn't be someone who was also looking for my brother because he'd been

256

scammed," Helen said. "You'd think he'd be happy we are trying to find David."

"I think it might be something worse than that. It might have something to do with one of the men who died in Victoria in August."

"You mean he killed David and doesn't want us to find out?"

"Or maybe he is David and doesn't want us to discover that maybe he killed one of the men."

"Oh." Helen was quiet for a while. "I really can't argue with you on that."

When they reached Paul's cabin, he was outside talking with a young woman. The horse was hitched to the wagon loaded with sacks of flour, sugar, and rice. There were also boxes full of cans of milk, oysters, and macaroni and cheese.

Helen made the introductions. "Miss Owens, this is Mr. Baxter Davenport. Baxter, this is Miss Pearl Owens."

"Set the valise on the boxes," Paul said. "Pearl will ride here on the seat with me. You two can ride on the sacks."

Baxter put Helen's bag next to a large suitcase and helped Helen climb into the back of the wagon. He scrambled up beside her. They settled in as best they could while Paul flicked the reins, and the horse started along the street.

It was a cloudy but warm day. They travelled through the streets of the town and then out onto a well-worn trail beside the

Klondike River. Baxter's head soon began feeling the effect of the movement of the wagon.

The trail was dry and dusty. It was busy in both directions with horse or mule-drawn wagons and carts loaded with sacks and boxes. Men and a few women carried bags of varying sizes as they weaved their way in and out of the carts.

"Those bags and boxes in the wagons headed back to Dawson are full of gold." Pearl turned slightly to talk with them.

"From the gold claims?" Baxter asked.

"Yes. The miners send their gold dust and nuggets to the Alaska Commercial Company store to sell to them or for safe keeping."

Baxter looked at the tents and cabins that dotted the Klondike River valley. The cabins were of various shapes and sizes and made out of any material the owner could find.

There was constant noise along the trail: people chatting or calling to each other, carts and wagons creaking and groaning under the weight of their loads, mules braying. Baxter and Helen were jostled around as the wheels hit bumps or dips in the road.

"This is Bonanza Creek," Pearl said as they turned and continued beside the creek that flowed into the Klondike River.

Baxter couldn't believe his luck as he looked around. He was in the famous

Klondike gold fields, and that thought took his mind off his headache. He regretted not coming last year, but the knowledge he probably wouldn't have been able to stake a claim when he got here lessened that regret. He doubtless would be like the majority of the men wandering the streets of Dawson right now: defeated and disappointed. Or maybe he'd have sold his remaining supplies and gone back to Victoria. But now he was riding beside the actual creek where gold was discovered.

He saw that Helen was just as enthralled as he. She turned to him.

"I can't believe I've actually made it all the way from England to see this." She paused. "Well, it was really to find my brother, but this is a bonus."

The four spent the rest of the ride talking. Baxter shared his story about his upbringing in Victoria and how he'd become a private investigator. Helen told Paul and Pearl about her brother being banished from England ten years ago and how he'd gone missing. He was the reason she was in Dawson.

Pearl told them how she had gotten a reporting assignment with the Halifax Morning Herald, her hometown newspaper, and had come north. She and her cousin, Emma, had made the journey to the town of Fortymile on the Yukon River to stay with Emma's brother, Sam, who had been in the north for five years with two of his friends.

Gold had just been discovered on Rabbit Creek, later named Bonanza Creek and Sam and his friends headed there. She and Emma bought a tent and supplies and followed them to where Dawson now sat. At the time, it was just a few tents.

Pearl had been sending articles and sketches about the gold rush to her newspaper ever since. Emma had married one of her brother's friends, and they'd headed back to Halifax in the fall of 1897.

Paul said he'd been in the north for five years. He'd originally come on a trip with his father. When his father left, Paul stayed in Fortymile. He had no desire to prospect for gold and had worked as a bartender and in a saw mill. When gold was discovered, he moved to Dawson and started working on the newly set up saw mill there. Like Pearl, he'd seen the town grow from a few tents to what it was now.

It was mid-afternoon when they arrived at Grand Forks. It was a smaller version of Dawson with buildings in various stages of construction, plus cabins and tents. Men also wandered the streets here as they did in Dawson.

Paul stopped in front of the Grand Forks Hotel. "You get rooms for the night while I deliver these supplies. We'll have something to eat when I come back, and then I'll take you to the Beckwith/Braddock claim."

Paul went around and helped Pearl off the seat while Baxter jumped off the back and aided Helen in getting down. Baxter picked up Helen's valise and Pearl's suitcase.

"I don't need a room," Pearl said. "I'll be staying out on the claim with my friend, Florence."

Baxter looked at Paul. "Will you be needing a room?"

"I'll be loading up with gold this evening, so will sleep with my horse and wagon. I've got my bedroll under the seat."

The three walked into the hotel, and Baxter set Pearl's suitcase beside a chair just inside the door. To one side of the lobby was a restaurant, and a door on the other side led to a saloon.

"I'd like two rooms," Helen said to the man behind the counter.

He looked from Helen to Baxter. "We have a small room reserved for women or couples. There are bunks for men in a large common room. You can pick whichever one is empty."

"We'll take them," Baxter said. He paid for the accommodation, then carried Helen's valise upstairs and placed it on the top bunk of the lady's room and went looking for his bed. The large room had twenty single beds in it, all made up with blankets and pillows. He'd have his choice of any of the empty ones when he returned.

* * *

Freddie hurried up the hill towards Paul's cabin knowing he would get his ride after all. He hadn't wanted to kill that detective because that would have had the mounted police scouring the town for the killer. But he knew he'd hit him hard enough to put him in the hospital for a few days.

And Freddie had a story ready about why he was showing up unexpectedly: a new dentist in town had asked him if he knew anyone who could supply wood for the dentist's office. If Paul asked him how he met the dentist, Freddie would say at his table at the Northern Saloon. Freddie rubbed his hands in anticipation. This was working out well. When that detective didn't show up, Freddie would ask if he could go instead.

Paul didn't have time to tell anyone that Freddie was riding with him. And if he kept his head down on the ride and got off before they reached Grand Forks maybe no one would be able to say who was in the seat beside Paul.

Grand Forks had spread out a bit, and there were a few miners camped along the road leading into it. He would tell Paul that one of those miners was a friend. He heard the man was sick and wanted to visit him. That way, he could get off the wagon before

262

it reached the town so no one would see him with Paul. And if Paul picked him up again at the same spot tomorrow, anyone Paul met in town would say he was alone.

Freddie still had his reservation on the riverboat leaving tomorrow afternoon. He figured he would ride to Grand Forks today and return tomorrow morning with Paul and his load of gold. On the way back, he would kill Paul, drive the wagon to town, unload as much gold as he could put in a large suitcase he'd bought, and board the boat just before it sailed.

Freddie thought it would be a day or two before Paul's body was discovered, another day for the police to decide what had happened and start asking questions. He reckoned that if someone did notice him with Paul and told the police, he'd be at least three days ahead of them. If things went right with transferring to a steamship at St. Michael, he'd stay ahead of them. And he would purchase a ticket on the first steamer leaving St. Michael, whether it was going to Seattle, Victoria, or San Francisco.

He also decided to change his appearance by shaving off his moustache and beard before leaving his cabin tomorrow. He'd even bought a hat to pull down over his hair to hide the colour.

Freddie had everything planned. He hadn't told anyone, not even Miss Mulrooney or the owner of the Northern that he was leaving. He had paid his rent for the week and booked his poker table for the rest of the month. Everything was going according to his schedule. He was almost at Paul's cabin when he saw Baxter Davenport and a woman walking up the hill ahead of him. Baxter was carrying a valise.

Freddie stopped dead in his tracks. They were still going to Grand Forks with Paul. How could that be? Davenport should be in the hospital. He had hit him twice, hard. He swore under his breath when he saw them stop at Paul's cabin. Paul's wagon was already full, and Pearl Owens was also there.

He watched as Pearl climbed up on the seat while the other two crawled into the back and sat on the sacks piled there. He couldn't believe it as he watched them drive away. He should be on the wagon. He had made so many plans, and now they were ruined.

Freddie turned and stomped down the hill to Front Street. Even though it was early morning, he needed a drink. Although the music and dancing quit anywhere between four and seven o'clock in the morning, the bars stayed open. He went into the Dominion and ordered a double whiskey. He downed it and ordered another. It was a good thing he hadn't said anything to Miss Mulrooney about leaving nor had given up his table at the Northern Saloon. After the two drinks, he went to his cabin. The suitcase was open on his bed ready for him to fill with gold dust and nuggets. He knocked it off and threw himself on the bed.

What did he do now? He had to leave Dawson, and soon. What if that man who chased him away last night was able to describe him to the police? What if they were looking for him right now? They would find out what he had done in Victoria if they arrested him. He was getting desperate.

He didn't know when Paul would be going to Grand Forks again and if that trip would coincide with a riverboat leaving Dawson. He knew it would be useless to wait for Paul to return tomorrow and try to convince him to come to his cabin before he deposited the gold at the bank. Paul had his own approach to doing things and didn't like deviating from his procedure. If he had gold to deliver, that was his priority.

Freddie banged his fist against the wall. He was so mad, madder than he'd ever been in his life. He'd worked hard to come up with this plan. Everything was arranged. But there was nothing he could do except try again next time Paul was going to Grand Forks. It had been in a casual conversation that he'd been able to ask Paul about this trip. It would be suspicious if he asked again, especially since he had never expressed an interest before.

Maybe he should steal what he could today from whomever he could and leave tomorrow on the riverboat. But then he wouldn't have the gold he needed to make a new start. He'd be right back to where he was when he left Victoria: homeless and penniless.

Chapter Twenty-Two

Mattie looked forward to her day off. After leaving Helen's valise in the dining room and saying goodbye to Helen and Baxter, she hurried to her bedroom and flung herself on her bed. She lay there basking in the knowledge that Helen wouldn't be calling on her for anything for the rest of the day and part of tomorrow. Her time was her own. She picked up the newspapers Helen had discarded and read through them, learning about the town through the articles and advertisements.

When she was sure that Helen and Baxter would have left the hotel, she went down and asked for hot water for a bath. And the best part of doing that was that she didn't have to heat and haul the water. It would be brought up and poured into the tub by someone else. And they would bring her a cloth and towel. She could act like the mistress this time.

Mattie put on her slippers and carried her clean set of clothes to the washroom, where water already steamed in the tub. She hung her clean clothes on a hook behind the door and undressed. After her bath, she would sort through Helen's and her clothes and send the soiled ones to the laundry.

With a grin, Mattie stepped into the tub and sank into the water. It felt so good to luxuriate in the warm water. There was no time limit. No one would be calling for her. She wouldn't have to quickly jump out and dress.

As the water cooled, she regretted not asking for more hot water to be brought up. She scrubbed herself with soap and the cloth, then stood and stepped out. She dried with the towel and put on her combination, a pair of blue bloomers she'd inherited from Helen, and the matching dress that reached just below her thighs.

Mattie slid her feet into her slippers, left the towel for the staff to take when they emptied the tub and hurried to her bedroom. She dropped her soiled clothes on her bed, then sat beside them and pulled on her stockings and shoes. She decided that if she wanted to enjoy the full extent of her freedom, she had to take her and Helen's clothes to a laundry first. There had only been a couple of days that she'd been able to do laundry on the boats as they were coming here.

She opened her trunk and took out three dresses and a combination. In Helen's room, she sorted through and brought out two skirts, two shirt waists, three dresses, and three combinations. There were also some dirty clothes in the trunks in Belinda's office she'd have to get.

It wasn't proper etiquette to display soiled washing in public places, but she couldn't think of any way to get the bundles of clothes down the street. She could try wrapping them in her shawl, but it wasn't big enough to hide them. She could make two trips if necessary.

Mattie hurried down the stairs to Belinda's office. She knocked on the door and entered when Belinda called, "Come in."

"Good morning," Belinda said, smiling at her. "How can I help you today?"

"I need to send some clothes to a laundry, and I'm wondering the proper way to do that here."

"I'll have a porter bring a bag to put them in, and then he'll take them there for you."

"He will?" Mattie couldn't hide her surprise. She wasn't used to someone doing her job for her.

"Yes." Belinda stood. "I'll summon him now. Where are these clothes?"

"There are some in my room, some in Helen's, plus I have to get a few from these trunks."

"Sounds like he might need two bags," Belinda said. "I'll go get him."

Mattie opened the top trunk and looked at the clothes she'd folded in it for laundering. She would not let a porter touch her and Helen's unmentionables.

The door opened, and Belinda came in with two large, white canvas bags. She set one by the door and handed the other to Mattie, who smiled gratefully. Mattie picked up the folded clothes and placed them in the bag.

"Do you know where the nearest laundry is?" Mattie asked Belinda as she worked.

"There is one just down the street run by a German lady and her three children. She arrived in town and immediately bought a controlling interest in a bath house. She partitioned the building with a laundry on one side and a counter for her daughter to sell cakes and ice cream and soft drinks like root beer and ginger ale on the other."

When the bag was full and the trunk nearly empty, Mattie pulled the drawstring on the bag and then closed the lid of the trunk. She tried lifting the bag, but it was too heavy.

She dragged it to the door. "Thank you, Belinda," she said as she opened the door.

A large man was waiting outside. "Let me take that, Ma'am." He reached in and picked it up with one hand.

"I'll fill this one on the second floor," Mattie said, picking up the other bag.

"I'll store this one behind the counter in the lobby and come up."

Mattie hurried up the stairs. She wanted to fill the bag before the porter arrived. This one wasn't as heavy as the first, and the porter had no problem throwing it over his shoulder and carrying it down the stairs. Mattie grabbed her purse and followed him.

They went out the hotel's front door and along Front Street to a smaller building sandwiched between two larger ones. The sign in the front advertised Laundry and Ice Cream. Mattie pushed open the door and held it for the porter. He set both bags on the small counter and turned to leave.

"Thank you," Mattie said, realizing she didn't even know his name.

An older woman came out from behind a curtain. She opened one of the bags to look in. "Just women's clothes?"

"Yes," Mattie said. Then she dared to push her luck. "I'd like these mended and washed." Mending was her job before she sent her mistress's clothes down to the laundry in the basement of their mansion.

"Yes, Ma'am," the woman said. She wrote on a piece of paper and gave it to Mattie. It had a number on it. Mattie noticed the woman's red and cracked hands and felt sorry for her. Washing clothes was not an easy way to make a living.

"They will be ready in two days," the woman said. "Would you like an ice cream?" My daughter is through there." She pointed to a doorway leading into another room.

"No, thank you." Mattie hesitated, but then she figured it was safe to ask about David. She doubted this woman would have had anything to do with him except wash his clothes. "Have you ever had a customer named David Gastrell come in?"

"I don't take names. I just give numbers for them to use when they pick their clothes up."

Mattie nodded and left the building. She almost skipped down the street. Her duties were done. She was totally free now.

She walked until she found a café. Helen had given her additional money to pay for the laundry and for any extras that might come up. Mattie decided that eating in a café counted as an extra. She'd never dined anywhere but at her parents' home and her employer's house. Even when she and Clara went on their afternoon jaunts, they'd taken cheese and bread with them. It was only on this trip that she became familiar with eating in a real restaurant.

The waitress came over with a menu. Mattie looked it over and decided on a sardine sandwich, a dish of stewed fruit, and hot chocolate. Cocoa and hot chocolate had been reserved for the upper classes for hundreds of years. Even when chocolates became mass-produced, the lower classes could not afford them. She'd made hot chocolate for Helen on cool days and some evenings before she went to bed. In all that time, Mattie hadn't drunk any. To eat or drink any household food other than what they were given for their meals was a reason for instant dismissal.

While she waited, she looked around at the patrons. They were mainly men. The two other women in the room were accompanied by a man. She was the only single woman. She looked at each individual man. It was like there was a dress code for them here in Dawson. Most of them wore black trousers, a white shirt, and a black jacket and had a beard and moustache or just a moustache. There wasn't a clean-shaven man among them in the room.

When he was fifteen, David had tried to grow a moustache and beard like Prince George, Queen Victoria's grandson. But his efforts at a beard had been in vain as he grew older. His beard had always been patchy and looked scruffy even though he had it trimmed by a barber. He'd had more success with his moustache, but his anger at not having a matching beard made him shave both off.

Mattie had heard Helen and Baxter talk about the moustache that David's landlady said he'd grown. He must have gotten over his anger about not being able to grow a beard.

The sardine sandwich was good, and she enjoyed her stewed fruit. While she savoured the hot chocolate she surreptitiously studied the men. Was one of them David? None had his light brown hair, though. Was one of them the man who had attacked Baxter? Baxter hadn't been able to describe him, so there were no characteristics or marks she could watch for; he could be anyone.

Mattie paid for her meal and went out onto the sidewalk. She was now afraid to ask anyone about David. How much did the attacker know about the search? Did he know that she and Helen were also here asking questions about him? Thankfully, being a maid and on duty most of the time, she hadn't been able to talk with many people, so she thought it quite safe to watch for David as she walked.

But she wasn't looking for a man of his size or someone with his hair colour or having his facial features. All those may have been altered as he grew older. So what she was looking for were his eyes. Helen described them as sparkling blue, but that didn't do them justice. Mattie remembered them as a sharp, dramatic blue that didn't show up in the photograph. Their deep, azure colour made a woman swoon when she looked into them, and many a woman had.

She knew she had to be careful if she found him. If he turned his charm on her, she wasn't sure if she could resist him, just as she'd fallen under his spell years ago. But she was older now and hopefully wiser.

Chapter Twenty-Three

After Helen, Baxter and Pearl ate Helen paid for the meals, and they went outside. Paul put Pearl's suitcase in the wagon. He helped her into the seat while Helen and Baxter sat on the back end of the wagon with their legs hanging over. The valley they rode through was bare of trees. There were just stumps and sparse brush.

"Trees covered this valley before gold was discovered," Pearl turned to tell them. "The miners cut all the trees down to build their cabins and for the fires used to melt the permafrost so they could dig down to the gold."

There was constant movement of men hurrying in both directions, some carrying sacks or equipment, others just walking. Cabins and a few tents dotted the area. Mounds of dirt and long rows of wooden troughs covered the hillsides and valley floor. Men were busy shovelling dirt from the piles into troughs, with water pouring out the ends.

"Those mounds are what the miners dug out of the ground over the winter," Pearl explained. "They used to be many times

275

higher than they are now. This past spring, the miners built the sluice boxes and set them up, so that water from the creek ran down them. Then they shovelled the dirt into the sluice boxes, and the running water separated the gold from the rest of the debris as it ran over the riffles."

"What are riffles?" Helen asked.

"They are narrow pieces of wood set crossways in the bottom of the sluice box."

"Here we are," Paul said, stopping the horse beside a cabin.

"Pearl!" A woman dressed in men's trousers and shirt dashed around the corner of the cabin.

Pearl jumped off the side of the wagon, and the two women hugged.

As Baxter helped Helen down, he looked around the claim. The logs of the main section of the cabin were faded and had moss and mud chinking to fill in the space between them. A new addition had been built on the back, and the logs still had the look of green wood. There was a slab door, and a burlap bag covered the one window. A second cabin was partially completed further away with a tent set up near it.

Baxter looked up at the blue sky and then the creek flowing by. Would he have liked this type of life if he'd managed to come here last year?

"Hi, Paul," the woman said.

"Florence." Paul dipped his head.

Pearl made the introductions. "Florence, this is Miss Helen Gastrell and Mr. Baxter Davenport. Helen, Baxter, this is my best friend, Mrs. Florence Braddock."

"Pleased to meet both of you," Florence said. "What brings you this way?"

"We are looking for my brother and have a few questions we would like to ask Dr. Beckwith," Helen said.

"And I've brought your bridesmaid dress," Pearl added.

"Oh. I'll take you to see Andrew, um Dr. Beckwith, and then I'll look at the dress. Come with me."

Florence led them along the creek to where two men were repairing part of a long sluice box. Both wore light shirts, dark trousers, and had hats on their heads. They stopped working as the three walked up to them

"My brother Andrew Beckwith and my husband Eugene Braddock. Andrew, Eugene, these are Miss Helen Gastrell and Mr. Baxter Davenport. Andrew, they've come to ask you some questions." She turned away, and she and Pearl hurried back to the wagon.

After they shook hands, Andrew asked. "Questions about what?"

* * *

While Baxter launched into the story of why he and Helen had travelled to Dawson, Helen watched Eugene, who had gone back to work on the sluice. His hat was pulled down over his eyes but there was something familiar about him. Had she seen him before? Had he been in Dawson in the past couple of days? Was he one of the hundreds of men she had stared at since they'd arrived?

"And we were wondering if he might have gone to you for medication or an injury." Baxter ended, handing Andrew the photograph.

"Can't say I remember him." Andrew shook his head. "But there were a lot of sick men when I was there. Probably still are."

"Yes, we spoke with Father Judge," Helen said turning from Eugene to Andrew. "The hospital is full."

Andrew gave the picture to Eugene. "You came here last fall. Did you meet up with this David on your travels?"

Helen started. Eugene had come here last fall, the same time that David was supposed to have come. Helen watched as he glanced at the picture. She hadn't noticed any reaction from him when her name was mentioned. Did he seem a little shocked when he saw the man staring back at him? She tried to see the colour of his eyes but his hat put them in shadow. She checked his right palm but couldn't see any scar from this angle. He did have a crescent-shaped scar on the back of his hand. David hadn't had one of those, but then it had been ten years. Anything could happen in that amount of time.

Could he be David? He was the right height, but he had a more muscular physique than she remembered David having. That could be because it looked like being a miner was hard work. He didn't seem to recognize her, but again she'd changed a lot since she was the eleven-year-old girl he'd last seen.

He would have known the name, though.

Helen wondered if Baxter noticed Eugene's reaction to the picture or if it was just her imagination. He didn't ask any other questions of him. She wished that Mattie had come. Mattie had worked in their house since she was fifteen, and David was about seventeen. She would have more memories of him than Helen herself. And he might recognize her.

"My father asked me to bring my brother a message." Helen watched Eugene. "It's important that I give it to him."

"I don't know him." Eugene barely lifted his head as he gave the photograph to Andrew and turned back to the sluice box.

Did he show some interest in her statement? Did he answer too quickly? She hadn't recognized David's voice in the four words he'd spoken. She couldn't think of anything else she could say except outright ask him if he was David. And she couldn't do that without more confirmation. If he hadn't wanted to admit that he was her brother now with her standing there, then all he would do was deny it if she queried him.

"Come back to the cabin and have some coffee," Andrew said.

Eugene continued to work as the others started to walk away.

"Are you coming, Eugene?" Andrew asked.

"No, I'll stay here. This has to be done."

Was he trying to avoid them? Helen wondered. It seemed strange and almost rude that he wouldn't want to entertain guests. But then, David hadn't really cared about other people. He also hadn't cared about working any more than he had to. If Eugene was her brother, he certainly had changed. Would their father have been willing to meet this new David, if indeed he was David?

How could she find out in the little time they were going to be here?

They got back to the cabin and found Florence wearing a beautiful pink dress, a sharp contrast to the trousers and shirt she'd had on a short time ago. While the men went to the fire pit to make the coffee, Helen stopped with the women.

"That's a lovely dress," she said to Pearl.

"Thank you." Pearl stood back looking at her friend. "I thought it would fit perfectly when I saw it."

"I wish I had mirror to see," Florence grumbled.

"You'll see when you come to Dawson for the wedding."

"Oh, didn't Andrew tell you? We're coming in on Tuesday for the grand showing of the animatoscope movie films."

"No, he never said anything."

"Maybe it's supposed to be a surprise. But I think I should take this off. I don't want to get it dirty." Florence and Pearl headed to the cabin. "Come with us, Helen," Florence said.

They entered the small cabin with its table and two chairs, wood stove, and shelves for canned goods, pots and pans, dishes, and cutlery. A hanging blanket covered a doorway on the back wall. Florence pushed it aside, revealing a double bed and a row of clothes hanging along one wall. She stepped into the bedroom and pulled the blanket shut but continued the conversation.

"Are you and Mr. Davenport going to watch the film?" Florence asked.

"I've been concentrating on finding my brother. I don't know anything about what's happening in Dawson."

"Yes, Pearl told me that you haven't seen him in years. Do you think you'll recognize him after all this time?"

"I'm not sure." Helen thought about Eugene. Maybe she could find out more about him. "How long have you and Eugene been married?"

"Almost two months." Florence pushed aside the blanket and came out dressed in her trousers and shirt again. She'd hung the dress with the other clothes.

"How did you meet?" Helen hoped Florence wouldn't think she was too nosy.

Florence looked at Pearl. "It was through Pearl and her cousin, Sam. Andrew had been very disappointed that we couldn't stake a claim when we arrived. That's why he set up his doctor's practice. Pearl and Paul brought Andrew and me out here to see what operating a gold claim was like and I met Eugene. He was working for Sam on his claim here."

"Is Sam coming here today?" Pearl asked.

"Not that I've heard."

"He doesn't live here?" Helen asked in surprise. "I thought this was his claim." He was one of the reasons they'd come. Belinda had told them he had been in the north longer than any others. He could have met David. Plus, he'd hired Eugene. He might be able to tell them more about him.

282

"He married a widow who has a claim further up the creek. He lives there now, and the two of them are working her claim. We've taken over looking after his claim here."

"Oh." Helen didn't think they had time to go see him.

"Where are you staying?" Florence asked. "I could get him to stop in and see you next time he's going to Dawson."

"We're at the Fairview Hotel. But we are leaving within a week."

"So you met Pearl at the hotel."

"Belinda suggested I speak with her. And she mentioned we should come out here and talk with Andrew and Sam." But it was time to get back to Eugene. "You and Eugene bought Sam's friend's claim."

"Yes. Donald married Sam's sister, Emma, and they went back to Halifax. Emma is with child now, and they decided not to return."

"Andrew said Eugene has only been here since last fall."

"Florence nodded. "He couldn't find a claim, so started working for Sam for a percentage of what he found."

"It looks like hard work."

"It is, but we love it. And we can't wait until Pearl and Andrew get married, and she comes out to help. But enough being inside and talking. That'll happen most of the winter." She picked up a plate with a towel covering a hump. "I made a cake this morning. Let's take it out and get some of that coffee."

Pearl found some cutlery and plates, and they went outside.

Helen asked for David's photograph and showed it to Florence. Maybe she would notice the resemblance between it and Eugene. If she did, she made no comment on it. She just shook her head while she cut the cake.

Helen did her best to hide her disappointment. They'd learned nothing on this trip, and it looked as if she was the only one who thought Eugene bore any similarity to David.

Chapter Twenty-Four

Mattie began walking along the crowded Front Street. It was early afternoon, so the saloons and dance halls were quieter than in the evening. Again, she was awed by how the men she met were courteous toward her. Even in their dirty and worn clothes, they were gentlemen. Then she saw an obviously inebriated man swaying his way down the sidewalk. The drunk headed in her direction. She stopped, wondering which way she should dodge to miss him.

A man stepped in front of her and guided the drunk to the side.

Mattie smiled her appreciation, and the man nodded at her. His eyes above his beard were a soft brown.

But the man didn't continue walking. Instead, he raised his hat. "Mr. Edmund Davies, at your service."

Mattie took in the medium-height, powerfully built man dressed in a white silk shirt with a starched collar, a necktie with a stick pin, and a silver waistcoat. This handsome man looked as if he had money, yet he introduced himself to her.

"Miss Mattie Lewis," Mattie said shyly. She was not used to men talking to her in such a polite way.

"Pleased to meet you, Miss Lewis. Are you new in Dawson?'

"Yes, I arrived with my…." Mattie didn't want to say mistress. She didn't want this man to know she was a servant. She didn't want to see the disdain and scorn in his eyes. She didn't want him to walk away, ashamed that he'd spoken with a woman of such low class. "I arrived a couple of days ago with my friends."

"Welcome to our humble city." Edmund Davies bowed slightly. "May I accompany you on your walk?"

Mattie was taken aback. She'd never had a man ask her to walk with him in public. But she'd been taught her place well. She wasn't supposed to be talking with such an impressive man, let alone walk with him. But, how to say no? That worry was taken away from her.

"Edmund, there you are!" a voice boomed. "I've been looking for you."

"Excuse me," Mr. Davies smiled at her. "Perhaps we can walk some other time."

Mattie watched Edmund and his friend head into the crowd, wondering if the polite man was the same one who had chased off Baxter's attacker. She shook her head. It didn't matter; she wouldn't be seeing him again. She continued on her quest along

Front Street. Despite being one of a few women in a sea of men, she felt no fear, not like in London. On their afternoons off, she and Clara always made sure they were home before dark. Some of the streets were not safe for a woman to walk at night.

Log and frame buildings of various sizes stood side by side, facing the Yukon River. In the block between King and Queen Streets were many saloons. She saw the Aurora Saloon where Baxter had gone that first night. Mattie counted four theatres and a number of saloons past King Street that also had a blend of dance halls and theatres. She marvelled at the names: the Northern, the Dominion, the Phoenix, the Combination Theatre, the Monte Carlo, and the Horseshoe Saloon advertising the Oatley Sisters in concert.

At each corner, Mattie looked down the side street. Most were just as packed with saloons, dance halls, and theatres. She saw three women come out of one of the dance halls. They flounced their way along the sidewalk in their fancy dresses and boas. They laughed and flirted with the men as they went by.

Again, she wondered if she should apply to work in a dance hall. It looked like the women were popular and made money. She'd heard they were paid for each dance, and many danced all night. They were also paid for every drink they convinced a man to buy. The big question was, what did it take to be an entertainer in one of the dance halls? What special abilities did the women need to have to be allowed on one of the stages?

She had to make up her mind soon. Did she want to leave Dawson, or did she want to stay? Helen and Baxter would have to go back to Victoria soon. The riverboats only ran until mid-September. They had to reach the mouth of the Yukon River before the river froze, or passengers would be stuck in a town somewhere along the river until spring.

Mattie decided that while watching for David, she would also check to see what businesses were already set up in Dawson and if any were looking for employees. She could start as a worker and open her own establishment once she was trained. After all, Belinda had started small.

After an hour of walking up and down Front Street and some side streets, she admitted that finding David in this mass of constantly moving humanity would be impossible. It would be easier for him to find her, she being one of the few women in town.

Was there a way of getting a message to him? The only one who Baxter had mentioned knowing David was Tom Chisholm, and it hadn't sounded as if Mr. Chisholm wanted anything to do with him. So there was no use talking with him.

Was there a bulletin board set up somewhere where she could place a message? Surely one of the big commercial stores must have a board as a courtesy to their customers. Mattie walked in the front door of the North American Transportation and Trading Company. She wandered around but didn't see any place where she could leave a message.

She went to the Alaska Commercial Company store. This time she found a bulletin board on each side of the King Street entrance. The boards were already overflowing with notes of different sizes and on various types of writing material. And there were notes tacked on the wall beside the boards. It would take all day to read every one of them, and a person would only do that if they were expecting someone to leave them a note. David wouldn't be.

Mattie sighed as she left the store. Baxter was the detective and she would leave it up to him to find David. Once they had found him, though, she would put her plan to confront him into action.

When she neared the docks, she saw a large crowd milling around. Men and a few women were standing on the wharves, while the rest stood on the hillside and others blocked the street. A band was playing *The Commodore Song,* and everyone waved enthusiastically to a couple on the departing riverboat deck, who waved in return.

"Must be someone important," Mattie mused.

She was thinking about walking to Second Street to continue to the hotel when suddenly, with a cracking of wood, one of the wharves gave way. Mattie gasped as she watched about twenty-five men and one woman plunge into the deep water. While they floundered, trying to keep their heads up, life preservers, chairs, and anything they could hold onto that would float were tossed over the side of the riverboat. Men on shore threw ropes at them while others scrambled into watercraft and rowed towards them.

Some men made it to shore on their own using the life preservers or grabbing hold of the ropes, while others were pulled into the boats. At long last, everyone was on shore. When the woman was dragged out, she stood dripping wet and began laughing.

Mattie smiled at her reaction to the dunking then walked the rest of the way to the hotel.

* * *

Baxter stepped out of the Grand Forks Hotel onto the boardwalk. While he was in the town, he would check out the saloons for David. David could be here just as easily as in Dawson. Both towns catered to the same type of people: lonely miners looking for fun and a way to spend their money.

They hadn't learned anything at the claim but stayed long enough for Baxter to try his hand at shovelling dirt into the sluice box. His heart jumped when he saw the amount of gold left after the water washed everything else away. He'd found a medium-sized nugget and the desire to buy a claim. The only problem was that he didn't have the money needed for the purchase.

Baxter started down the walk. Here, as in Dawson, there was the constant noise of construction: hammers pounding, men yelling, saws cutting. One large building had the North American Transportation Company sign on it; a small building beside it housed a photographer. Further on, there was another hotel, and Baxter counted three cafés and three saloons. Also like Dawson, many people had set up businesses in their tents. He wondered what Mrs. Lowe would tell him if he went to have his fortune told. Would she say he was destined to stay here and find gold, or would she tell him a dark cloud hung over him, and he should be careful? He touched the scab on his head. That he already knew.

He continued his walk, looking at the men as he passed them. None of them paid any attention to him. They had their places to go, whether back to their claims, a café for a meal, or a saloon. He had thought he could wander all the streets of this small town looking for David, but now knew he couldn't. It was too spread out and was getting late. Plus, the walking hadn't helped with his aches.

Baxter walked to the nearest saloon. The music and conversations were loud as he stepped in the door. He went to the bar, ordered a double whiskey and wandered around the rooms. The saloons here were no different than those in Dawson. Men gambled using their pokes as collateral, drank whiskey, and danced with the girls. He scanned the tables looking for anyone who might resemble David, but it was difficult. Beards and moustaches interfered with getting a good look at their faces.

Baxter bought some chips and sat at one of the tables. He might as well win some money while here.

Chapter Twenty-Five

It was eerily quiet when they arrived back in Dawson the next afternoon. No saw mill screeching, no pounding of hammers, no music. Pearl had asked Belinda for a few days off and stayed at the claim, so Helen rode beside Paul. She looked at him in surprise.

"It's Sunday. Everything closes down from midnight Saturday to seven Monday morning."

"The silence is glorious."

Paul drove the wagon to the Fairview Hotel.

"Thank you, Paul," Helen said as he helped her climb down. She was sore and tired. Even though she had ridden on the seat, it had still been a bumpy ride.

Baxter slid off the wagon box and picked up her valise. "Yes, thank you for the ride. It was impressive to see the gold rush in action."

Helen and Baxter walked into the hotel. She just wanted to have a bath and lie down. Although it had been exciting to see the creek where the gold had been discovered, she was frustrated that they had learned

293

nothing from Dr. Beckwith. And on top of that, Baxter had said he didn't think Eugene was David.

"There aren't any similarities that I can see," he had stated when she brought it up.

"Miss Gastrell," the man behind the counter interrupted her thoughts. "I have a message for you." He held up an envelope.

Helen took the envelope and opened it. The date on the sheet of paper inside was today's. She read it out loud for Baxter.

Dear Miss Gastrell.

Today the man Miss Van Buren and I thought might be your brother, David, returned. He had another proposition for us. I told him we would think it over and let him know tomorrow. If you could come over about ten he will be here.

Regards

Mrs. Hitchcock.

Helen grinned up at Baxter, buoyed by the new information. "Maybe we've found him."

"Maybe," Baxter smiled back. "I'll go with you tomorrow in case there is any trouble."

Before going to her room, Helen ordered hot water for her bath. She needed it after the dusty ride. She and Baxter climbed the stairs.

Baxter deposited her valise on the floor in front of her door. "I think it's time we tried a different restaurant. I'll stop by for you later." He continued to his room.

Helen knocked on Mattie's door. "I need you to take a clean outfit from my trunk and my toiletries to the washroom for me," she said when Mattie opened it. "I've ordered water for a bath. While I'm in there, you can unpack my valise."

"Yes, Miss."

Helen stretched out in the tub of warm water. Going to the gold claims had been a distraction, but her mind kept going to her father and his death. She hadn't seen him on his deathbed. She hadn't said a final goodbye. So it didn't seem real, and she hadn't been able to cry yet. Maybe that would happen when she saw his grave.

After her bath, Mattie entered the room and helped her dress. "I want you to come with us tomorrow to visit the ladies in the big tent," Helen said as she put on her light brown skirt. "They have a man going there who they think could be David."

"Yes, Miss."

Helen wondered if she was imagining the slight change in Mattie. Sure, she still did her job as flawless as ever and she still was polite when she spoke, but she seemed to be lacking the usual deference in her tone. What had Mattie been doing while Helen was searching for her brother? What had made her change so subtly?

"I'll be dining with Mr. Davenport soon," Helen said when she finished dressing. She opened the door of the wash room and went back to her room.

Mattie gathered up Helen's soiled clothes and followed. She placed them on the foot of the bed and found Helen's brush. Helen sat awkwardly on the edge of her bed while Mattie brushed her hair, then twisted it into a bun. They had just finished when there was a knock at the door. Mattie opened it.

"What a wonderful silence," Helen said as they stepped out onto the boardwalk. "I can't believe the people here have gotten used to all the noise."

"Yes. I agree."

Even though the businesses were closed, the streets still teemed with men. Now they had nothing to do: no whiskey to drink, no gambling, no shows to see. They had to find something else to occupy their time for a whole day.

"What do you have planned for the rest of the day?" Helen asked as they walked long the boardwalk.

"Well, since everything is closed, I thought I would wander through the tents up on the hill. Maybe David is living in one of them. You could come too, if you wish."

Helen smiled to herself at his last statement. She had thought his attitude had changed towards her since her father's death and this was proof. He was finally treating her like an equal partner in this investigation.

"I hadn't thought about doing something like that," Helen said. "But it's true, he has to live somewhere. And as long as we do it in daylight, we should be safe."

When they finished their meal, they walked to Queen Street and headed towards the sea of white tents that occupied the flat land behind the wooden buildings and rose up the hillside. The tents were cramped side by side with little space between not following any street pattern. Men sat in groups in front of them and talked. Helen noticed some had bottles of whiskey beside them and cups in their hands.

"This might be useless," Baxter said, after a few minutes of picking their way between tents and around men on the ground.

"Yes." Helen was uncomfortable walking in this part of town. It seemed like they were invading the men's privacy. Everything they had was stacked about the tents or could be seen through the open flaps. And it was sad to see the defeated expression on many of the men's faces.

"You might have a better chance without me," Helen said. "You'll be able to wander freely and ask questions where you will."

"I'll walk you to the hotel and come back."

* * *

The screeching of the saw mills and the hammering of the workers was back in full force the next morning as Helen, Mattie, and Baxter walked down to the river.

"I didn't learn anything new," Baxter explained on the. "No one had heard of a man named David Gastrell, and none of the men I asked recognized the picture."

"Maybe this morning will be more fruitful," Helen said. "We need to learn something about him soon. I don't want to leave without some news to take back to my family."

Helen found Jim to row them over to West Dawson. On the other side, a pile of logs on the ground looked like someone was going to build a cabin beside the big tent.

Helen hoped they were not too early as they walked up to the tent's open flap.

"Hello," she yelled.

"Come in," Edith Van Buren beckoned. "Mary is busy with her writing right now. She'll be with us in a few minutes."

Helen could see Mary Hitchcock bent over the desk in the far corner.

"This is Baxter Davenport and my maid, Mattie Lewis. Mattie has worked in my parents' household for years and has a better chance of recognizing David than I do."

Edith led them to the table and motioned them to sit in the chairs. Helen and Baxter sat down while Mattie stood. Suddenly a man stuck his head in the tent.

"We've come to say goodbye."

Helen swung her head to look at him. He was short and overweight. Definitely, not her brother.

Mary Hitchcock put her pen down and came over as three men stepped into the tent.

"Thank you, ladies, for giving us the directions to where your claims are on Bear Creek. We're on our way to stake our claims there, also."

"Well, good luck, Sirs," Mary said, adding with a grin, "And remember, you each owe us a million dollars if they pay."

"Hopefully, we make enough."

They all tipped their hats and walked out.

"I'll be finished in a few minutes," Mary said, going back to her desk.

Helen could see the men through the open flap as they strapped heavy packs on their backs and headed to the river.

"Is a million dollars the going rate for helping someone find a claim?" Baxter asked.

"No," Edith laughed, shaking her head. "That was just Mary's joke. They offered the usual half interest in their claims, but we're not interested in that. We have our own claims and someone working them. That's

299

all we need. We just wanted to help those high society men, who are used to attending debutant balls and luncheons at their clubs, find claims."

Mary came over to the table. "May I see the photograph again?"

Helen handed it to her, and she and Edith studied it. "The man gave his name as Charles Gilroy. He'd learned we brought many magazines, illustrated weeklies, and novels for us to read. Since we will be leaving for the winter, he was willing to sell them for us. We asked him if he had cash to pay for them, and he said no. He wants us to give them to him, and he'll sell them for a small percentage."

"That doesn't sound like something David would do. He had broader aspirations, bigger ideas on how to make money."

"Maybe he's desperate right now."

Helen nodded. "You could be right. There seem to be a lot of men in dire straits here."

"Yes, the rich eat steak and caviar while the poor live on scraps of bread."

"Hello," a man's voice said from outside the tent.

Excitement built in Helen's stomach. Was she about to see the brother who'd left when she was eleven?

Edith walked over to the opening and said. "Please come in."

She led a middle-aged man over to where they sat. Helen watched him walk behind Edith. He was about David's height and had light-coloured hair with some gray in it. He looked older than she'd expected. Was he David? Could he have aged that much in ten years?

"Mr. Gilroy, this is Mr. Davenport, Miss Gastrell and Miss Lewis."

"Good day, Ladies," Mr. Gilroy said to Helen and Mattie and shook Baxter's hand.

"Hello," Helen said, greatly disappointed. He hadn't shown any reaction to her name. She glanced over at Mattie, who studied him.

Mr. Gilroy turned to the two women. "Have you made up your minds about me selling the magazine and novels for you?"

Mattie looked at Helen and shook her head.

"Are you sure you don't have any cash to put up?" Mary looked at Helen as she asked the question.

Helen gave a slight shake of her head. Neither she nor Mattie knew the man.

"No," the man said sadly. "I was hoping you'd let me do it on commission because I'm in need of money."

"We're sorry we can't make a deal with you," Mary said.

Mr. Gilroy stared at her for a few moments, Helen thought he might protest, but then he just nodded and left the tent.

"So he's not David," Edith said.

"I'm quite sure he's not," Helen said. "But there was something about him that bothered me. I just can't put my finger on it."

"Oscar Gilroy was one of the names used by one of the three men who died in Victoria last August," Baxter said.

"Yes." Helen nodded. "That's right."

"I will make tea, and we shall have some cake." Edith left the room.

"I've been hearing stories that you are going to set up a bowling alley and animatoscope," Baxter said while they waited.

"That has been our plan," Mary answered. "But they are still on the riverboat *Rideout*, which finally arrived two days ago, a month after we did. We've been told by the customs official that we owe more taxes and duties on our household goods, lusuries and food. In the meantime, we are looking for a suitable building for the bowling alley. We are also discussing operating our animatoscope with a couple of theatres." She smiled ruefully. "We have a list of men who want to run them for us and share in the profits."

"We've heard that another one has arrived in town and will have its first showing tomorrow evening," Edith said as she came back with a tray. "All this waiting for that steamer has cost us our advantage."

Helen was in awe of these women and their spirit and daring. They travelled the world together, seeing historical sites and meeting famous people. They came here on an adventure and were ending it by hiking over the Chilkoot Pass.

Sure, she had travelled extensively on the Continent, but that had been with her family. Coming to Dawson had been her first trip where she made the decisions. And she found she liked having control.

"Is someone building a cabin beside you?" Baxter asked.

"We are to hold our goods over the winter," Mary said. "But that isn't the easiest thing to do around here. The price goes up when anyone knows something is for the grand ladies, as we are known. All our neighbours pay twenty dollars a day for horse and man to do any work for them, but for the big tent, twenty-five dollars is the lowest price."

Helen was amazed at the number of times she'd heard of men pulling scams on people. For some reason, she thought David was the only one capable of such things, but from what she'd heard, many men like him were here.

After their tea and cake, the three said their goodbyes and returned to Dawson.

"I'm going to the saloons again," Baxter said as he stepped off the small boat. He turned and offered Helen his hand.

"Do you think it wise?" Helen took his hand and stepped out of the skiff. "Someone out there doesn't want us to find David."

"I don't plan on being in any dark areas tonight. And with all the men around, I'm sure he won't try anything in the light."

"Be careful."

Helen watched Baxter go. He seemed eager to get to the saloon even though it was only afternoon. She didn't know how he did it. Even with a sore head, he was out looking for David. Of course, he was getting paid for it, but it still didn't seem like he took any time off.

She was finding sleuthing to be a hard job. She was tired of asking the same questions over and over again, of showing David's picture with the same explanation to everyone they met. And she certainly didn't like that they now had to check over their shoulders for an attacker. The excitement had worn off, and the realization that being a detective was very different from what she imagined sank in. Solving a mystery wasn't easy.

Suddenly, there was a hue and cry down by the docks and the blowing of a steam whistle. "Booooat!" came the now familiar cry. Helen looked towards the river and saw a riverboat towing a barge snug up to the dock. Men on the boat threw ropes to those on the docks to tie up with two other riverboats already there.

Helen wondered how many men were going out on those three boats. She'd heard that thousands of men had already left the town in the past month.

Chapter Twenty-Six

"What did you do while I was gone to Grand Forks?" Helen asked as she and Mattie walked up to Front Street.

"I explored the streets and some of the stores."

"Did you find anything worthwhile?"

"Lots of beautiful clothes, jewellery. Did you know there are approximately sixty stores of various kinds in this town?"

Helen looked at Mattie in surprise. "How do you know?"

"I've read advertisements for about thirty-five of them in the newspapers and counted others mentioned in articles and reports."

"Does that include the saloons, dance halls, theatres, cafés and laundries?"

"No. Just the ones that offer goods for sale."

"Where would you suggest I look for souvenirs?"

"What type are you looking for? You don't have much room in your trunks."

"Then I might have to leave something behind." Helen smiled at the look of disdain on Mattie's face. She never liked that Helen so easily discarded anything she didn't want. "Or if you have room in your trunk, I can give you a couple of dresses."

That seemed to mollify Mattie, and she smiled back. "I would suggest buying some gold nuggets from a bank or one of the miners. They are small and easy to carry and would represent the gold rush."

"Yes," Helen said slowly. She hadn't thought about that. Her ideas had been jewellery for her mother and sisters and a gold pan for her brothers. But the jewellery and gold pans in Dawson had come from places in the south. They hadn't been made here in the Canadian north. But a gold nugget would have come from the earth here.

"I like that idea," Helen smiled at Mattie. "But I still want to look through the stores just in case I see something else. Plus, David might be shopping. After all, he must eat and buy clothes or food."

"We can start here," Mattie said as they stopped in front of the three-storey Alaska Commercial Company building.

"From the look of the number of customers, this seems to be the central point of the town's business area," Helen said.

Helen entered the building with Mattie following. There were rows of offices behind a counter. Clerks wandered in and out of the offices or helped customers at the counter. Could David be working here? If he had changed his attitude, maybe. She studied the clerks, wondering if one of them was David. Most had their heads down, examining the papers in their hands as they walked or were hidden by the customers they were helping. Helen looked at Mattie.

"No," Mattie said. "I don't see him."

Helen nodded, and she and Mattie continued past the counter to a large area of shelves stocked to overflowing with goods. They walked through the various departments but Helen found nothing that appealed to her as souvenirs.

"Let's go to the second floor," Helen said.

They climbed the steps and found the men's section. Helen looked around the large room. There were a couple of salesmen helping a few men who were shopping. None looked familiar. Again she glanced at Mattie. She was watching one man, but then she shook her head.

With a sigh, Helen checked through the men's clothing. There were heavy miner's shirts and trousers and gentlemen's fancy dress shirts and suits. Stetson hats with wide, flat, brims and high, straight-sided crowns with rounded corners were interspersed with Knox hats having narrower brims and creases in their crowns.

Helen looked at the hats as souvenirs for her brothers but decided they were no different than those she'd seen in Victoria.

They represented all North America, not just the Yukon or the Klondike.

They carried on to the housekeeping and lady's departments but found nothing of interest. Helen was impressed with the store as they descended the stairs. She'd read about other gold rushes in North America and the towns full of stores and shops that sprung up seemingly overnight. They'd disappeared just as quickly when the gold was depleted, or there was a new discovery somewhere else. This store had a feeling of permanence like it would be here for years to come. So maybe Dawson City would still be here after this gold rush was over.

They left the store and continued along Front Street. Signs in windows or banners tacked above doors advertised transport companies, gold dust buyers, dentists, lawyers, photographers, outfitters, and more.

Gold! Gold! Gold! One sign read while others advertised *Fine Diamond Work! Watches! Cigars!*

From what Helen learned since coming here, Front Street had the most expensive real estate. Less expensive lots were along the cross streets like King, Queen, and Princess. Those who wanted to be part of this affluent part of Dawson filled the spaces between larger buildings with canvas-covered wooden frames, like a small five-foot-wide fruit stand they came across.

The stand opened onto the boardwalk, with the fruit displayed on a table. Helen stopped and bought two oranges. She gave one to Mattie, and they sat on a bench to eat them.

A thought hit Helen as she looked at the men walking by. Had David seen her or Mattie on the street or in a store over the past few days? What if he was the one who had attacked Baxter? A shiver ran through her like someone walking over her grave. She never thought about him watching her or Mattie. She'd only thought about them finding him.

Helen checked to see if anyone was attempting to hide behind a post or corner of a store. She sighed with relief when no one skulked around in the shuffling crowd of men. It made her feel a little better.

She was still amazed at the contrast among the men going by. Some, dressed in filthy, torn clothes, walked beside men in suits and top hats. And many of them were talking and laughing with each other. There was no class difference here. Then she realized something. All these men came here to find gold. Maybe they all dressed in dirty clothes at one time. The only difference between them now was that some struck it rich, and some didn't.

They finished their oranges and continued their walk. There were other small booths squeezed between the wooden buildings displaying crumpled clothes, torn sacks of flour or rice on tables and used tools, and cooking pots hanging from hooks.

Helen and Mattie stopped at a few dry goods and entered two furniture stores but found nothing small enough for a souvenir.

"There is quite the selection in the stores, isn't there?" Mattie said.

"Yes," Helen agreed. "Some buildings are primitive, but the merchandise is comparable to what is available in London. But it's getting late, and I've had a long day. I want to buy a newspaper, eat, and retire to my room."

* * *

"Look what I won last night," Baxter said when he met Helen and Mattie the next morning. He waved some tickets at them.

Helen took them. "These are for the opening of the animatoscope moving pictures show tonight."

"Yes." Baxter looked smug as he pulled a chair over and sat down. "My four eights beat his three kings."

"And Pearl, Andrew, Eugene, and Florence will also be going," Helen said thoughtfully. She looked at Mattie. "You'll come with us so you can take a good look at Eugene Braddock. Even though Baxter says no, I think Eugene looks a lot like David."

"Yes, Miss," Mattie said respectfully, although her heart beat fast. Would she be seeing David tonight? What would his or her reaction be?

"And I must take both letters with me to show him."

Mattie watched the excitement on Helen's face. Even though she hardly remembered him, she looked forward to seeing her brother.

"I wonder who we can give the fourth ticket to," Baxter said.

While Baxter and Helen mulled that over, Mattie finished her breakfast.

"Excuse me, Miss," Mattie said, standing. "I'll go tidy your room. Will you be needing anything else?"

"No," Helen said. "Mr. Davenport and I will be checking all the laundries and bathhouses in the town to see if David frequented any of them. I don't know when we will be back."

"Yes, Miss." Mattie's heart soared as she hurried up the stairs. She had the next few hours free to look for work.

Mattie entered Helen's room, picked up her nightgown and hung it up. She made the bed, then folded yesterday's newspaper and took it to her room. She turned to the *Want Ads*.

One young woman placed an ad looking for a job as a bookkeeper. Another was from a woman who wanted to work as a cook in town or the mining area. Mattie could do the same, except she had no training in either of them. And she doubted there was a calling for a lady's maid in this town.

Disappointed, she continued reading the newspaper. She saw what she was looking for in Real Estate. For Sale: half interest in the best-paying café in Dawson. Apply at this office.

Mattie wondered which café and how much was required for the half interest. Her savings weren't very much compared to the gold and money that exchanged hands here every day.

Mattie tore the ad out of the newspaper and set the rest aside. She would read them this evening. Now she needed to go to the newspaper office. She wore a white shirt waist and a light green skirt that reached her ankles. She put on the matching light green jacket, picked up her purse, and left her room.

She quickly crossed the lobby and exited the hotel. She wasn't sure if Helen and Baxter were still in the restaurant, but she didn't want them to see her leave. She didn't need to be answering any questions.

Mattie walked to the *Klondike Nugget*'s office and entered.

"May I help you, Miss?" the man behind the counter asked.

"Yes," Mattie used her best cultivated voice, wanting to sound as if she was worthy of his respect. "I would like to know more information about this ad." She set the torn paper on the counter.

"Just a moment." The man went to the desk behind him and opened a ledger. He turned a couple of pages. "Ah, yes. That is for a Mrs. Perkins. Her café is on Duke Street. It's at the north end of the town just off Front Street."

"Thank you," Mattie said. She picked up the piece of paper and left.

She walked through the crowd to Duke Street and saw a small building with the word *Café* above the door. Outside, a man and woman seemed to be in an argument. Two young boys were near them, and a small crowd had gathered to watch. Mattie crept closer, not sure if they had anything to do with the restaurant.

"I spent the entire morning looking for my boat," the man said. "I thought it was stolen and was going to report it to the mounted police when I saw your two boys leisurely rowing it on the river." He glanced pointedly at the boys. "I could have had them arrested for thievery."

The boys cringed and looked down at their shoes.

"I'm very sorry, Mr. Conner," the woman said, wringing her hands.

"You'd better give them a good talking to. If there was any trouble on the river, they could have drifted to Fortymile, and no one would be the wiser."

"I promise this won't happen again, right boys?"

"Yes, Mother," they both answered.

"It better not." Mr. Conner turned and stomped away.

The woman slapped the boys on the sides of their heads and shooed them through the open door into the restaurant. The crowd slowly dispersed, the fun over.

Mattie waited a few minutes then entered the building. It was dim inside after the bright sunshine.

"Do you wish to sit at a table?" the same woman came up to Mattie. The boys were nowhere in sight.

Mattie hadn't thought about eating, but maybe ordering something would make it easier to talk with her.

"Yes, please. And I'd like a cup of tea."

"Anything to eat?"

"A muffin."

"Yes, Ma'am." The woman bustled off. She went through a doorway that Mattie assumed led to the kitchen.

Mattie looked around the room. It was small, and the walls were made of logs. Two pictures hung on one wall, and the other was bare. There was one window and the open door for light. But the tables all had clean white tablecloths on them and a vase with one flower in it. It was a nice touch, but it didn't look like it was the best-paying café in Dawson.

The three customers were all men. She studied them, wondering if one could be David. They all had dark beards and dark hair. She smiled to herself. It seemed she couldn't look at a man in this town without wondering if he was David. It was important to her that they find him before Helen and Baxter returned to Victoria. She didn't like the idea that if she stayed, she would always have to be careful, that she might run into him or the attacker one day.

Mattie took the newspaper ad from her purse and set it on the table. The woman came back with a tray. She set a pot of tea, a cup and saucer, and a muffin on a plate on the table. This was the first time Mattie had been served a pot of tea instead of just a cup. She liked it.

The woman spotted the piece of paper. "Have you come about the ad?"

"Yes," Mattie said. She held up the pot. "Do you have time to join me?"

"I'll get me a cup." The woman hurried to the kitchen and returned with a cup and saucer. She set them on the table and sat across from Mattie.

"My name is Miss Mattie Lewis, and I've come from London, England." Mattie didn't think it was necessary to give any more of a background. "I'm staying at the Fairview Hotel while looking to find work here in

Dawson or a business to invest my money." She knew she sounded snobbish, but she was enjoying her role as a potential businesswoman in search of a partnership.

"I'm Mrs. Alice Perkins. I've been here since the spring and started out baking bread and making pies to sell out of my tent. I did well enough to buy this lot and building and open this café."

Mattie poured the tea. She didn't know whether it would be impertinent to ask the next question, but it was important.

"Do you have any ledgers to show your income and expenses that I may look at?" Old Mrs. Gastrell had always insisted on seeing the books of the business she and her husband started, even after handing it to her eldest son. When her eyesight became too bad to read them, Mattie read them to her. Mattie now knew what constituted a good month and what didn't.

"No, I can't be bothered writing everything down. After paying my bills, I go by how much money I have left over."

"And how much is that?" Mattie took a sip of her tea.

Mrs. Perkins shrugged. "Depends on the month, but I can tell you that there hasn't been a time yet that I haven't had money in my pocket at the end of the month."

"Why do you want a partner then?" Mattie had thought it would be because she was in debt.

"Twice the hands to do the work means twice the work gets done. I could serve more customers, bake more muffins, pies, and bread and make more soups and stews. I stick with the cheap basic food that the men here like. None of this fancy caviar or stewed clams for me."

"Do you think you will have more customers if you make more food?"

"I'm already turning them away in the evening because I've run out of food. I need someone to either help me or make it possible for me to hire a helper."

"How much do you want for half interest?" Mattie wished she had a better idea of how much Mrs. Perkins made.

"Before I answer that, I would like to ask you some questions."

Mattie nodded and bit into her muffin.

"Why do you want to be a partner in a café here? Do you plan on staying, or is this just some whim?"

"If I find the right business, I wish to stay here."

"Do you know how to cook and clean?"

"Yes, I've been doing that most of my life."

"Oh?"

Mattie knew she would have to tell Mrs. Perkins the truth. "I'm a lady's maid. I've come here with my mistress. I'm good at cleaning and a quick learner, so I could bake or cook anything after a little training."

"Why do you wish to leave her employ?"

"I want something different. I've been a servant most of my life."

"I can understand." Mrs. Perkins nodded. "I worked in a laundry for many years to support my sons. When I heard about the gold rush, I decided to come here and start my own business. It turned out very well for me. And to answer your question, by my figuring, half of my café is worth five hundred dollars."

Mattie did her best not to gasp. She didn't have that much money. By her calculations she had one hundred and twenty-five Canadian dollars. She was so disappointed.

"I'm sorry that I wasted your time." Mattie stood. "How much do I owe you?"

"Five dollars." Mrs. Perkins said. "Would you like to discuss it more? Maybe we can come to an agreement."

"I wish I could, but I just don't have that much money." Mattie put a five-dollar bill on the table.

"Could you ask your mistress for a loan?"

Mattie stopped. Could she?

"I'll have to think about that." Mattie walked to the door. She turned and addressed the room, although she looked at Mrs. Perkins. "Do you know a man named David Gastrell?" She watched in her peripheral vision for movement in any of the men. While they looked up at her, none of them made any effort to speak up.

"Are you looking for him?" Mrs. Perkins asked.

"My mistress is. He's her brother."

"No, I don't know him."

"Thank you," Mattie said and went out the open door.

She was almost in tears as she walked along the boardwalk. That was her only chance to start a new life. From the lack of want ads, there wasn't any work here for her. She would have to accept Belinda's offer or quickly find something in Victoria before Helen sailed to London. If she didn't, she would have to go back with Helen and be a maid for the rest of her life.

Did she have the nerve to ask Helen for a loan?

* * *

On the way back to the hotel, Mattie looked for help wanted signs in the windows of businesses. Not everyone put an ad in the newspapers. She didn't have the courage to speak with Helen about a loan, so she had to find something else because she wanted to stay here. She liked that she was treated like a lady by the men here, that no one looked down on her because she was just a lady's maid. She liked the freedom she felt when she walked the boardwalk. She would accept Belinda's offer to work as a waitress if nothing else. That way, she would have a job until she found herself a business.

When she reached the Alaska Commercial Company Store, she didn't see a sign but wondered if she should go in and ask. Suddenly she was jostled from behind, and she started to fall. Her stomach gripped in fear. Was she being attacked like Baxter?

A man hurried forward and caught her. "Are you hurt?"

"No," Mattie said a little shakily. She looked around to see who had pushed her. No one seemed intent on watching her. Then she realized she recognized the voice. She looked up at Mr. Edmund Davies. "I'm fine, thank you."

Mr. Davies lifted his hat to her. "May I walk with you, Miss Lewis?"

Mattie hesitated. It was frowned upon in England for a woman to be in the company of a man she didn't know. But here, there seemed to be no such restrictions. Although this was the second time he'd come to her aid, he was still a stranger. But she'd done a lot of things here that she'd never do at home. And she would add walking with Mr. Davies to her list.

"Yes, Mr. Davies, you may."

He smiled as he held his arm out to her, and she slipped her hand through his elbow as if she'd done it many times before.

They walked in silence. Mattie liked the feel of her hand on his arm, a new sensation to her. It also gave her a sense of security.

"I understand you came to the rescue of a friend of mine, Mr. Davenport."

"Ah, yes, the man in Paradise Alley. You'd be surprised how many men are robbed there."

Mattie decided not to tell him the truth about the attack. "How long have you been in Dawson City, Mr. Davies?" She needed to make conversation and wanted to know more about the man who had just saved her from a nasty fall.

"I arrived in 1896 from Circle City. I struck gold on a claim on Eldorado Creek."

"Then you are rich," Mattie blurted out before she could stop herself.

"I guess you might say that. I have made some money from my claim."

Mattie was suddenly in awe that she was walking with a rich man treating her like a lady. She liked being in his company.

"And you, Miss Lewis. What brought you to Dawson?"

Mattie was tongue-tied. What should she say? To tell the truth that she was here with her mistress would cause this man to drop his arm and walk away.

"I've come to see about entering into a business."

"And what type of business do you have in mind?"

"I'm thinking of maybe a restaurant."

"Well, there are certainly enough men in town to feed." Mr. Davies smiled at her.

Mattie liked his smile. It lit up his eyes. She wasn't sure what his age would be, but she thought he wasn't much older than she.

Mattie now had no desire to look for wanted signs in windows. In fact, she felt it best for her to return to her hotel room. She didn't want to say or do something that would show she wasn't the businesswoman she pretended to be. Plus, Helen would be wanting her soon.

"I'm staying at the Fairview Hotel."

"Then that's where we shall go."

They continued along the boardwalk, and when they reached the hotel, he disengaged his arm and held the door for her.

Mattie swept past him into the lobby. "Thank you for escorting me."

"My pleasure." Edmund Davies gave a slight bow and touched his fingers to his hat. "Maybe we'll meet again soon." He strolled back out onto the boardwalk.

"I see you've met Mr. Davies," Belinda commented from behind the counter.

"Yes." Mattie walked over. "He seems like a nice man."

"Be a little careful of him. He's a gambler who has made and lost a fortune in the past year. He's a lady's man and falls in love easily. He buys women anything they want, from clothes to caviar. Right now, he's engaged to one woman who left to go Outside to visit her family. While she's gone, he's seeing another."

"Outside?" Mattie asked.

"That's what we call the rest of the world. Anyone who leaves here is going Outside."

"Well, he was a perfect gentleman with me."

"Just be cautious. I wouldn't want you misled by him."

"Thank you."

Mattie hurried up to her room, disappointed that Mr. Davies seemed no different than David. Were all men like his? Then she remembered Mr. Gastrell. He had been stern but fair with his family and his staff. She knew it had taken a lot of thought on his part to send David away and that he'd regretted having to do it. But with his knowledge about what type of son David was, plus his suspicions that he was a killer, he couldn't have let him stay.

Chapter Twenty-Seven

Later that afternoon as they prepared for the moving pictures show, Mattie couldn't concentrate on helping Helen dress. She was worried about facing Eugene Braddock. She had been just as worried when they went across the river to see Miss Van Buren and Mrs. Hitchcock. The man they met there had definitely not been David, but what if Mr. Braddock was? What would she do? What would he say if she identified him? Would he yell at her, leave, or try to deny it?

She took a deep breath to steady her nerves. Just as she'd done with Charles Gilroy, she would check Eugene Braddock's general features and look into his eyes and she also had to get a good look at the palm of his hand. For she knew the true story of how he'd gotten it.

One evening, when she was seventeen and he nineteen, David had snuck up on her when she was alone in the kitchen. He'd put his arms around her from behind and nuzzled her neck as he had before. She liked that and wished she could believe him when he said he loved her. But she knew deep down that he didn't, and she wasn't going to be one of those women who fell in love with a sweet-talking man only to have him leave her. She didn't want to be like the girls she had heard about.

She turned and kissed him a long lingering kiss as they had done before. But that evening, he tried to force himself on her instead of stopping when she asked him. She fought him off and snatched up a knife. He reached out to grab her wrist, and she slashed his palm. Seizing his hand to stem the blood, he rushed to the sink, turned on the tap and plunged his hand under the cool running water. The water immediately turned red as it ran down the drain. Mattie took a kitchen towel and wrapped it tightly around his palm.

Without a word, David left the kitchen, and Mattie cleaned up the blood from where it dropped on the floor and in the sink. She told no one as she hurried to her room. The next day she heard he was telling everyone he cut his hand while chopping wood.

Mattie knew so much more about David than she'd told anyone, so much more that she wanted to tell Helen before she met her brother. She thought she should warn Helen. Maybe it was time to reveal the secret Mattie had kept all these years.

"Your father sent David away for many reasons," Mattie began. She didn't care if she used David's first name instead of calling him Mr. Gastrell as was required by all the staff.

"Oh?" Helen paused in putting on her combination.

Mattie wasn't sure how to tell her then blurted out, "Your father thought he was Jack the Ripper."

"What?" Helen gasped and turned to her. "Why would he think that? How do you know he thought that?"

"I overheard him talking with one of his friends. They were having a drink in the library, and the door was partially open. I was walking by with a tray to take to your grandmother."

"And you eavesdropped?"

"No, Miss." She certainly wasn't going to admit that. "He was talking very loud. He was very upset, almost crying."

"Why did he think David was the Ripper?"

"According to the papers, the police thought the killer had some medical training, and David spent two years at Cambridge College studying medicine."

"And that's the only reason?"

"David was out on all the evenings those women were killed." Mattie helped Helen into her mauve dress.

"That's not proof," Helen shook her head. "I don't believe it."

"The murders stopped after David was sent away."

* * *

Baxter dressed in his black trousers, white shirt, and burgundy waistcoat. He looked forward to this evening's performance as he hadn't seen a moving picture for a long time. They were all the rage in Victoria, and he and his mother had gone to a few.

And tonight might be the last night of his investigation. While he hadn't seen the resemblance, Helen was quite sure that Eugene Braddock was her brother, and he was glad that he'd been able to win the tickets for them to attend the movie. Time was running out for them. They had to think about going back to Victoria. After being in Dawson for seven days, they so far hadn't been successful at finding much out about David Gastrell. The only clues he found were that a man named David had worked at the Aurora Saloon, and maybe the same man had gone to Atlin. If that man was Helen's brother, then there was no way of them finding him. Baxter wasn't about to head overland on foot since there was no road or direct waterway between the two places.

He sure admired these men who lived here. They packed up their belongings and moved to wherever they wanted. That lifestyle had a certain freedom, but he was glad he'd come. After seeing the conditions, he was happy that he hadn't made it last year as planned. This was not the life he wanted. He chuckled. He probably would be like most of the men here, selling his outfit so he could go home again.

There was another clue, the attack, but he didn't know what to make of it. It could be David himself trying to scare them away, or someone who killed David and didn't want them finding out, or it could be for some other reason they didn't know.

Baxter pulled on his jacket and left the room to check his hair in the mirror in the washroom. He should have gotten it trimmed, but other than that, he looked pretty good. He knocked on Helen's door.

Mattie answered. He couldn't pinpoint what was different about her, but she seemed to have an air of confidence about her. She wasn't the meek lady's maid anymore.

"Are you ladies ready?"

"We are, Mr. Davenport," Mattie said. "I just have to get my shawl."

She walked next door to retrieve it while Helen stepped out behind her. Baxter held his arm out to Helen, and they went down the stairs, Mattie following.

They walked the short distance to the theatre where the movie was being shown. A large throng of people lined up at the door awaiting admission. They hung on the edge of the crowd for the doors to open. Baxter looked over the mass of people.

"I don't see Dr. Beckwith, Miss Owens, or Mrs. and Mrs. Braddock," he said to Helen. "Maybe they've changed their minds."

"Oh, I hope not. Mattie must meet Mr. Braddock. I have to know if he's my brother."

"If they don't come, I can take Mattie to their claim to see them."

"Leaving me here won't do me any good," Helen said. "We can both go with her."

Baxter looked at Mattie. What did she think about being talked about as if she wasn't there? She stood slightly behind Helen as a good servant should, waiting to be told what to do.

The doors opened, and they started moving slowly forward. At the door, Baxter gave their three tickets. He'd given the fourth to a man he'd seen on the street earlier today. He'd looked so forlorn that Baxter thought he could use some cheering up. The man thanked him profusely before hurrying away with the ticket clamped securely in his hand.

The room was full of benches and chairs. A large white sheet hung at the front. They were jostled from all sides as they worked their way to a bench in the middle of the room. Baxter again looked around and finally saw Pearl Owens and Dr. Beckwith. Mrs. Braddock was with them but not

Eugene Braddock, although there was an empty chair beside Mrs. Braddock.

Baxter tried to catch their attention to let them know he and Helen were there. When that didn't work, he pointed them out to Helen.

"They're over on the other side and three rows back from the front row."

Helen looked at them. "Eugene isn't with them."

"But there is a chair for him." Baxter stood. "I'm going over to speak with them. Maybe suggest we meet for coffee or tea afterwards."

"Yes."

Baxter wove his way through the men and women looking for places to sit or who stood visiting before going to their seats. He could feel the excitement in the crowd. This was a big event in their lives.

Baxter reached the row where they were sitting and worked his way down to the empty chair. He started to sit when Florence quickly placed her hand on it. "It's saved for my husband," she said, then looked up at him. "Oh, Mr. Davenport. Good to see you again. Do sit down."

"Hello, Mrs. Braddock, Dr. Beckwith, Miss Owens." Baxter sat down. "Miss Gastrell and I are on the other side. We are having coffee after the show. Will you join us?"

Florence looked at the others. They nodded. "That would be very nice," Florence said to Baxter.

"Would the restaurant in the Fairview Hotel be fine?"

"It would."

Baxter nodded and returned to his seat. He wondered where Eugene was. He had come with them, and they expected him.

The lanterns dimmed, and the crowd started cheering.

"The Haverstraw Tunnel was built in 1882 in New York," the man running the animatoscope explained before starting the film.

There was a whirling noise from the animatoscope and the words *The Haverstraw Tunnel* appeared on the screen. The cheering increased.

The scene began by showing the train tracks ahead and the trees and fields beside them. Filmed from the front of the engine, Baxter felt like he was actually riding the train. Then there was a tunnel, and everything went dark when the train entered. When the daylight appeared, everyone gasped as a man crossed the tracks just ahead of the train. They travelled beside the Hudson River, and then the screen went dark.

There was a moment's silence then the audience erupted into loud cheering and whistling and clapping.

"Run another one! Run another one!"

Soon another picture started. This time the words *Boxing Cats* came on the sheet. Two cats, each wearing gloves, came on and began boxing at each other. It ran for only a couple of minutes before the screen went dark again.

"Let's see a real fight," one man yelled.

"Yeah, where's the Corbett-Fitzsimmons fight I heard about?"

"It's a long film and will be tomorrow evening's show," the projectionist said.

The next film was titled *Annabelle Serpentine Dance*. It showed a woman holding her long flowing skirt out to the sides. She kicked her bare legs high, which got the men whooping and whistling. She swooped her skirts up and down as she moved to her right and left.

"Run it again!" someone yelled above the hooting and shrieking when the film stopped.

The projectionist obliged and ran four more short films before the evening ended.

* * *

As they pushed their way through the crowd leaving the theatre, Mattie became separated from Helen and Baxter. She wasn't worried, though. She knew they were meeting at the hotel.

333

She dodged around groups of men standing in front of the theatre, talking and laughing about the films they had just seen. She watched where she walked, not wanting to trip and fall or collide with anyone. But in such a packed area, that was impossible. Suddenly a man was in front of her, and she barely avoided running into him.

She stopped dead. David's tiepin was in his tie.

Memories came flooding back: the day she and Clara had gone to the jewellery store in London, the contemptuous way the owner asked them to leave; Clara laughing as she held out her hand when they were halfway down the street. In it was the diamond and pearl tie pin she'd stolen.

Mattie had been shocked and scared. She looked back over her shoulder, expecting the owner to come running down the street after them.

"Teach that snooty owner to treat us like dirt," Clara said.

"What are you going to do with it?"

"I'm going to give it to David?"

"David?" Mattie couldn't believe what she'd heard. "Why David?"

"Because he's been courting me, and he says he loves me."

"Oh, Clara." Mattie was at a loss for words. How could she tell Clara that David said that to every girl and woman he met? And he only had one reason to tell them that.

"I know he's courted a lot of women, but he told me I am different, that he wants to marry me."

Mattie's memory flipped ahead to Clara crying over David leaving her behind when he went to Canada. "I begged him to marry me as he'd promised and to take me with him," she cried.

Then Clara told Mattie that she was with child, and had nowhere to go. She knew she would lose her job and couldn't return to her family. And now Mattie had found David. Now she could make him pay for what he had done to Clara.

She raised her head expecting to see David's dynamic blue eyes but instead looked into the cold, grey-blue eyes of a stranger. She was stunned. He was wearing David's pin but he wasn't David. Mattie and the man stared at each other for a moment then the man put his hand on the pin while he gazed intently into her eyes. They both realized that she knew the pin didn't belong to him. A jolt of terror ran through Mattie at the rage on his face. She tried to back away but was caught by the throng of men. She couldn't move. The man grabbed her arm.

"Let me go." She tried to pull away, a deep fear in the pit of her stomach.

"You're coming with me." He dragged her through the crowd.

Mattie knew she must do something. "Help! Help!" she yelled, trying to be heard over the noise of so many voices. "I don't know this man!"

The men closest to them turned to look.

"Leave us alone," the man scowled at them.

"Please help!" Mattie shouted louder. "He's going to kill me!"

"Let her go." A man stepped in front of them.

"She doesn't want to go with you," said another.

A group circled them. Then one of the men stepped up to the man with the tiepin and punched him in the face. He staggered back, letting go of her arm. Mattie jumped away from him. The man hit him again, knocking him to the ground. "That's for Stanley."

Suddenly Baxter and Helen were at her side. Helen put her arm around Mattie while Baxter went to the man's side and stood with him over the stranger.

The man who saved her turned to her. "Are you fine?"

She looked into his eyes, and her heart skipped a beat as it had so many years ago when she was young. "David?"

"Hello, Mattie." He looked at his sister. "Hello, Helen."

"Oh, my," Helen gasped. "I knew it. I knew you weren't Eugene. I knew you were David."

The man on the ground began to rise.

"David, he has your tiepin," Mattie said quickly. "The one Clara gave you."

"Yes, I saw it." David punched the man again. "This is Alexander Hughes, or maybe he's going under the name Freddie Alden, or he could even be Cyril Green. Whichever name he is using, he's the man who killed my friend, Stanley Noland, in Victoria."

Chapter Twenty-Eight

Helen sat and looked around the table. To her right was Baxter, and to her left was Mattie. Her brother David/Eugene, her sister-in-law Florence, Pearl, and Andrew completed the circle. It had been a busy evening. The mounted police had arrived, and after Mattie explained that Freddie had grabbed her arm and tried to force her to go with him, they arrested him. When David told them he thought Freddie, as he called himself, was the man who killed his friend Stanley in Victoria last fall and the tiepin he wore was proof, the police asked the four of them to go to the barracks and explain.

There David told the constable how he and his friend Stanley had been ready to sail for Dawson last fall. But the morning they were supposed to leave, Stanley never showed up with their tickets. David looked for him and found out about the discovery of Stanley's body a day later. He went to identify him and asked about his money and their steamship tickets. They were missing.

Also missing was David's tiepin, which he'd lost in a poker game to Freddie a few days earlier. Stanley had promised to win it

338

back for him, and Stanley was so good with cards that David knew he would keep his word.

"If you contact the Victoria police, you will find that last fall, a Stanley Noland was found murdered," David said.

"And I can vouch for that." Baxter stepped up. "I'm a private investigator from Victoria, and I know for sure that the body of a man named Stanley Noland, who also went under the names Charles Fairfax and Oscar Gilroy, was discovered in a grove of trees. The police still haven't found the man who killed him."

"If you check the passenger lists for the steamship lines for last fall, you will probably find that a ticket belonging to Stanley Noland was used the day before his body was found," David continued. "I believe this man, Freddie Alden, used that ticket to come here."

Of course, Freddie Alden denied everything, even his treatment of Mattie, but the police locked him up. The four of them had to go back to the police barracks in the morning and explain everything again, giving further details.

It was now after midnight, and they were eating pie in the Fairview Hotel restaurant. David was telling them his story.

"Before I begin, I want you to know that I told Florence the truth about my life before we married, so what I'm saying isn't a surprise for her. After your visit, I told Andrew and Florence everything. They all know the story I told them and everyone else about having grandparents in Victoria who gave me money to go and seek my fortune is a lie.

"I grant that I wasn't the nicest person when I lived in England, and I wasn't much better when I came to Canada. I scammed people out of their money. I cheated at poker. I even turned to robbery for a while. When I settled in Victoria, I realized that it wasn't the type of life I wanted. I tried taking the straight and narrow path but must admit I strayed quite often. Then I became friends with Stanley, and we decided to come here." David paused and took a deep breath.

"When I discovered he'd been murdered and our tickets and his supplies were missing, I looked for his killer. But I had no skills at finding who did it, so I decided to come here anyway. I didn't know for sure if his ticket had been used by the killer or sold to someone else until I saw my pin on Freddie's tie tonight. Freddie and I were acquaintances, and I lost my pin to him in a game. I sincerely regretted that because it had been given to me by a special person, and Stanley said he would get it back for me.

"I know he kept his word because the police questioned Ernest at the saloon where Stanley worked. Ernest confirmed that Stanley won it back in a game before he started work that night. It was missing when he was found. The police figured whoever killed Stanley also had the pin.

"I borrowed enough money from another friend to catch a steamship north a week later. I still had my supply of food to take with me. I didn't know if the murderer came here, so I changed my name to Eugene Braddock. I thought I might be able to learn if anyone was bragging about killing someone, or I might even see my pin. Stanley being murdered made me realize I was leading a dangerous life. Plus, I guess I was finally growing up. I found a job working on a gold claim for Pearl's brother, Sam, and got bit by the gold fever bug. I worked hard, so didn't get into Dawson to look for Stanley's murderer very often. I was saving my earnings to buy my own claim.

"Then I met Florence and wanted to marry her. I lost all thoughts of revenge."

"Why didn't you send for your allowance?" Helen asked.

"My anger at our father for sending me away never lessened, and I took his money out of spite. Then when I arrived here I decided to cut all ties with him. And like I said before, I had finally grown up."

"Did he accuse you of being Jack the Ripper?" Helen asked.

"How did you know?" David looked shocked. "I didn't think anyone knew."

"I overheard your father telling a friend," Mattie said quietly.

"I tried to convince him I wasn't, but he wouldn't listen. That my own father would think that of me hurt more than being sent away."

Helen noticed that he didn't ask how their parents or any of their siblings were doing. She took the letters from her purse.

"I went to the post office, and there was a letter addressed to you from Father. It arrived four weeks ago. Didn't you check for any mail from him?"

"I thought about it, but I seldom made it into Dawson, and when I did, there always was a crowd outside the post office. I had my own money now, and I wasn't interested in his allowance or what he had to say."

Helen slid the letter across to him. He stared at it, then slowly picked it up and looked at the open flap. He looked at her.

"I wasn't sure if I would find you, so I opened it."

David read it over and then reread it out loud so everyone could hear.

My son David.
I hope you are in fine health and enjoying your time in the gold fields. Because I haven't heard from you since you left Victoria I have sent Helen to contact you in Dawson to make sure you are alive and well. She will be arriving the latter part of August.

This is not a request for you to come home, nor is it a letter of forgiveness. You still are not welcome here.

Your Father
Algernon

"Nothing new," he grunted as he tore up the letter.

"Mother also sent a letter addressed to me." Helen pushed it over to David.

"If it's addressed to you, why do you want me to read it?"

"Father died almost two months ago. Mother added a postscript at the bottom, which I believe is meant for you."

David opened the letter, quickly scanned it then read the bottom. "If you find David, please tell him to come home." He set the letter down and wiped his eyes. "I have missed Mother."

* * *

It was late morning when Mattie, Helen, and Baxter returned to the hotel from the police barracks. After hearing the full story about the death of Stanley Noland, the superintendent decided that one of his men would escort Freddie Alden to Victoria and explain the situation. David wrote everything down and signed the paper to be given as evidence, along with the tiepin, against

343

Freddie. Baxter would pick up the pin after the trial and mail it back to David in Dawson.

Mattie wanted to speak with David in private. She had things to tell him, things he needed to hear. But most of all, she wanted to hit him. For, even though he claimed to be a changed man, he still needed to know how his actions affected other people in his parent's household. But he had gone back to the hotel he was staying in to tell the others what the police had decided.

Baxter turned to Helen. "It's been a pleasure working with you," he said.

"Thank you. And I've enjoyed my stint as a detective with you."

Mattie smiled to herself as Helen blushed a little at his statement. She still thought they would make a good couple. Maybe on the trip back to Victoria….

"I have all the voyage home to write up a detailed report for Mother." Baxter walked towards the saloon door. "Right now, I'm going to have a drink to our success. And I might do a little gambling, too, just for the fun of it."

"I'll tell Belinda that we will be checking out as soon as we can book passage back to Victoria," Helen said. She dug some money from her purse. "Mattie, will you go buy some oranges from that fruit seller we visited a few days ago."

"Yes, Miss."

Mattie was torn as she walked down the boardwalk to the fruit stand. It was time for them to leave, and she had to tell Helen she was staying. She hadn't realized how that decision would affect her. Yesterday it had been a thought, today it was real. She wasn't going back to England.

Mattie was picking through the oranges when she felt someone beside her. She looked up into David's strikingly blue eyes. They hadn't lost any of their charm.

"Hello, Mattie," David said. "May we talk?"

She wondered if she should yell at him now or wait to find out why he wanted to speak with her. After all, that was the reason she'd come to Dawson. She had to confront him about Clara.

Mattie nodded then paid for two oranges and put them in her purse. She followed David to a nearby bench.

"I'd like to ask you about Clara."

Mattie was surprised at his request. "You remember her?"

"Yes." David smiled. "I was sweet on her."

"You promised to marry her." Mattie could feel the anger building in her.

"I did and I wanted to, but Father would have nothing of it. He may have treated his household staff better than other employers, but there was no way any of his children would marry one of them."

Mattie stared at David. Clara had been right when she said David loved her. "What of the two women your father paid off?

"They were before I realized I loved Clara. When Father decided to send me away, I begged him to let me take Clara with me, but he refused." He paused. "How is she?"

Mattie had waited all these years to exact vengeance on David over what he had done to Clara. She had waited for him to show up on his parent's doorstep so she could tell him how Clara stole the tiepin because she loved him. She wanted him to know that Clara had risked getting caught and being sent to jail and losing her job for him. She had wanted to yell at him that he had taken advantage of a naïve young girl. But much of that anger was gone. He had loved Clara and wanted to be with her.

"She found out she was pregnant after you left."

"Oh."

"She was afraid of losing her job like she'd heard so many women did if they got pregnant or sick. I tried to convince her that your father was different, that he would probably give her some money and send her home. But she was terrified of her parents' reaction." Mattie took a deep breath. "So, instead, she committed suicide. She put rocks in her coat pockets and threw herself into the Thames River."

David gasped. He looked at her, stricken. "Oh, my god. I shouldn't have left her behind. I should have found a way to book her passage with me." He dropped his head in his hands.

Mattie reached out and touched his shoulder. "I'm sorry."

David was quiet for a few minutes then he lifted his head. "I didn't want to come into Dawson to see the moving pictures and possibly see Helen again. I wasn't sure I wanted contact with my family. But Florence convinced me that I should at least think about it. After all, Helen is my sister, and what happened to me wasn't her fault. I was surprised to see you three in the pictures, and I kept my distance, but when I saw Freddie grab you, I knew I had to help."

"I'm glad you did. And you have made Helen very happy by admitting who you are. Will you be going to England to see your mother?"

"That, I don't know yet." David stood. "I must go. Florence and I have to change our names to Gastrell on our marriage licence and our claim. Then we have to get ready for supper with Helen. Thank you, Mattie, for telling me about Clara."

"Goodbye," Mattie said and watched him walk away. With a sigh, she went back to the hotel. She saw Helen talking with Belinda at the desk. It was time to tell Helen she was staying and ask Belinda for the job.

347

"Miss Lewis," a voice called.

"Mrs. Perkins." Mattie was surprised to see her.

"You said you were staying at this hotel, so I thought I would come and see you. Have you found the money to become my partner?"

"No, I'm afraid I haven't."

"What's this about being a partner?" Helen said, coming over. "A partner in what?"

"A partner in my café," Mrs. Perkins said. "She answered my advertisement in the newspaper and came to see me."

Helen looked at Mattie, surprise on her face. "You want to stay here in Dawson?"

"Yes, Miss, I do," Mattie spoke carefully. "I've been a domestic servant for most of my life. I want something different. I hoped to find work or a business that I could buy into, but I don't have enough money."

"Oh, Mattie, what will I do without you?" Helen had tears in her eyes. "You've always been part of my life."

"I know, Miss." Mattie didn't know what else to say. She reached out and took Helen's hand. Memories of all the years watching her grow from a baby to this beautiful young woman flooded her. She looked into Helen's eyes, imploring her to understand. "You have a full life ahead of you as a doctor when you return to London while I only have my dreary life as a maid to look forward to."

Helen nodded slightly. "I understand." She pulled Mattie in a hug. "I will miss you terribly."

"I will miss you, too." Mattie felt a lump in her throat as she hugged Helen back. This was something they hadn't done since Helen was young.

Helen let her go and turned to Mrs. Perkins. "How much are you asking for a half share of your business?"

The End

Readers we need you.

Please leave a review, even a one liner counts, and has a big influence on our future sales.

***Joan Donaldson-Yarmey's books
published by BWL Publishing Inc.***

Canadian Historical for Adults and Young
Adults
Rushing the Klondike
Romancing the Klondike
West to Grande Portage
West to the Bay

Mysteries
Sleuthing the Klondike
Gold Fever
The Travelling Detective Series

Holiday Romance
The Twelve Dates of Christmas

Joan Donaldson-Yarmey was born in New Westminster, B.C., Canada, and raised in Edmonton, Alberta. Over the years she worked as a bartender, hotel maid, cashier, bank teller, bookkeeper, printing press operator, meat wrapper, gold prospector, warehouse shipper, house renovator, and nursing attendant. During that time she raised her two children and helped raise her three step-children.

Since she loves change, Joan has moved over thirty times in her life, living on acreages and farms and in small towns and cities throughout Alberta and B.C. She now lives in Edmonton with her husband and one cat.

Joan began her writing career with a short story, progressed to travel and historical articles, and then on to travel books. She called these books her "Backroads" series and in the seven of them she described what there is to see and do along the back roads of British Columbia, Alberta, the Yukon, and Alaska. She has now switched to fiction writing and is proud to be one of Books We Love Ltd published authors.

Rushing the Klondike, Romancing the Klondike, West to the Bay, and *West to Grande Portage* are Joan's four Canadian Historical novels for adults and young adults.

She has had three mystery novels, *Illegally Dead, The Only Shadow in the House,* and *Whistler's Murder* published in what she calls the "Travelling Detective Series". They come in a boxed set. In her stand-alone novel, *Gold Fever,* she combines mystery with a little romance. *The Twelve Dates of Christmas* is a holiday romance.

https://www.bookswelove.com/donaldson-yarmey-joan/

http://thetravellingdetectiveseries.blogspot.com/

https://www.facebook.com/writingsbyJoan